WITNESS PROTECTION

EVERNIGHT PUBLISHING ®

www.evernightpublishing.com

Copyright© 2019

Stacey Espino

Editor: Karyn White

Cover Art: Jay Aheer

ISBN: 978-0-3695-0014-4

ALL RIGHTS RESERVED

WITNESS PROTECTION

The darkness clung to her like shadows refusing to move on.

—*The Initiation* by Sam Crescent

WITNESS PROTECTION

WITNESS PROTECTION

Stacey Espino

Copyright © 2019

Chapter One

Men ran up and down the hall outside her bedroom, their heavy footfalls making the glass in her windows rattle. Her father would be pissed tonight. He hated when his men let business get too close to home. She expected at least one of his hired guns would be executed to make an example, to instill fear in the others.

Always with the fear.

Sophia could practically hear his speech already. What was worse than everything, was the fact she'd become immune to the violence. It was ingrained in her life, and her father did little to hide his business from her. He believed not teaching her his native Russian tongue would be enough to keep her in the dark, but she wasn't so naïve.

A barrage of gunfire rang out downstairs.

Sophia didn't flinch.

She sat on the window bench in her bedroom, looking down at the cars driving by, wishing she was being whisked to someplace far, far away. But, no, she was here, practically a damn prisoner in her own home.

Sophia had everything money could buy. If only there was a price tag on her freedom. She walked over to her dresser and picked up a framed picture, running a finger against the glass, smiling at the memory. It was her graduation, and her father had pride on his face, his arm around her shoulders … God, how she missed those days.

It was soon after the picture was taken when things changed.

Once she started maturing, he grew distant, saying she looked too much like her mother. He was convinced she'd become a whore like her and began accusing her of trying to sleep around. Men on his payroll who showed too much interest suddenly disappeared, never to be heard from again.

So, most of her time she was home, under careful watch, unable to embrace her independence. She lost herself in reading, studies, and her passion had always been painting. One corner of her room was a mess of canvases, easels, and unfinished projects.

At twenty-four, she still didn't know what the fuck real life felt like. Some days she wished she'd never been born, that she'd been slaughtered along with her mother. Taking her own life had infiltrated her thoughts more and more over the years. It both disturbed and fascinated her. Her imagination was the only thing keeping her sane.

She set the picture back in place, next to one of her many Russian dolls. Whenever her father became especially cruel, he'd bring her a new one the next day as some kind of peace offering. Her collection was growing. It seemed guilt was stronger than love. No matter how beautiful or priceless, the collection only represented the pain it was meant to cover up.

More gunshots.

Sophia rolled her eyes.

Maybe a stray bullet would end her misery. Would her father regret being an asshole once she was dead?

Her door burst open. She gasped and whirled around.

"*Come!*" Hawk motioned for her to take his hand. He was out of breath, a sense of urgency in his voice she'd never heard before. He was one of her father's enforcers and the babysitter who constantly kept tabs on her activities.

"What is it?"

"We have to go. Right now, Sophia." He took a couple brisk strides into the room and wrapped his hand around her wrist, yanking her along with him. She stumbled, half protesting. The scent of gunpowder stung her nose when they emerged into the hallway. He switched hands, holding her wrist with his left hand so he could pull out a Glock with his right.

"Tell me what's going on," she said.

"Hush."

He navigated down the hallway toward the massive winding staircase. The stairs always reminded her of fairy tales. When she'd been younger, she would pretend to be a princess trapped in a castle.

Today was more of a nightmare.

A body lay sprawled out near the final steps, blood pooling, dripping down like a morbid waterfall.

She bolted to a stop, digging in her heels.

"Not now, Sophia. Your father wants you safe. Let's go," said Hawk, his hand still shackling her wrist. There was no way she could escape from him. The man was built like a brick shit house, solid muscle and covered in ink. One of her father's top enforcers. But she wasn't afraid of him, even though everyone else seemed to be.

As much as she wanted to protest, she allowed him to lead her down the staircase. He kept his gun at the ready, aiming at every new angle as they descended. Another man lay dead in the foyer, and several of the stained-glass panels had shattered, colorful shards of glass scattered over the white marble. There was commotion coming from the back kitchen, garnering Hawk's full attention. He opened the coat closet in the foyer. "Get in there. Don't move until I come back. I have to find your father."

She crouched down, and then he closed the door, blanketing her in darkness. It didn't take long for the air to turn stale. Her legs began to cramp. Sophia imagined that she was one of those dead bodies, *her* blood soaking the marble. Her father would probably curse because she'd stained the porous tiles. When she was a kid, he forever gave her shit when he caught her painting in the foyer. But she loved how the stained-glass made her skin turn to rainbows.

Time seemed to stand still.

How long had she been inside the closet?

The sound of her own breathing drowned out all the sounds, claustrophobia setting in. Sophia opened the door an inch to let in some fresh air. She took a deep, cleansing breath, savoring the cool air filling her lungs.

That's when she saw movement in the library.

The double doors flung open, and a man she'd never seen before dragged her father out by the back collar of his suit jacket. Like a dog. Her father's nose was bloodied, and she'd never seen him so afraid. Now that she thought about it, she'd never seen fear in his eyes.

"This is the end of the road, Vasily." The man pressed the muzzle of his gun to her father's head. "No more playing God. It's time to meet your maker."

He pulled the trigger.

The spray of blood was surreal, the body collapsing heavily to the floor. Sophia gagged, her stomach roiling, her vision blurring. She let go of the closet doorknob and it swung outwards, the hinges making the slightest squeak. The murderer's head whipped to the side, their eyes meeting. Her jaw dropped, and she froze, too terrified to move or think.

He only managed to take one step before bullets came flying at him from the back of the house. The monster didn't seem fazed, still staring at her with those evil eyes. He lifted his gun, pointing it directly at her. She held her breath, everything seeming to play out in slow motion.

A bullet grazed the gunman's face, and he brought his free hand up to cup his cheek. He cursed and ran out of the foyer just before Hawk and Vladimir raced out the front door after him.

Her adrenaline rush made her dizzy. She still couldn't move, and only gasped small mouthfuls of air as the blood from Vasily Morenov's body slowly spread out toward her like spilled paint. She wondered what colors she'd have to mix to recreate the crimson hue. Her mind began to fracture, the room slowly spinning. So many images flooded her mind, a kaleidoscope of moments now lost to memories.

He can't be dead.

Her father was the only family she had. He was invincible. She should be horrified … but somehow, she only felt numb.

"Sophia!" The voice was muted, as if she were hearing it from under water. Was she drowning? It felt like everything in her life was being washed away. When her body was hoisted into the air, reality came rushing back, along with all the sharp sounds—shouting, car doors, alarms. "Sophia, snap out of it!"

Hawk carried her through the hallway to the back of the house. She wrapped an arm around his neck to hold on, her body bouncing up and down as he jogged the rest of the way. She slipped in and out of reality, old memories merging with the present. It was Hawk who'd rushed her out in his arms on her eighteenth birthday when the FBI raided the house during her party.

Her father had handled everything, like he always did.

Now he was dead.

Using his shoulder, Hawk rammed open the emergency door, and set her on her feet next to one of the black BMWs. "Get in," he said before helping her fasten her seatbelt. It seemed so trivial. Worrying about a seatbelt when so many men had just lost their lives. How many other daughters had lost their fathers tonight? Had any become orphans like her?

Hawk slid over the hood to get to the driver's side. He checked the clip of his Glock before replacing it in his shoulder holster.

"Cops are coming," said Vlad, standing in the open doorway.

"Deal with it. I need to get Sophia somewhere safe."

"Any idea who it was?"

Hawk shook his head. "He's a lone wolf. There's no contract on Morenov's head. If there was, I'd already know about it."

"How the hell did some nobody take out that many men?"

Hawk ran a hand through his hair, pacing back and forth. "*Fuck!* I should have been there."

"What the hell happened?" asked Vlad.

His jaw twitched. "He told me to protect Sophia. Last I saw him he was safe." Hawk pounded his fist on the roof of the car, making her jump in her seat. "I can't believe he's gone."

"We'll find out whoever did this. Where you taking the girl?"

"I have no fucking clue."

****

Hawk backed out of the driveway, then spun around once on the roadway, the tires squealing when he floored the gas. He still wasn't sure where he was heading. His mind was a fucking mess.

Vasily was dead.

That man was the only father figure he'd ever known. Now he had nothing.

Vasily had taken Hawk in when he was ten years old, raised him, taught him to fight, to protect the Morenov Empire. He owed everything to Vasily, and he had no clue what would become of his life now. He was thirty-two, and he'd never held a legal job. All he'd known was a life of crime, his focus on protecting the family. Hawk was one of the few men his boss trusted with his daughter. She'd been his full-time ward since she turned eighteen.

He remembered his passenger, looking to the side to check on Sophia. Her father was dead. Nothing he could do would bring him back. Nothing he could say would fix this shit.

One thing for certain, he'd never let anything happen to Vasily's only daughter. He'd die protecting her.

"Sophia, talk to me."

She stared straight ahead, not moving, not speaking. Her eyes were glazed over as if a million miles away.

"Say something, goddammit."

Nothing.

He swerved to an alcove on the side of the highway, putting the car into park. Hawk shifted in his seat, and cupped her face with both hands, giving her a jostle. "Sophia!"

He never knew what to expect from her. Some days she was tough as nails, all strength, even challenging her father, and others she'd crumble just hearing a car honk. Growing up in one of the biggest crime families could really do a number on a person.

Her lips parted, and she slowly focused on his eyes. His heart went out to her. She was an orphan like him now, and fragile like a china doll. He half expected her to shatter in his hands.

"Hawk."

"I'm here, baby. I won't let anyone hurt you. I promise." She was in shock. No tears, no fear, no panic. "Did he see you? The man who shot your father, did he see you?"

She swallowed, making eye contact again. Sophia nodded. *Fuck.* In their world, witnesses had a seriously short shelf life. That bastard would come looking for her. He wouldn't stop until she was dead. Hawk had to get her somewhere safe until he could figure things out.

"Okay. No problem." He turned around and tapped his fingers on the steering wheel. No way would he freak her out and tell her how much danger she was in. He had to keep cool.

Hiding out at one of their many properties around the city wouldn't be smart. That gunman had just taken down nearly a dozen of the city's most renowned killers. Morenov only kept the best close to home. He'd have to use cash and get them in a high-rise hotel under a fake name. He pulled back onto the highway, heading for the city center.

"He's dead, right?"

They'd been driving for a while. He was surprised to hear her voice. "Yes."

"Are you sure?"

Considering Vasily's brains were splattered all over the fucking foyer, there was no doubt in his mind. "I'm sorry," he said. "Fuck, I'm so sorry."

"This can't be real. How can this be happening?"

"It's all my fault. I should have been there," he said. If he didn't have to protect Sophia, he'd probably have swallowed a bullet to end his own guilt. "After everything he's done for me, I wasn't there when he needed me most."

She returned to her trance, not disagreeing with him. He didn't deserve her forgiveness, and he doubted she'd ever offer it.

Hawk drove.

When they arrived at the hotel, he held Sophia's hand and left the car with the valet. The Morenov princess was used to the best, so they couldn't just stay at any dive. He pushed through the glass doors and headed to the check-in desk. The massive chandeliers offered dim lighting to the spacious lobby.

"I need a room for me ... and my wife."

"How many nights will you be staying with us?" The man at reception looked to be late twenties with an English accent.

"I don't know. At least a week. I need something high. Something private."

The guy nodded, looking at his computer screen. Sophia held his hand in a death grip. "Is she okay?"

Hawk looked over at Sophia. She was pale as a sheet. "She's not feeling well. Can we speed this along?"

"Do you have a credit card for our files?"

"No. I have cash." He reached into his inside jacket pocket, careful not to reveal his gun, and pulled out a stack of hundreds. He slapped them on the counter. "Consider this my security deposit. I need a key card."

Hawk had been raised in a world where money and power talked. It was ingrained into every fiber of his being. He was used to getting his way, no matter the cost.

By the time the elevator stopped on the top floor, Sophia was wobbling on her feet. He scooped her up into his arms and carried her down the hall to their penthouse suite. Once inside, he kicked the door shut and brought her straight to the bedroom. He laid her down on the king-sized bed, removed her flats, and tucked her in.

"Get some rest," he said. Hawk gave her a kiss on the forehead and closed the bedroom door behind him. Once alone, he exhaled, wishing this was all a nightmare he could wake up from.

He began to pace, rubbing behind his neck as he tried to focus. Only hours ago, he'd been sitting back in one of Vasily's custom leather chairs, enjoying a Cuban cigar as they shot the shit about an upcoming distribution meeting. He could still hear Marco laughing, and remembered Enon telling them his wife just had a baby.

They were all dead.

Hawk braced a hand on one of the floor-to-ceiling glass panes, blowing out another breath as he stared at the streets below, the people rushing around like ants. He didn't know what he was dealing with, so couldn't be too safe. Hawk still wasn't foolish enough to believe being forty floors up meant they were untouchable.

He'd only caught a glimpse of the shooter. Dark brown hair, shaved at the sides, long on top, and a tattoo crawling up his neck. He had to be around 6'4", wearing black jeans and a dark sweater. Still, not much to go on.

All Vasily's top men were dead. There was just

him and Vladimir left. The other hired guns didn't live in the mansion because Vasily didn't trust them enough to be under the same roof as Sophia. And they probably didn't give a shit that their boss had just been assassinated. There was no second in command, no plan of action if Morenov was taken out. Hawk liked to think of himself as a son, but that had always been his own wishful thinking.

He pulled out his cell and called Vlad.

"Yeah."

"What happened with the cops? You find out anything?" he asked.

"Everything's been dealt with for now. The cleaning crew is coming for the bodies. Where'd you take the girl?"

"Don't worry about her. What about the shooter?"

"I checked the security footage. He's professional, all right. Maybe a private hit? Something personal? No fucking clue."

"Okay. Call me if you have anything new. I'm going to lay low until we know more about this fucker."

"Watch your back." Vlad ended the call.

He put out the "Do Not Disturb" sign and locked the door after checking out the hallway. He was fucking paranoid. At least Sophia was safe. Hawk took off his coat and holster, dropping them on the kitchen island. He opened the crystal decanter on the bar and poured himself a glass of hard liquor, knocking it back in one shot. This was not how he planned his day.

Hawk peered in the bedroom, then slipped inside. Everything had to revolve around Sophia now. She'd always been her father's number one priority; now she had to be his. He sat on a chair near the side of the bed, staring at her in the dim lighting as she slept.

She was fucking stunning.

A sleeping angel.

And he was a sick bastard to even think it.

Her long, blonde hair spilled over her shoulder and pooled on the mattress as she cuddled up on her side. The gentle rise and fall of her chest calmed him. After the most stressful days, a visit with her always soothed his beast. He'd been her bodyguard for as long as he could remember. Once she turned eighteen, Vasily insisted she be watched twenty-four, seven. He became obsessed that his daughter would humiliate him, become some kind of raging whore. But Hawk knew Sophia. She wasn't anything like her mother, or her father. But the older she became, the more he saw the life in her eyes ebbing away. The sadness was there even when she smiled, but it wasn't his place to question anything. The last thing he needed was for her father to become suspicious of him, too.

It was better to keep his thoughts and desires locked away. Now that her father was dead, she'd probably hate him. He wasn't sure he could ever prepare himself for that, but he deserved it nonetheless.

He stood to leave, but Sophia reached out her arm. "Don't go."

Hawk sat on the edge of the bed, the mattress dipping. "I thought you were sleeping."

She rolled to her back and looked up at him. "I don't want to be alone."

He brushed the stray hairs from her face. Her lips were slightly swollen, but there were no tears in her eyes. "I'm not going anywhere."

Chapter Two

Cayden tugged off his hoodie and tossed it in the bathtub. He leaned over the white pedestal sink in the bathroom to examine the damage to his face in the mirror.

"Motherfucker!" The bullet had grazed his cheek, leaving a burning gash that would leave a nasty scar. He poured alcohol on a facecloth and blotted the wound, gritting his teeth from the jolt of pain.

Everything about today was fucked up.

His jobs weren't usually so damn sloppy, but this one had been personal. He should have ended that piece of shit quick and easy, but he drew out Morenov's suffering, and it cost him big time. Not only did he nearly get his head blown off, but he'd left a witness behind.

He'd just made his kill, and then that fucking girl had to throw a huge wrench in his plans. His only target had been the kingpin; the others were just collateral damage. They should have stayed out of his way. Cayden had nothing personal against the girl either, but he couldn't leave a witness alive, an unspoken rule in his line of work. He had a reputation to uphold—every hit had to be clean.

The blonde had been curled up in the bottom of a closet, her big, dark eyes staring straight at him like a deer in the headlights. He had no doubt she'd be able to pick him out of a line-up. It pissed him off that he had to leave her breathing, but he'd find her if it was the last thing he did. Cayden had ways of finding out information.

He tossed the rag into the tub with his hoodie and cracked his neck to each side as he left the bathroom. Cayden dropped down on the sofa, resting his legs on the coffee table. He leaned his head back, draping his forearm over his eyes.

He'd done what he set out to do. Shouldn't he feel better than this?

Cayden had cameras set up around Morenov's house. He'd been doing recon for over a week before he made his move. Once he'd finished the job, the first thing they did was whisk his witness away. They'd only hide the girl from him if she was important.

He'd replayed the security videos over and over since arriving home. He sat up and hit play again, zooming in on her face. It took him a while to realize it was Morenov's only daughter. He'd never seen her come or go and could only pull up a few old pics online. Vasily's right-hand man had taken her. Cayden had placed trackers on all the cars, so he couldn't hide her from him for long.

His plan slowly took shape.

He'd wait them out, give them a few days to think he'd moved on. Then he'd wait for them to make a mistake, striking when they least expected it. He'd break her neck or put a bullet in her brain. It didn't really matter how it was done.

The cushion next to him jostled as his cat jumped up to join him. He ran his hand over her back. He'd taken her in as a stray over four years ago. "Hey, Rosie. How was your day? Better than mine, I hope."

Talking to a fucking cat.

This was what his life had come to.

He chuckled to himself, not willing to focus on how shitty things turned out for him. He was good at what he did, and the work paid well, but he was thirty-five now. Blowing his money on bitches and partying no longer held the same appeal. Then again, with Frank Almeida and his family gone, he had nothing left to hold onto, no reason to behave.

He leaned over the coffee table and began disassembling his handguns. Cleaning his weapons kept him focused. And right now, his mind was a mess. A drip of blood landed on his hand, then another. Cayden got up and slapped a few bandages over the wound on his cheek. It would have to do. He didn't visit hospitals, and he needed to restock his medicine cabinet. After the bloodbath last month, he was fresh out of everything.

Cayden needed something to eat, and some noise to clear his head. He pulled on his jacket and put a full clip in his handgun before tucking it into the back of his jeans. After locking the door, he jogged up the concrete stairs from his basement apartment. A siren sounded in the distance, cats shrieking nearby. The stench of the sewer greeted him when he got to the sidewalk, only the scant streetlights illuminating the neighborhood. He lived in the ghetto, one of the seediest shitholes in the city.

That's the way he liked it.

Being under the radar, nobody to bother him, was how he chose to live. The reputation of the area didn't scare him—he was worse than the bogeyman.

He walked down the street to Bruno's Pizzeria, the bells chiming against the glass as he entered. The entire neighborhood consisted of Mom-and-Pop shops struggling to survive. There were more and more stores boarded up over the past couple years. Small businesses couldn't afford to pay the extortion payments.

The scent of pizza made his stomach rumble. The lights, the voices, the laughter—it all brought back bittersweet memories of what he'd lost.

"Cayden, what can I get you?" asked Bruno.

He sat down at one of the small two-person tables and pulled out his smokes. He tapped the pack, then lit up, taking a deep drag. "Usual."

"You got it."

The numerous conversations were a comforting backdrop as he watched the cars drive by from the front store windows.

He knew Amelia approached before she spoke. "Hi, Cayden. I'm sorry to hear about—"

"It's fine, Amelia. I don't need to hear about it." He sure as fuck didn't need to rehash this over and over. A month may have passed, but the pain and anger still brewed inside him like it was yesterday. He'd become more reclusive, bitter, and pissed off with the world. Morenov's death helped, but nothing could fix what was broken inside him.

"Sorry. Can I do anything to help?" She sat down on the free chair. She wore purple sweats, her hair up in a messy bun.

"Drop it." He took another drag and leaned his head back, exhaling above him. Holy shit, he was just hanging on by a thread.

"We could go to a movie or something. You know, get your mind off everything," she suggested.

He clenched his teeth together. Cayden wasn't sure what the fuck it was about him, but the bitches wouldn't leave him alone. He'd made it clear he wasn't available, but that didn't stop them. They weren't after his money, because as far as anyone knew, he was dirt broke.

He valued his privacy.

"We've been through this," he said.

She reached for his face. "What happened?" He grabbed her wrist before she could touch him.

"No touching," he said, shaking his head once in warning. "I nicked myself shaving."

"Order's ready, Cayden!" Bruno shouted from behind the counter. He was busy making pizza with his wife and teen son. The delivery drivers frequently came and went with orders. It was nice to see their place doing well.

He stood up and approached the counter, snuffing out his cigarette in one of the ashtrays. "Smells good," he said. Cayden set a twenty on the counter.

"You okay?" Bruno pointed to his cheek, his hands covered in flour. His son came and took the money, leaving his take-out box in its place. Cayden always took his food to go.

"Nothing serious," he said. "How's business been?"

"It's good. I can't complain, right?"

He grabbed his box and forced a smile. "I'll see you soon. Take care."

Amelia ambushed him just outside the doors. She was cute or could have been. The girl was messed up on crack and turned tricks on the side to support her habit. You couldn't pay him to go near her. "Why you avoiding me, Cayden? Are you seeing someone?"

"No, and I have no plans on changing that." He walked around her. "Trust me, you don't want a man like me. Be smart and worry about getting your own shit together."

Cayden had come from the bottom, just like Amelia, just like a lot of people living in the area. One difference set them apart—he wasn't addicted to any of that shit they were on. It was Frank Almeida who'd made sure he kept on the straight and narrow, and even though he was gone, Cayden was old enough to know better. The only escape he needed was some booze, cigarettes, and killing.

His cellphone rang during his walk back home. "Yeah."

"There's only one left in the house." It was Randy. They'd been friends since they were kids.

Cayden used him for information once in a while. He always needed cash. "No cops."

"Good. I'll have to pay our friend a visit."

"You need me to tail the girl?"

"No. She'll be easy to find. You did good, Randy. We'll have a drink soon, eh?"

"Sure." Randy hung up. Cayden had been avoiding everyone lately. His mind was focused on revenge, and he wouldn't be himself until the job was done.

His witness had to die.

****

Sophia sat up in the bed.

She was alone.

It took a few moments for reality to suffocate her. It hit her like a blow to the chest, stealing her air and making her nauseous.

Why couldn't she stay in blissful ignorance forever?

The visual of her father's blood flashed in her head again, in perfect detail, and she tried to shake the image away. She bolted up to her feet, rushing to the window to pull back the drapes with both hands. The morning light stung her eyes. She exhaled, thankful for the morning, the new day, but she was still completely lost.

Hawk had brought her here, whisked her away in the night. Had he saved her from the same fate as her father? She wasn't sure if that was a blessing or a curse. Life as Vasily Morenov's daughter was a lonely one. But without her father, she had no identity, and wasn't sure where she fit in. She'd been segregated from the world—tutors, private lessons, no socialization. It had been done for her safety, but she knew it all boiled down to her father's need for control.

Now she only had Hawk.

Why did he even care about her now that his boss was dead? She'd expected him to run, to leave her to fend for herself. Had he really cared about her all these years or was he just doing his job? Sophia was terrible at reading people.

She'd had a secret crush on her father's hired babysitter but didn't think much of it since he didn't reciprocate her feelings. He was eight years older, and he'd been around since she could remember. It had only been the past five years or so that he'd become a regular fixture in her life. Her father trusted him, but Hawk was nothing like Vasily.

He wasn't a monster.

A few months ago, Hawk had agreed to be the subject for one of her paintings. It had taken almost a year of begging. He sat on a stool near her window, so the lighting was just right, looking too big and out of place in her feminine bedroom. She'd called the painting *Dark Angel*, but she never told him that. He was a mix of light and darkness, good and evil intertwined. His eyes were the color of caramel, his dark hair lightly brushed off his face. As she painted, she memorized the strong line of his jaw, the fullness of his lips, and the conflict in his eyes.

She was twenty-four.

A woman.

Sophia's body reacted to the spicy scent of his cologne, and she couldn't help but notice how his shirts pulled tight around his biceps. He worked out in the basement gym almost every day of the week, and his dedication showed. His shoulders were corded with muscle, his arms hard and toned. Sometimes she'd catch him coming up the stairs in just his gym shorts, and she'd pretend not to see. She noticed everything, and she still remembered.

Hawk was always strapped, and for some reason it made her hot. Sophia hated guns ... or tired of them. Weapons and Hawk did crazy things to her libido. Her father would never entertain her having a relationship with any man, never mind one of his staff. He expected her to die a virgin, an old spinster who'd never known love.

Now she had no rules to follow ... only her own.

Sophia left the bedroom and found Hawk lost in thought, sitting in a reclining chair facing the floor to ceiling windows. He stared off into space, still like a statue.

They were high up, higher than she'd ever been. She tentatively walked closer to the glass, a mix of fear and awe. From her vantage point, the city looked like a piece of art, the architecture and blue of the sky tempting her to capture it on canvas.

He must have heard her, turning his head in her direction. "You're up."

"Where are we?"

"Someplace safe." The chair swiveled, and he faced her. "Are you hungry?"

She shrugged.

"There're bagels and muffins on the counter. Picked them up this morning. I know you hate coffee, but there's tea."

Sophia wandered around the room, not sure what to think or feel. "Why am I here, Hawk?"

He narrowed his eyes, his head tilting to the side. "I'm keeping you safe."

"From what?"

"You said that guy saw you. That means you're a witness. It's not safe to be home."

"Why are *you* here?"

He stood up, the leather chair creaking. Hawk approached her, holding her arm so she paid attention to him. "What do you mean?"

She scoffed. "You're out of a job, aren't you? I mean, your boss is dead. You don't have to babysit me anymore."

"You think this is just a job? Vasily was like a father to me. He *saved* me. I owe him everything."

Her father didn't deserve to be a martyr. "You don't owe *me* anything."

"You're his daughter. The last thing he told me was to protect you. That's exactly what I plan to do, Sophia."

"So I'm a prisoner here, just like I was at home?"

"I'm not following."

She turned away from him, heading to the kitchen. "Never mind."

It pissed her off that he was still loyal to her father. And she was even angrier that he still showed no interest in her besides duty. Less than twenty-four hours ago she'd watched her father killed before her eyes.

She held her stomach as she recalled the blood.

An ocean of blood.

How should I feel?

She felt like a ticking time bomb. The little girl inside her cried out, desperate and empty, craving her father's affection. She needed more time to prove herself worthy of his love, but the sands in the hourglass were empty. The woman was angry, angry for the years of control, the growing resentment, and the constant comparisons to the mother she'd never known. Vasily Morenov hadn't died yesterday, not for her. He died years ago, as soon as she stopped being a child. Her father made her associate being a woman with something dirty, something that made her unlovable.

Any chance to earn his love ended with that one bullet. Had the man with the hard, blue eyes stolen her father's chance at redemption or given her a gift?

"Do you want to talk?"

"There's nothing to say," she said.

"Pretending nothing happened isn't going to make it go away. What you saw … no one should have to see that. Especially you."

"Especially me? Why is that, Hawk?"

Did he think she was weak? A delicate flower? Her bitterness seeped to the surface. This wasn't her, but she couldn't stop herself.

"Because you're special."

Tears welled up in her eyes for the first time. She turned away so he wouldn't see. Why couldn't her father love her? What the fuck would it take to make him proud?

"Sophia?"

She shook her head. "Leave me alone. Please."

Of course, Hawk refused to listen. He tugged her shoulder, spinning her to face him. "Let it out. Your father just died. You're allowed to grieve."

"You don't understand. I feel nothing. How can I grieve for a man who hated me?"

"Don't say that."

"It's the truth!"

"He loved you, Sophia. You were all that mattered to him."

Her sinuses burned as she fought back her emotions. "Bullshit! He cared about money. About control. He had to be the best at everything."

"You were his *printsessa*," he whispered the words.

She shook her head, hot tears running down her cheeks. If he said one more thing, she'd lose it completely. Sophia knew the cold, hard truth, and it hurt more than anything. Her father had been cruel, distant, and made her life miserable.

She wished things had been different, but part of her was happy he was dead.

And that fact broke her heart.

Chapter Three

Two days.

Hawk finally understood how Sophia must have felt being held captive in her own home. Being holed up forty floors from the city streets, with no end in sight, was making him more stir-crazy by the hour.

"Will there be a funeral?"

He turned to find Sophia standing in the bedroom doorway, her hair wrapped up in a towel. Talking with Sophia had been a balancing act of truth, white lies, and finding the right words to not upset her. "Anything public wouldn't be safe. We've talked about this."

"So, what happened to him then? Was he dumped in the trash?"

The cleaning crew would have disposed of all the evidence, including bodies. He wasn't prepared to tell Vasily's daughter that there would be no body to bury. It was the world they lived in, one of violence and sin. "It'll all be handled. Nothing for you to worry about."

She came over and sat on the arm of his chair. The cityscape lit up the night sky, disguising the fact it was past ten in the evening. From their vantage point, the views were stunning. He could sit and stare for hours— he had been.

"What's going to happen, Hawk?" Her whisper sounded like a worried child.

"Just a little longer. I want to keep off the radar for at least a few more days."

"And then what?"

He'd love to know. A huge responsibility had been thrust on him the moment Morenov was assassinated. Hawk couldn't just drop Sophia off on her doorstep and wish her well. As long as the killer was loose, he'd want his witness dead. Either in a week or a year from now, at some point Sophia would pay the ultimate price.

The mansion was the only place he'd called home. Both their lives were in a toss-up, but he had to keep control, had to convince her that he knew what the fuck he was doing.

"Then we start over."

She shifted on the arm of the chair, pulling the towel off her hair. It unraveled over her shoulder, still damp from her shower. The scent of strawberries perfumed the air. She'd given him a list of must-haves that he'd picked up for her. "I'm not sure I'll know how to do that. My father never let me do anything for myself. It's going to be a harsh wake-up call."

"I've seen you give your dad's crew shit before. Hell, I can hardly get you to listen to me. You're tougher than you think."

She shook her head. "I don't feel very strong right now. There's so much on my mind. It's overwhelming."

He rested a hand on her knee. She wore an oversized t-shirt as her pajamas. "Now's not the time to worry. You've been through a lot. Just try and rest."

"What will *you* do after?"

"I'll have to get work. Probably contracts." He shrugged. Hawk didn't have much time to worry about himself when Sophia's life was in danger.

"Where will you go?" she asked. "Are you staying at home?"

He smirked. She was too damn cute. "Like you said, my boss is dead. It's not my home anymore."

Sophia frowned. "Of course, it's your home. You've lived there my whole life."

"It's different now. I'm not family. I'll have to go my own way."

"No, Hawk. You can't leave me. Everyone's gone. There's no one left." She slid down off the arm of the chair onto his lap, then wrapped her arms around his neck. "Please don't leave me." The heat of her whispered words lingered on his neck.

Holy shit, he was in a hard place.

This wasn't some fucking fairy tale where everything would go back to normal once the dust settled. Her father was a major kingpin with a lot of enemies. Sophia may be his daughter, but Hawk was nothing—just another hired hand with a price on his head. Once she was safe, he'd have to start a new life away from her.

"You're just emotional. Trust me, you'll be fine."

She pulled back and scowled. "I'm not emotional. I'm broken. You're all I have."

He exhaled, deciding now wasn't a good time to argue with her. She'd been through the wringer, so he'd humor her tonight. Hawk pressed her head back to his chest and gently brushed the hair off her face.

"Your heartbeat is strong," she said. She toyed with the buttons on his shirt. The room was dim, only the lights of the cityscape giving the walls a scant wash of light. She tucked her knees up onto his lap, cuddling up like a kitten.

It wouldn't be easy to walk away. Sophia had been his full-time ward for the past six years. Even before that, she'd been a fixture in his life since he moved into the house. He came to the Morenov home when he was a little boy, so they'd grown up under the same roof. Only he wasn't family, and he slept in the staff's wing, and never felt like he truly belonged. Her father had pitied him, taking him under his wing rather than leaving him on the streets.

Sophia missed her father and looked to Hawk for

security. The fact that unwholesome thoughts kept creeping in his head pissed him off. He was a twisted bastard to look at Sophia as anything but a little sister. She was innocent, untouchable, and mourning her father. Either he was getting cabin fever or he needed a stiff drink to drown his fucked-up desires.

"You should get to bed," he said.

"It's not even late. Let's do something," she said. "Can we go out for a little while?"

"You know we can't."

She sighed and slipped off his lap, walking to wall of windows. At first, she'd been afraid to get too close. Now she pressed both palms to the glass above her head and rested her forehead on the window. "I used to watch the cars from my bedroom window. I'd give each person a story and try to guess where there were going. It's too far up here. I can't see their faces."

Sophia sounded lost. A feather on the wind.

"I wonder what would happen if I jumped from this high up," she said. "When I hit the road, would my blood run crimson like my father's?"

"Sophia…"

"Just wondering." She twirled back around, mischief in her eyes. "How many people have you killed?"

"Who said I killed anyone?"

She paced in front of the windows. "I know a lot more than you think. My father thought he kept me in the dark, but I'm not an idiot. I even picked up Russian over the years, enough to get the gist anyway."

"He was protecting you."

"So, how many, Hawk? How many lives have you taken?"

He wasn't going to play games with her. What was the point? "Too many to count."

Her mouth opened slightly. She was probably surprised he answered her. "Can I see your gun?"

He shook his head.

"Please…" Her pleading reminded him of the many times she tried to get him to pose for one of her paintings. It was hard to refuse her anything.

Hawk pulled out one of his pistols, removed the clip, and checked the chamber before holding it out to her. She smiled, sauntering over to the chair.

"It's no fun without the bullets."

"You're not getting bullets."

She huffed and took the gun with her to the window, examining it every which way. "So many cars." Sophia held both arms straight and lined up the sights. "They wouldn't know what hit them," she said, aiming at the street far, far below.

He got up and headed to the bar, dropping an ice cube into a clean glass with a clink before adding the liquor. Carrying his drink, he joined her at the window. "So, you're a killer now?"

"Maybe."

He humored her. "Who do you plan on killing? The man who murdered your father?"

"I haven't really thought about it." She held the gun to her temple and pulled the trigger. The empty gun clicked. "I was mostly considering doing myself a favor."

Hawk snatched the gun away, some of his drink sloshing onto the tiles. "What the fuck do you think you're doing?" He tossed the gun onto his chair and grabbed her wrist. "That shit's not funny."

She had no fear of him.

Sophia smiled, a mix of sadness and insanity. "Don't you ever think about it? Ending it all? I have. It's been on my mind for years."

He dragged her with him to the bar so he could set his drink down, but then he thought better and swallowed it in one shot. Fuck, he'd been ready to bite the bullet after the massacre at the mansion. He was still breathing because of his responsibility to Sophia. "I don't want to hear to talk like this again, do you understand me, Sophia?" He held both her shoulders, giving her a little jostle. "I'm not risking my life here for nothing."

"No one's asking you to stay. Why don't you leave?"

"Stop testing me," he said. "We have a few more days cooped up in this suite. It could be worse."

She exhaled and slipped away.

He wished he could fix her, fix everything. She was a mess, and he had little to offer in comfort. She took one of the oversized cushions from the sofa and dropped it in front of the windows, then sat cross-legged on it. "You must think I'm weak," she said, not looking at him. "Maybe I am. I don't know. It would be nice to be you, Hawk. Strong, fearless, invincible."

"Is that what you think?"

"It's what I know. All Dad's men were terrified of you."

"Not you."

Protecting the Morenov Empire had always been his passion. He loved Vasily and would do anything he asked. The crime boss personally trained him, ensuring he could kill without remorse, and take a beating without breaking.

He paced back and forth.

"Hawk?"

"Yeah, baby?"

"Want to know my biggest fear?"

He jutted his chin, motioning for her to continue.

"Being alone. Stupid, isn't it? I mean, considering

35

I've spent most of my life alone." She turned and looked up at him this time. "Are you afraid of anything, Hawk?"

He thought about it briefly. "Just one thing." Her curiosity piqued, her eyes widening as she awaited his response. He'd been raised to be fearless, cutthroat, and ready to die for the family. Not much gave him pause. Weaknesses were dangerous for men in his business, giving others something to exploit.

"Please tell me," she said.

"Losing *you*."

****

Cayden took a bite of his hero sandwich as he scrolled through the video surveillance images on his phone. It was time to pay Vladimir Sokolov a visit. Vasily's man was holding down the fort, still loyal to the piece of shit. Cayden had been biding his time, but it was the night to even the score. Morenov's Russian princess had witnessed him kill her father. He couldn't leave her alive. Since she was the old man's only child, he'd consider it a service wiping out the bastard's bloodline.

They were hiding the girl in an overpriced hotel for the past five days.

Penthouse suite.

Nobody could hide from Cayden. He'd get information from Vladimir, set his plan into motion, and then kill the witness. It had been over a month since Vasily ordered the hit on Frank Almeida and his family. Although Cayden was having a fucked-up time getting over his grief, he was certain it would be easier to move on once the loose ends were tied up nicely.

"You're coming over for dinner tonight, Cayden. No arguments," said Frank.

"And what does Mrs. Almeida have to say about that?"

Frank looked at him as if he'd grown a second

head. "She loves you like her own son. Be over at six."

Family was an enigma to him. He always felt like an outsider, not knowing how to behave. For some reason, the bakery owner took Cayden under his wing.

"I've never been invited to dinner. Am I supposed to bring something?"

The old man smiled. "Just yourself."

He tried to keep busy with new contracts but couldn't get his head in the game. Memories of that girl in the closet kept haunting him. Her dark eyes were filled with shock and disbelief. He wasn't one to go out of his way to kill innocent bystanders, but she was complicated.

Cayden finished his dinner, then shrugged on his heavy holsters. He had a one-man arsenal strapped to his body, and his trunk had everything he'd need to set his plan into motion. After tonight, he hoped his concentration would return once he no longer had to obsess over his witness.

This chapter of his life needed to be closed.

He tugged on his jacket to keep discreet and slung his duffel bag over his shoulder before leaving his apartment. He jogged up the stairs and walked down the street toward the alleyway where he rented a garage.

He'd grown up in this neighborhood. One of his grade schools was just up the street, and he'd lived in a few of the houses during his foster care years. Some of his friends asked why he stuck around. His memories were fucked-up, but they were all he had. Most people took having roots for granted. Cayden had nothing, so he kept holding onto the little history he had. Now that the Almeida family had been wiped out, he'd never felt so unsettled. Nothing grounded him, and he didn't give a fuck about anything. His darkening thoughts scared him.

The most dangerous man in the world is the one with nothing to lose.

He understood that now.

The alleyway was dark shadows, only one outdoor light giving him enough illumination to get the key in the lock. There were some punks doing a drug deal fifty yards away, but, for the most part, people left him alone.

He was anonymous, invisible, forgettable.

Cayden had been orphaned when he was a few months old. According to the stories, his mother was killed in a retaliation hit, and his father, an Irish gangster back in the day, went out in a blaze of glory. There were a lot of rumors floating around, but none of them did him any good. Thanks to their fucked-up Children's Services, he wasn't adopted out to a childless couple looking for a baby to love. No, he was shuffled around to foster and group homes until he was fifteen and had had enough of the bullshit. Life on the streets wasn't easy, but his saving grace came over a decade later in the form of Frank Almeida. Without him, he'd likely be dead or in jail.

He reversed his car out of the garage, checked on his prized Harley, then locked up. The route to Vasily's was etched on his brain. He hadn't returned since that day, but his perfect hit had become messy. It was time to clean shit up.

As he drove, he called Randy. "Hey."

"You're alive."

"Sorry I haven't called. Been busy."

"What do you need?" asked Randy.

"I can't call you now?" He could hear the resentment in his friend's tone, and he hoped after today things would settle into a new normal. He had some bridges to mend, and he needed to get his head right.

"You want something."

"Nothing right now. I'm cleaning up that loose

end tonight. Shit could get ugly if that prick doesn't cooperate. Stay by your phone." He didn't anticipate much trouble with Vladimir, but if he had to kill him, he'd need Randy to get a cleaner over to the Morenov mansion.

"I'm always here."

He turned off his phone and returned it to his breast pocket. Darkness provided the cover he needed. Cayden parked in an abandoned building lot behind the house. His surveillance put Vladimir in the study with a couple guests. They hadn't been there an hour ago.

Fucking shit.

He watched the grainy footage from the camera he'd set up in the corner by the ceiling. One of the whores knelt in front of Vladimir, sucking his cock. At least his target was preoccupied, but Cayden didn't need more problems. If he had to kill them all, he would, but it was always a last resort.

Cayden picked the lock at the back of the house and slipped inside unseen. The alarm was turned off, probably thanks to the unexpected visitors. He remembered these hallways from the day he'd taken his revenge, the day he executed Vasily Morenov for killing the only family he'd ever had.

The man was pure evil.

The Almeida family were honest and hard-working, murdered for being unable to pay the growing amount demanded by Vasily's men for having a store in their territory. Cayden had no clue Frank had been paying them off for years or he would have put an end to it a long time ago. But driving himself crazy about a past he couldn't change wouldn't help him now.

Revenge helped.

He stood outside the office for the longest time, listening to the women giggling and that sick bastard talking dirty in Russian. Cayden looked down by his feet. The white marble was pristine, the stained glass replaced with a regular tinted window. It was like nothing had happened here five days ago. He turned his head and looked at the closet in the foyer. How had he not noticed her there?

His blind rage had stolen his senses. Frank had always taught him that anger was a weakness, to never react when he was pissed off, but to take a breather until he could act with a level head.

He kicked the double doors, and they burst open, splinters of wood flying in every direction. With his gun trained on Vladimir's head, he pointed to the exit, hoping the bitches would be smart and get the fuck out. They screamed, ducking their heads as they rushed away, leaving half their clothing behind. Their heels clicked along the marble until all was silent again.

"So, you're the one who killed Vasily. Who are you anyway?"

"Nobody."

"Who paid you? Why are you doing this?" Vladimir had to be pushing sixty, with a heavy accent. One of Vasily's old school goons.

Cayden ran a hand through his hair. The top was getting too long, falling in his eyes. "This isn't twenty questions. Unless you want to join your boss in the great beyond, I suggest you get your ass up and start walking."

He did as told, zipping up his pants and heading out of the office. Cayden came up behind him, his gun constantly trained on his head.

No more mistakes.

"What will you get out of killing me? I'm nothing to you."

"If you shut the fuck up, maybe you'll get out of this alive. Right now, we're going to my car, nice and quiet like."

They exited out the back doors and walked across the parking lot to where he'd left his car. He opened his trunk and pulled out a set of cuffs, securing Vladimir's hands behind him. Once he had him in the passenger seat, they hit the road.

"Where are we going?" asked Vladimir.

"You know where we're going."

The car was eerily quiet. The glow of the streetlights flashed across the dashboard every few seconds as he drove toward the highway.

"She's innocent."

Cayden grit his teeth. He didn't want to hear this now. Killing the witness was a necessity, not a pleasure, even if she was Vasily's bitch daughter.

"You don't have to kill her."

"We both know how this game works. Your girl watched me pull the trigger. That has to be remedied," said Cayden.

"You'll never get to her. Hawk is expecting you."

"No, he's hoping I've move on, but he doesn't know me very well. From my experience, every man is ready to give up his soul to save his own ass."

"Not Hawk. He'll die protecting Sophia."

Cayden cringed. He didn't want to hear her name or anything else about her. He liked his hits to be as impersonal as possible, and he chose to block out the details.

When they reached the city, he parked on a quiet side street near the hotel. "Now, you're going to call Hawk and tell him you have some important information for him. Tell him you want to meet at the coffee shop right over there."

"I won't do it."

Cayden twisted a silencer to the end of his

41

handgun, taking his time as the other man watched. He pressed it to the side of Vladimir's thigh and immediately pulled the trigger. No second chances. The man screamed and arched, his hands still locked behind his back. "You'll bleed out, so I suggest you get to a doctor ASAP. Of course, you're not getting out of my car until you do exactly as I told you. No games. No fucking this up. Listen, Vlad, I know where your parents live. I won't think twice about paying them a visit. Your mother just finished crocheting your Christmas gift. Not a fan of the navy blue, personally."

"Bastard."

"Yeah, you're right about that. We good to go?"

"I'll do it," he said.

Everyone had a weakness. He unfastened the cuffs and waited for Vladimir to make the call. When it was done, Cayden took the man's phone and smashed it on the dashboard. "I'm dropping you off at the clinic on the corner. Best of luck, old man."

STACEY ESPINO

Chapter Four

It had been almost a week since they'd checked
into the hotel. Sophia's emotions had been scattered, but
she began to accept her new reality. There was no other
choice.

She'd rented a movie and crashed on her bed to
watch it. "Hurry up, Hawk."

A few minutes later he stood in her doorway,
wearing just his black pants, eating an apple. "I'm not
watching that shit."

"You promised. It's not as fun watching a movie
alone." She was sick and tired of doing everything alone.
If she could convince Hawk to join her, all the better.

His body was ripped to perfection. Did he even
realize how tempting he was to women? To her? Even at
rest, casually leaning against the doorframe, his abs were
toned, his shoulders strong and thick with muscle.

He tossed his core into the garbage can near her
dresser and came into the room. He'd been sleeping on
the couch all week, despite her offers to share the bed.
She patted the mattress beside her and ruffled the
mountain of pillows for him.

"You're lucky we're trapped in here." Hawk sat
on the bed, the mattress sinking as he lifted his legs and
settled on the pillows. He was so big next to her, his skin
golden against the white sheets. And so much ink.

She lost interest in the movie.

"What do all these tattoos mean?" she asked.
Sophia sat up and crossed her legs, running her palm
down his chest. She swallowed hard. His skin was warm
and firm, and her body lit up from just touching him.

He looked up at her, resting his hand over hers to
still her movements. "I guess they tell a story. Badges of
honor, mistakes, memories." Hawk leaned up on one

elbow and led her hand down to the side of his stomach. "Your dad gave me this one."

She appreciated art and knew each picture had to have meaning. Sophia pulled her hand away and looked at the small abstract skull. "He actually did it himself?"

"A long time ago."

Sophia had no clue her father had an artistic bone in his body. He'd always been a complete mystery. He'd never spoken to her about himself or his past. Although he never demanded she stop her painting, so maybe he understood her passion. She ran her finger over the picture, trying to capture a piece of the father she knew so little about.

"It's my most cherished piece. It'll always remind me of him."

She scowled at that. Her feelings toward her father were volatile and mixed. And Hawk's loyalty to a dead man was getting old. "Maybe I'll get one myself."

He shook his head, running the backs of his fingers down the length of her arm. It felt way too good. "No way. He'd never approve."

"He's gone, Hawk. I make my decisions now."

"Guess I'll have to take his place."

She wanted to retch. "You want to be my daddy?"

"I want to take care of you. Besides, you're perfect the way you are. A tattoo would only ruin that." He tapped her lips with his finger, and she hadn't realized they were pursed. She was tired of being treated like a child, especially by Hawk. "No more pouting."

She grabbed his wrist and made him cup the side of her face with his palm. Sophia closed her eyes and leaned into his touch, not letting him pull away.

She loved him.

Had for years.

But he only thought of her as a responsibility, a child needing supervision.

She turned her head and kissed the inside of his rough palm. Instead of lecturing her, he shifted to his side, pushing up on his elbow until they were almost face to face. His chest rose and fell, on the brink of control. He gently cradled the back of her head and pulled her closer.

Is this actually happening?

Sophia parted her lips and sighed when they kissed. She'd been waiting for this forever. He was slow, gentle, and deliciously thorough. So much better than her fantasies. Hawk pushed himself higher until his weight was braced on his hand, his big ribs pushing her backward to the mattress. She felt as if she was being consumed, swallowed whole by his much larger frame.

This was exactly what she wanted, what she'd been dreaming of.

She ran her hand over his shoulder and down his back, needing to feel him, wanting him all over her. Never wanting tonight to end.

He trailed kisses down her neck—soft, gentle kisses. The scent of his musky cologne was an aphrodisiac. His skin felt almost hot, and the tenderness of his touch had her entire body aching. Sophia craved so much more.

"Hawk…"

"You've always been my weakness, Sophia."

Her body thrummed, her heart leaping in anticipation. She held his shoulder and leaned up to kiss his jawline. Sophia whispered in his ear without a second thought. "I love you."

His body tensed, and he grabbed a handful of the comforter until his knuckles turned white. He dropped his head, taking deep, measured breaths. "I'm sorry. I've got to go."

He rushed from the room.

"Hawk!"

What had she done wrong? Disappointment and shame assaulted her until her eyes welled with tears. Her father's constant suspicions, and now Hawk's rejection, made her feel dirty.

It had been too good to be true. Too perfect. It had to come crashing down, like everything else in her life.

Hawk had been coming and going more often lately, like he couldn't stand the sight of her. Maybe he was getting cabin fever and those perfect kisses were meaningless.

They'd been staying in the same suite for five days. He'd been sleeping on the sofa every night since their room only had one king bed. Hawk was probably regretting his decision to babysit her for so long.

The most exciting thing they'd done was play cards or watch movies at night. This whole thing was ridiculous. No one was after her, and Hawk was being overprotective like he'd always been. Her father was controlling her from beyond the grave, but she did as Hawk instructed, and didn't leave the suite.

Sophia used the alone time to take her evening shower. It had been her habit for as long as she could remember, and helped her sleep at night.

She closed her eyes as the warm water flowed over her hair and body. Her showers were more than getting clean; they were her therapy. She imagined all her worries and all the blood in her memories washing down the drain. Her nightmares hadn't let up. They'd start with her painting in the foyer as a little girl. They'd end with blood coating the white marble and her father's dead eyes staring back at her.

Now she had a new problem. Hawk had awakened something inside her. Her entire body was on fire, craving Hawk's touch again. Craving so many filthy things. He was strong and gentle in equal parts, and she wanted him to use her, to make her his. They'd crossed that invisible boundary, and, for her, there was no turning back.

She stepped out onto the mat and dried off with the oversized bath towel. The mirror had fogged up, so she wiped her hand across it. She kept telling herself she couldn't wait to leave, to get back to normal. But what was normal now? Life would never be the same again. Maybe she'd stay in this hotel room with Hawk, avoiding reality forever.

It was a nice thought.

She smoothed cream all over her body and dressed in a fresh t-shirt and yoga pants. Her choices were limited. Since she never left the suite, it was all about comfort. Sophia grabbed her brush from the top of the dresser and sat on the edge of the bed to start combing out the small knots.

Brushing her hair had always been soothing for her. She'd imagine her mother doing it, everything in vivid detail, right down to the feeling of tender love. Of course, it was all fictional, her imagination giving her a little taste of what she'd never had. Her mother was killed when she was born. There wasn't even a picture to keep. She'd only had men in her life—her father, his hired hands, Hawk.

The mirror in front of her was massive with an elaborate carved gold frame. Everything about their penthouse suite was luxurious right down to the smallest detail. Back home, her father insisted on all the finer things in life. Material things failed to impress her.

She heard Hawk return a while later. Her heart

began to race, and her cheeks flushed hot, remembering the taste of his kiss. She didn't want him to be mad at her, to blame her for seducing him. What she wanted was to continue where they left off. She'd probably just end up apologizing and stifling her true emotions.

Her hair was nearly smooth, so she hurried up to finish, wanting to look her best. A dark shadow appeared in the reflection of the mirror. He'd come into her room. What would he say to her? Her breath caught in her throat, her pussy aching. She swore she'd spontaneously combust.

"Hawk?"

He didn't answer her. She got up to check but didn't even get a chance to turn around before a rough hand slapped over her mouth from behind.

Hawk would never hurt her.

"No screaming." It was a man's voice. A deep whisper that she knew would haunt her forever. Was it one of her father's enemies? The man they were hiding from?

When he turned her, forcing her to walk forward, she saw him in the reflection. Those blue eyes, and now a scar on his face.

It was *him*.

Her father's murderer.

He was going to kill her.

Only a few days ago, she'd been ready to die. Wanted to die. Now, faced with certain death, panic washed over her.

She tasted blood as her lips and cheeks pressed unforgivingly against her teeth. He held his hand over her mouth so tight she swore she'd have bruises on her face.

How would she get out of this alive?

Hawk was gone, and she had nothing to protect

herself with. This was the man who managed to decimate a house full of trained killers. She was no match.

"We're leaving this room, and you're going to keep your mouth shut or I'll fucking kill you. Understand?" She nodded her head. "If you try to signal someone, I'll kill them, too."

She left the room for the first time in five days. The hallway was empty. He removed his hand, and she instinctively reached for her cheeks, gasping for breath. The barrel of a gun dug into her back as he prodded her toward the elevators.

Once inside, he pressed a button on the elevator panel and stood against the back wall, her body poised in front of him. She was frozen in fear, unsure what move she should make. Wondering if she was about to join her parents. When the door chimed, he jabbed her in the back again, so she got out into the hallway and kept moving.

"Inside," he said after using a keycard to open a door halfway down the hall. She hadn't even paid attention to the floor they were on, too terrified to think straight. He gave her a firm shove, and she stumbled into the room, nearly falling before catching her footing. This suite wasn't as elaborate as the one she had with Hawk. It was smaller, simpler, with regular windows rather than the massive glass wall with the breathtaking view.

The killer had been in the same hotel all along.

"Please don't hurt me," she said. "I won't say anything. I haven't said anything."

He looked her up and down without saying a word. The stranger shrugged off his jacket, hanging it on the back of a chair in the dining area. He was even more strapped than Hawk, guns and extra clips filling the numerous holsters and pockets. She didn't dare move an inch.

His back was to her as he stared out the window

into the night. "Nothing personal," he said. He pulled out one of his guns, checked the clip and tightened the silencer, then held it straight by his side. The muscles in his forearm flexed. She was transported back to that day, the day he pulled the trigger and ended her father's life.

This was it.

He was about to assassinate her. End her life at only twenty-four.

"You killed my father. I'd say that's personal." He was going to kill her anyway, so she wasn't going to beg for her life.

The fact she spoke up must have surprised him because he turned around to face her. "Your father was a monster."

"I agree."

He tilted his head, his eyes narrowed. "Then why do you care?"

"He was still my father. My only family," she said. "Why did you kill him?"

The stranger paced in front of her, his hand tight around the handle of his gun. It pissed her off that she found him attractive. He wasn't the usual overweight thug her father contracted. This guy was younger, harder, and had an intensity in his eyes that made her breath catch.

"He took something from me. Something precious."

"And killing him brought you peace?"

His face was a blank slate. He would have made a fortune as a poker player. It looked like he was about to say something, but he chose not to. He re-holstered his gun, and she released the breath she didn't realize she was holding.

Maybe she could talk her way out of this.

"I don't know who you are. I don't know your

name. How can I be a threat to you? Isn't it enough that you took everything from me?"

He licked his lips, bracing both hands on the small table as he leaned over it. An elaborate tattoo crept up his neck. "An eye for an eye. I did what I had to do."

"My father killed someone you love?"

He scowled. "He wiped out an entire family. Decent people. Innocent people. Now he's paid with his life." His voice dripped with emotion, getting angrier as he spoke.

Goosebumps prickled her arms.

"Then why kill me? What have I done to you?"

"You're your father's daughter."

Her eyes filled with angry tears. She wouldn't cry and give his asshole the satisfaction. "I'm nothing like my father! And you're no better than him if you kill me. Think about that."

He smirked for just a second, then rummaged through a duffel bag on the table. He pulled out a pair of cuffs and a length of chain. Her heart raced, the adrenaline rush making her dizzy.

She needed Hawk to make everything better.

"This way," he said. Once inside the bathroom, he handcuffed her hands in front of her and linked the chain, securing it around the pedestal of the sink before locking it. "It may not be what you're used to, *princess*, but a toilet and water is more than you deserve."

He closed the door behind him, leaving her in the dark bathroom.

"Fuck you!" she shouted once alone.

She sat down on the closed toilet seat. The scent of disinfectant irritated her nose. How would Hawk find her here? What did this man plan to do with her? Why hadn't he killed her yet? So many thoughts clouded her head. She could hear the contempt he had for her in his voice. He didn't even know her, judging her because she was a Morenov. She wasn't a murderer. In fact, she had nothing to do with her father's illegal business. If anything, Sophia was a victim herself, a prisoner in her own home. This stranger had already tried and convicted her based on her father, and she hated his judgment.

Sophia was grieving, still processing the feelings of hurt and resentment she had for her father. Her time with him had run out, so there was no chance to fix things, no chance to make amends. It was all this stranger's fault.

She lifted her arms, the heavy chains clattering, reminding her of criminals in the old castle dungeons. But this was no fairy tale, and no prince in shining armor was coming to the rescue. She should have known her life would end this way. Her father kept her locked away so his enemies couldn't use her in retaliation. Why did they care about her now that he was gone?

Sophia wanted to get out of this alive, but there was no reasoning with this man. He hated her, and if she was still breathing, he probably planned something worse than death.

****

"Where the fuck are you?" Hawk shouted when Vlad's answering machine clicked on for the tenth time. He wasn't in the coffee shop, and he'd stopped answering his cellphone. Hawk hoped he hadn't skipped out for a piece of pussy after asking him to meet up. After twenty minutes, he left the shop, looking to the right and left of the street.

How had he found his location in the first place?

If Vlad had found him, anyone could.

When he peered up to the penthouse suite of the hotel next to him, his thoughts went right to Sophia. They were supposed to watch a movie together, but his self-control around her was shot. He'd crossed the line and couldn't let it happen again. Sophia had cracked through his barriers, and he'd changed everything between them. How could she trust him again after he'd given into his desires?

It was so easy to forget the outside world when they were holed up alone together.

Things were getting too domestic between them. These breaks were becoming essential to his sanity. If he stayed locked up with her twenty-four-seven, Hawk was sure he'd lose his heart. Probably already had.

Sophia was too off-limits for him to even have such impure thoughts. Vasily would be rolling over in his grave if he knew the things swirling in Hawk's head.

He'd be giving Vlad shit later, but he wasn't going to wait another minute. Sophia had been alone long enough. He made his way up the elevator of the hotel, back to the suite. They'd been on lock down for days. Tomorrow he'd check them out and decide what to do next.

The suite was quiet. He wondered if Sophia had decided to go to bed and skip the late-night movie.

He gently pushed open the door to check on her, but the light was on and she wasn't there. "Sophia?"

Her brush was on the floor and the blankets were bunched up on one side. He bent down and picked up the brush, smelling her strawberry shampoo. Hawk frowned, not liking where this was going. The bathroom was still humid from a shower, so she couldn't have been gone long.

"Sophia!" He checked the rest of the suite, nausea setting in when he realized she was nowhere to be found. Maybe she'd gone to look for him. Taken a walk for a change of scenery.

He knew it was bullshit.

She wouldn't have left on her own, not after he told her to stay inside.

Hawk took a deep breath. He was probably overreacting.

His cell rang. "Yeah," he shouted.

"It's me. I'm calling from a clinic. The bastard shot me. He's going after Sophia," said Vlad.

He dropped his arm to the side, the phone still in his hand. The impossible reality took shape, and it terrified him to the core. How would he find her? The killer wasn't there to play games, just level the playing field. He didn't want a prisoner. He wanted Sophia dead.

"Vlad, she's already gone."

"Oh, shit. I'm sorry. He knew things, Hawk. Knew where she was. The guy's good."

He hung up. There was no sense talking with him. Vlad had failed him, led him away from his ward to save his own ass. The only person he could trust was himself.

He rushed down to the lobby, grabbing the man behind the counter by the collar, nearly pulling him over the granite barrier. The gasps around him brought back some of his sensibilities, and he released him. "I need to see security footage of the lobby. Do you have cameras in the elevators? Hallways?"

"Sir, if you're not with the police department, I can't help you."

Hawk clenched his teeth, his jaw twitching. There were too many people staring. He'd have to break into the security room himself or call in a few favors. He had to find Sophia before it was too late.

He winked at the man. "Sorry about the shirt, eh?"

It was night now, and darkness was his friend. But he needed a lead. She could be anywhere. When he started to think of the things that bastard could be doing to his sweet Sophia, he nearly retched, pushing the images away before they drove him crazy. When he got to the front of the hotel, he ordered his car from the valet and waited, his mind in a million directions.

His cell went off.

"Sophia?"

"It's Vlad. I'm on a public line. I got the license plate, not that it'll help. There was a pizza box on the backseat. Bruno's Pizzeria."

"Get another cell then text me the number." He hung up. Hawk was too pissed off with Vlad to talk now. The license plate wasn't going to get him anyway. A professional would have a dozen fake plates on hand.

The pizza—that was a different story.

If he could track that bastard, he'd make him pay for touching Sophia. Bring a shitstorm of pain to his front door.

He sat in his car once the valet brought it to him, searching up Bruno's Pizzeria on his phone. The location wasn't what he expected. It was in a rundown part of the city known for its high crime and drug infestation. It was under the Morenov umbrella. They had a lot of informants in that area because junkies were always ready to spill for quick money.

Hawk drove out to the seedy part of the city. It would be a cesspool at his time of night, all the criminals coming out to play. He only had one thing on his mind.

Bruno's Pizzeria was a beacon in the darkness, several patrons inside. The first "R" was burnt out on the sign, but the place looked better than most businesses on the street. He sat in his car, watching the people inside through the large glass windows.

After nearly half an hour of observation, he exited his vehicle and went inside the pizzeria. The scent made his stomach rumble, and sounds were everywhere—

orders and shouting from the kitchen, several conversations from customers, and the game on the television. No one took notice of him, which was always good in his job.

A teen boy behind the counter met eyes with him. "I'm looking for my friend. He was in here recently. Poor bastard got a bad cut to his cheek. Have you seen him around?"

"You mean Cayden?"

"Yeah, Cayden. We were supposed to meet up."

"Sorry, haven't seen him in a few days."

He nodded, keeping casual. "You wouldn't know where he lives, would you?"

The kid shrugged. "No clue. Maybe he'll be in soon. You can have a seat, if you like."

"Thanks."

Shit. At least he had a name—Cayden. Hawk rolled the word over his tongue, memorizing every syllable. It belonged to the man he planned to gut like a fish.

He noticed a woman looking at him from the corner table. Hawk approached her, pulling out a chair. She was easy to read, a local whore, no doubt.

"You know Cayden?" she asked.

"Old friend of mine. He never told me he had a hot girl like you hidden away." The woman blushed. Judging by the track marks on her arms, she was a hardcore user. He pulled out his wallet from his back pocket and slapped a fifty on the table. "Do me a favor and let me know where he lives. He probably forgot we were supposed to meet up."

She eyed the cash.

He slid it toward her.

"I'm sure he wouldn't mind," she said. "You're his friend, after all."

"He'll be happy you helped me out."

Once he had the address, he crossed the street to his car, driving the few blocks to Cayden's house. If he hurt one hair on Sophia's head, he'd make him die nice and slow.

The house was in disrepair, a real shithole. He didn't bother to hide his car. His heart raced, and a blind rage built up inside him. Hawk parked in front and went to the first door, noticing there was an apartment number. For a professional, he couldn't imagine the guy would actually live here. Maybe that junky had given him the wrong information.

He checked the mailboxes and noted "C.W." for the basement apartment. It could be Cayden's. He'd give it a shot because, at this point, he had nothing to lose. Hawk descended the concrete stairs and picked the lock. He drew his gun and pushed the door open.

Silence greeted him.

He flicked on a light.

Hawk had the right apartment all right.

There was a gun cleaning kit and empty clips on the coffee table, an overflowing ashtray, and countless pics of Morenov's place, layouts, security footage, and headshots. He bent down and picked up a picture of Sophia. She was a lot younger in the pic, but those big dark eyes stared back at him. He folded the photo and put it in his pocket, not wanting the bastard to have anything of Sophia's.

A cat peeked at him from behind the sofa. Hawk refocused, checking out the rest of the small one-bedroom apartment. He found more weapons, boxes of ammo, high-end surveillance equipment, and a kitchen full of booze.

No sign of Sophia.

He rummaged through more paperwork,

discovering "C.W." was short for Cayden Walsh. Did it even matter if he could track down every aspect of this fucker's life? If he killed Sophia, nothing would matter. He wouldn't be able to bring her back from death.

He punched his fist through the drywall, savoring the sting on his knuckles. He'd had one duty—protecting Vasily Morenov's daughter. Vasily was dead, and he had no fucking clue how to find Sophia.

Hawk dropped down on the sofa, trying to think like Cayden. Where would he take her? Why not just assassinate her in their penthouse suite and be done with it? Did he plan on torturing her?

"Fuck!" he shouted.

He wasn't sure how long he'd sat there, wondering if she was alive or dead.

His cell went off. "Yeah."

"Antonio Baretti Jr. My condolences for your loss."

The Baretti family had been rivals to the Morenovs for as long as he could remember. They constantly fought for territory, contracts, and supremacy. The fact the piece of shit was calling Hawk after Vasily's death was an insult.

"I thought you'd be celebrating."

"I'm not an animal. I had great respect for Vasily. That's why I'm calling."

"Oh?"

"You're hiding his daughter. I'd like to extend an offer of help in finding Vasily's murderer."

Hawk didn't buy it. Men like Antonio Jr. didn't live for good deeds. It was always about money and power. He was just like his father. "You're just doing this out of the goodness of your heart?"

"Friends are better than enemies, wouldn't you agree?"

"Cayden Walsh. He has Sophia. You bring her back to me alive, we can talk about friendship." He hung up the phone and took a deep breath.

He'd head back to the hotel and look for more clues. The video feed in the lobby would give him something he needed, he was sure of it. They may refuse to help him at the hotel, but he didn't plan on asking this time.

Chapter Five

The next morning, Cayden turned on the coffee maker, then took a cold shower. He should have woken up in his own bed, but he'd fucked up once again. This was supposed to be simple. Kidnap the girl, bring her to the room he'd rented, then finish the job.

He never hesitated when killing.

Numbing his emotions came easy for him during hits, no different than turning a light switch on and off. It was a safety mechanism he'd learned as a kid to survive being tossed from one shitty foster home to another. Some much worse than others.

He expected Sophia to cry and beg for her life. In fact, he'd been envisioning it all week. Instead, she challenged him. What was it about her that kept toying with his head? She was an innocent, but she was also Vasily Morenov's daughter. She was a complete contradiction.

Time wasn't on his side. Eventually her men would track him down, so he needed to deal with his problem. A problem of his own making. He pulled a smoke from his pack and lit up, taking a deep drag.

It didn't matter how cute and feisty she was, the girl had to go. He knew that. It was bullshit that he was second guessing himself this late in the game. He'd envisioned pulling the trigger, and it was pure satisfaction. The reality was nothing like the fantasy. Sophia wasn't what he expected of a mobster's daughter.

His cell vibrated. It was Randy.

"Your line secure?" Cayden asked.

"Yeah. You never called yesterday."

"There were no issues with our friend. He gave me what I wanted."

"Is it already done?" Randy asked.

He didn't answer at first. It was fucking embarrassing. "Not yet. It will be in about two minutes."

"I'd hold off. We have a bit of a complication."

Cayden leaned against the wall, exhaling clouds of smoke as he tried to ease his nerves. "What's the problem?"

"There's a hit out on you. Hot off the press."

He stood straight. "What the fuck? Who?"

"Antonio Baretti. The Morenov family probably paid him to get the girl back and make you disappear permanently."

"So they know who I am..." He said it more to himself, wondering where he'd fucked up. Vasily was dead, so who was pulling the strings now? He hadn't left any breadcrumbs behind. "Where did I screw up?"

Randy scoffed. "You're losing it, buddy. I'm just suggesting keeping the Russian princess alive so you can use her as a bargaining chip. Or not. That spoiled rich bitch wouldn't think twice about ordering your death."

It pissed him off that things had turned down a new, more inconvenient, path.

"Check out my place, will you? I want to know what they know."

"I'll head there now." The line went dead.

After tossing his phone on the bed, he went to the second bathroom off the living room. He stood in front of the door for the longest time, wondering what he was going to do with a hostage. Cayden rarely took people for ransom. He preferred find and eliminate contracts. Playing babysitter didn't suit him, but he also felt a sense of relief after Randy suggested he keep her breathing. Nothing made sense lately.

When he finally opened the door, he expected to find her curled up on the floor asleep. Instead, he had to duck to avoid being hit with a chunk of porcelain.

She screamed, rushing out toward him like a miniature gladiator. The pedestal sink was in pieces, blood specks splattered on the white tiles.

There goes my security deposit.

His body didn't even budge when she tried to strong-arm him. Cayden easily subdued her around the waist, hoisting her off her feet and smacking the porcelain from her hand. She thrashed, throwing up her legs to try and unbalance him, kicking against the walls. He forced her onto the sofa and pressed her face down, his knee on her back.

"Settle down."

"Get off me!"

He hadn't finished dressing, only wearing his jeans. What he wanted was to shove the barrel of his gun to her temple so she'd shut the fuck up. He flipped her around and shackled her wrists above her head. "You think you can escape? Think you can overpower me?"

She shifted her head from side to side, practically foaming at the mouth.

"Lucky for you, you're more use to me alive than dead at the moment. That can change, so calm the fuck down."

"You're hurting me!"

He eased his weight off. "We're leaving here. I don't want any trouble out of you."

"I won't go anywhere with you."

His patience was shot. He hadn't even had his cup of coffee yet. Cayden grabbed a handful of her hair, keeping her head bent over as he walked her to his bedroom. She stumbled and whined, struggling with her cuffs. With his free hand, he picked up his handgun from the dresser. He pushed her backwards, so she fell onto his mattress. Then he braced one knee on the bed as he leaned over her, the gun to the side of her head. He practically got a hard on knowing how close he was to blowing her brains in.

"You know how this works, sweetheart. I pull the trigger. You die. That what you want?"

She shook her head, her fire petering out to nothing.

About damn time.

"This is the situation. I don't want to be here. Because of you, I have half the city hunting me down. And I've missed my morning at the gym, so I'm extra cranky."

"You shouldn't have kidnapped me."

He tightened his grip on the gun, not appreciating her tone, and tempted to end this right now. "No talking." He stood back up, tucking his weapon in the back of his pants. Cayden removed her cuffs and chains. "Don't fucking move."

She lay there on the bed, rubbing her wrists, and watching him pull on a t-shirt and attach his harnesses. Staying in the hotel was too risky with a hit on his head. He needed to get off the grid for a while. Cayden had to gather information, and then he'd pick off his enemies one at a time until things were back to the status quo. He liked to live in the shadows, so knowing his name was public threw him way out of his comfort zone—and he put all the blame on Sophia Morenov.

He tossed one of his long-sleeved shirts at her. "Put this on. There're cuts all over your arms, and I don't want any attention drawn to us."

She sat up and did as told.

"Who's in charge now that your father's gone?"

When she didn't answer, he finished tugging on his jacket, then strode to the bed and grabbed her upper arm, giving her a sharp jostle. "Listen, princess, if you keep being difficult, I can make this very unpleasant for you."

She scowled. "Like killing my father and kidnapping me? I spent the night on a bathroom floor. What more do you have in store?"

Cayden smirked without humor. "Use your imagination."

Getting her out of the hotel without being noticed could end up badly if she made a scene. Considering how difficult she'd been, he didn't trust her to behave. If he killed her now, he'd have less baggage. He also wouldn't have collateral.

Decisions. Decisions.

It wasn't even nine in the morning, and the day was already fucked up.

He packed his duffel bag, shoving everything inside, grabbed his phone, and double checked the room. Before anything else, he needed to clear his head. He grabbed her by the shirt and led her to the kitchen, pushing her down into an empty chair.

Cayden ran a hand through his hair as he searched the cupboards for a mug. He needed coffee … and another smoke.

"It's me," she said.

Her voice surprised him. With his coffee now in hand, he sat down at the opposite end of the table. "What are you talking about?"

"My father's gone. That puts me in charge. I was his only child."

He lit up a cigarette, savoring his first drag as he examined the girl. She was twenty-four. And looked nothing like her father.

"You're not the one who put a hit on me. You were with me all night. There's someone else. Was it lover boy up in the penthouse suite?"

"He's not my boyfriend. And you shouldn't

smoke. It's bad for your health."

He exhaled, leaning over the table. "*You're* bad for my health."

The room was quiet. He sipped his coffee, going through his plan on getting them out of the hotel. He'd have to call in some favors. Antonio Baretti was head of a bigtime mafia family with a huge reach in the city. Cayden was a lone wolf.

"My father kept me locked up for my safety. He said men in his business with loved ones were fools. They were easy to exploit."

He set his mug down with force. "You referring to me, sweetheart? You think I fucked up by having people in my life I cared about?"

She shrugged.

"I did everything right. No family. No woman. They weren't killed because of me. But that didn't make it any easier."

"This is still revenge. When you love someone, it makes you weak," she said.

He grit his teeth. "And you're cold as ice, aren't you, princess?"

"Don't call me that."

"You're the Morenov princess, no? Or wait, you're the queen now, aren't you? You call the shots."

She glared at him, and if looks could kill, he'd be dead and buried. "I have nothing to do with my father's business, and I have no interest in starting."

"What do you want then?"

She paused, her mouth opening, but no words came out. Then she answered. "Love."

Twenty years ago, he probably felt the same way.

But Cayden had given up on love a long time ago.

****

She wasn't sure how long he was gone, but

Sophia heard the moment he came back in the suite. Her breathing picked up, but not from fear. There was something dark and brooding about her captor. He'd killed her father, so she should hate him. She did hate him. But there was more. She could see the hurt in his eyes and hear it in his voice because his pain reflected her own.

He pushed open the en-suite bathroom door. "Get up."

He'd cuffed her and left for about twenty minutes. Now he was back carrying a plastic bag from a pharmacy. He slid off his jacket, tossing it on the other end of the long double vanity, then began opening a box. She couldn't see with his wide back blocking her view. It smelled like chemicals. Her nerves picked up as she wondered what he planned to do to her.

"What's your name?" she asked.

"You want to know the name of the man who killed your father?"

"Yes."

He did a sideways glance towards her. "Cayden." She was shocked to get an answer from him. His voice was deep, and he never rushed his words. He reached in his pocket for the keys to the cuffs and released her wrists. "Take off the shirt."

She narrowed her eyes. "What for? You told me to wear it."

"I don't want it to get wet. Lose the shirt for now."

Sophia tugged it off, leaving her in her original t-shirt, and waited. Her arms were all scratched up from the porcelain shards. He patted the toilet seat, so she sat on it as instructed. Was he going to torture her? He was too good looking to be this evil. Then again, she'd never known a good man.

He draped a towel around her shoulders, then stood behind her, pulling her long hair free. When he ran his hands over her hair, his fingers smoothing out the knots, she tensed.

It shouldn't feel this good.

"Don't move. Unless you want this shit in your eyes." She heard a squirting sound and then cool liquid spilled on the top of her head.

"What is that?"

"They'll be looking for a blonde chick," he said. "You're about to go brunette."

She reached up and touched the top of her head, then looked at her fingertips. "Black? You're dyeing my hair black?" Sophia shouted the words.

"Relax. It's temporary color. You'll be back to your beautiful self in…" He leaned over to read the box on the counter. "Three to five washes."

He massaged her scalp with his strong fingers, gathering up her hair, coating it all in the sticky black dye. The smell made her eyes water. But she could only focus on the fact he'd called her beautiful, and he sounded like he meant it. Stupid to even feel flattered.

The man was a murderer.

Every man she knew was a murderer.

Her life was more fucked up than she realized.

"Okay, over the sink." He washed out her hair in the oversized bowl sink, the water turning black as it swirled down the drain. When he turned the water off, she wrapped the towel around her hair, scared to see herself in the mirror.

She removed the towel shortly after, her long blonde hair now deep black. The reflection didn't look like her. But she always did feel lost in her own skin.

Cayden used his thumb to remove a smear of dye from her temple. "It brings out your eyes," he said. She looked like a witch. He tilted her chin up, taking a good look at her new disguise. "Why don't you have blue eyes?"

She swallowed hard, her head still tilted upwards. Her father had blue eyes, but she took after her mother's dark brown. It bothered her that she didn't even have a picture, like her mother never even existed, but her father assured Sophia she was the spitting image of the woman she never met. It was the reason he turned on her when she'd matured. "I take after my mother."

"I never found anything on a Mrs. Morenov. She in hiding or dead?"

"You're blunt." She stepped back, twisting her head from side to side in front of the mirror. "I never met her. She died when I was a baby."

"Childbirth?"

"She was murdered. My father raised me."

He hopped up and sat on the counter. "Being an orphan isn't as bad as it sounds. Trust me, parents are overrated."

She ground her teeth. He couldn't make that argument when he was the one to make her an orphan. "You kill your parents, too?"

Cayden wet his lips, stared at her for a few tense breaths, then left the room. He called back. "Put the shirt back on and dry your hair. We're leaving in ten minutes."

Sophia leaned over the counter and stared at the stranger in the mirror. What was going to happen? Was Hawk looking for her? Was Cayden going to kill her?

Hawk had believed she was in danger. He said a hitman never left a witness alive as a rule. No matter how calm and human Cayden appeared, she knew for a fact that men in her world could turn their emotions off and do the vilest things imaginable. Trust was for the weak.

Once she'd blow dried her hair and freshened up, she joined Cayden in the kitchen. He was ready to go, his duffel bag already slung over his shoulder, his dark hair slicked loosely back.

"As of right now, we're a nice happy couple. No making eye contact with anyone. We just need to make it to my car in the sublevel. Understand?"

"And if I break the rules?"

He glared at her, the devil in his blue eyes. "Do you really want to test me?"

She kept quiet.

As soon as they were in the hall, she could taste freedom. Surely, he wouldn't make a scene if she made a break for it in the busy lobby. He held her hand, a little too tightly, as they walked to the elevator.

This time she paid attention.

They were on the ninth floor.

The elevator opened with a chime and one businessman stood in the corner. Cayden squeezed her hand harder, making her cringe, and tugged her close to his side. She hadn't realized how tall he was, so close in size to Hawk. If only Hawk was there now, her rock, he'd kill Cayden without a second thought and keep her safe.

She was tempted to meet eyes with the man from one of the mirrored panels. Would she be able to signal him? Would he even be able to protect her from a trained hitman? She'd probably just get him killed.

The elevator stopped on the third floor, and a tall woman with a red suitcase on wheels joined them. The clickety-clack of her luggage came to a rest as she settled near the far panel, facing them. Sophia was sure the woman could read her mind, hear her screaming for help even though her lips hadn't moved. If only she could make eye contact...

Cayden must have sensed her thoughts, or felt the growing tension, because he reached around and grabbed her ass, pulling her tight to his body. With his free hand, he cupped the back of her head and kissed her hard on the mouth. He had the faint taste of cigarettes and mint gum, but it was the brutal way he possessed her mouth that left her spineless in his arms.

The elevator kept dinging, but she didn't care. Her eyes were closed, her mind a million miles away. When he finally pulled away from her, she was speechless and stunned. She turned around—the elevator was empty, and they were on the parking level.

There would be no chance to make a scene in the lobby.

He grabbed her hand. "Come on, let's go. Almost there now."

She touched her lips as they rushed through the lonely parking level. How could he not be affected by that kiss? What the hell was happening?

Her father had kept her locked up like Rapunzel in a tower, so she had no experience with men, even at twenty-four. She wasn't good at reading people and had no street smarts or social skills. Her expertise was in university texts, painting, and the ins and outs of life in a fucked-up crime family. She was numb to killing, death, and weapons, but a simple kiss had managed to unravel her.

It was only her second kiss.

She licked her lips, trying to compare the gentle kiss from Hawk and the demanding one from Cayden. They were both perfect, leaving her raw and aching for more.

He pushed his fob, and a car dinged, the lights flashing briefly. Cayden opened the passenger door, moved some things off the seat, then motioned for her to sit. Were those bloodstains? He rummaged in the trunk before sitting in the driver's seat.

"Where we going?" she asked.

Cayden didn't answer her.

He started the engine and reversed out of the parking spot, paid at the exit, and then they were gone. Driving farther and farther away from the hotel, and Hawk, and everything she knew.

Chapter Six

Hawk rewound the security footage again, zooming in on Sophia and Cayden Walsh. They were only visible for seconds, exiting the elevator and leaving through the parking doors on the lower level. The bastard had his hand on her. And he'd changed her hair. Her gorgeous blonde hair was now pitch black, or maybe it was a wig. Hawk almost hadn't noticed them. It was Cayden's neck tattoo that caught his attention.

He slammed his fist down on the desk, the pens and papers jumping "Look at her, Vlad. Look what's he's done to her." The older man braced a hand on the back of his chair, watching the screens as Hawk played the clip again and again. "He's going to pay for this."

"Antonio's men will find him. It's what they do," said Vlad.

Hawk shook his head. "Why are they wasting their time and resources to find Sophia? Just to make peace? With who? It's not like the Baretti family to go out of their way if they aren't getting paid."

"Maybe they've changed their ways. Death can change a person."

He scoffed. "Are you fucking kidding me? I don't like any of this. Vasily didn't raise me to be a fool." He tapped his fingers on the desk. He hadn't gotten any sleep last night. He was too strung out, his mind scattered. "I have no idea where he's taken her."

"If he hasn't killed her yet, that's a good sign. As long as he's using her as a hostage, we have a chance to get her back alive."

Alive was one thing, but there was a lot a man could do to a woman and still leave her breathing. Hawk didn't even want to think about anything happening to his girl. The poor thing just lost her father, and now he'd let her down. He should have stayed with her and watched that damn movie, but he'd been weak—she alone made him weak.

He stood up and rolled out his shoulders. The security guard was still out cold, hunched over in the corner. He'd been lucky just to get pistol-whipped.

No sleep.

Sophia missing.

Hawk was going to crash hard.

He didn't trust the Baretti family, and one of his informants said a bigtime gang leader wanted Sophia dead. He was waiting on more information. So now there was a price on *her* head. Didn't they realize she wasn't a player? With Vasily dead, his empire died along with him. Hawk had no intention of running the business, and he knew Sophia wanted nothing to do with it, and she never had. Why couldn't they all celebrate that their biggest rival was out of the picture and leave them the fuck alone?

"I've already done what I can. That fucker uses a credit card or shows his face in any public place, I'll know. I'm going to get a drink, and then I'm getting some sleep. I'm no good with my head in the clouds."

"Yes, rest. Call me when you find out anything," said Vlad.

He nodded. "You still staying at the house?"

"We wouldn't want looters."

"Spread the word that Sophia isn't taking over the business. This power struggle is going way too far. Vasily's barely been dead a week, and the vultures are coming from every corner of the city." Hawk adjusted his jacket, then left the security office, looking both ways in the hallway before heading to the emergency door at the back of the hotel.

He walked down the strip, looking for the first

bar he could find. Hawk occasionally used alcohol as a vice, but he preferred the gym. Right now, with Sophia gone, he needed to forget it all. There was nothing more he could do until Cayden made a mistake … and he would.

It was just a matter of time.

After entering a dive bar, he found an empty stool at the counter and pulled out his cell. He ordered his first two drinks and called his informant. The place was noisy enough that no one would hear or give a shit about his conversation.

"Anything new on the hit?"

"Dollar amount just went up. Three million. Dead or alive," said Danny, one of his long-time informants.

"Why do they care about Vasily's daughter? She's not in the business," he said.

Cayden wasn't his only problem. Sophia was a shining target to every power-hungry bastard in the city. He knew of at least one credible contract for her life.

"She's the heir to an empire. That's a threat to a lot of dangerous people. So far, it seems only one has made a move."

"Send me the name of whoever put out the hit. If you don't know, find out," said Hawk. He put his phone in his breast pocket and swallowed the glass of mind-numbing alcohol, then the second. He tapped the counter for a refill, already feeling the burn all the way to his stomach.

Protecting Sophia was going to be a full-time job. If he got her back, it still wouldn't be over. Would they ever be in the clear? It didn't matter to him. He wanted to be her protector, and a hell of a lot more. Hawk needed to drink enough to dull his desires, to strip away every nasty thought in his head.

Sophia was his ward, not his woman.

Her father had entrusted her care to him, when no other man would do. That responsibility meant a lot to Hawk. The Morenov patriarch had saved him, given him a second chance at life.

He didn't deserve the honor. Vasily should have looked the other way.

****

Cayden hadn't been out to this end of the city in ages. He owned a few properties, but this one was the shittiest of them all. He bought the abandoned warehouse eight years ago to use as his headquarters when he was hired for a series of elaborate hits. He'd transformed the basement into a makeshift apartment, and he'd lived there for months. He still came by once in a while when he needed to ghost for a few days.

Before heading on the highway, he'd blindfolded Sophia. He didn't need her knowing any more about him than she did. His home had already been infiltrated and knowing that prick had been in his personal space rubbed him wrong. He still wasn't sure how he'd been tracked. Vasily's right-hand man was next on his shit list. He'd kill the bastard for free, just for putting him through this runaround.

He pulled up to the warehouse, the gravel drive crunching under his tires as he did a slow crawl. No sign of intruders, no cars, no life for miles. Many of the small square window panels had been broken, the big, industrial building an eyesore with the cityscape in the distance.

Cayden cut the engine and walked around to the passenger side.

Last time he came here, Frank Almeida had been alive. Now he was babysitting the daughter of his murderer. If there was a woman he should hate, it was Sophia Morenov.

Randy had been right, of course. This bitch wouldn't think twice about signing his death warrant. She'd probably been dreaming about it since witnessing her father's death. But that wasn't his fucking problem—an eye for an eye worked just fine for him.

"Get out."

She touched her blindfold. "Can I take this off?"

"No, leave it on." He grabbed her arm and pulled her along. She stumbled on the uneven drive, letting out little gasps each time she thought she might fall.

He liked to fly solo, and this dead weight had not been a part of his plan. Maybe he should make a fucking statement and send lover boy one of her fingers each week. That would put him in his place. Hawk wouldn't want his prize once Cayden fucked her up enough.

He unlocked the door and turned off the security system, punching in his code before locking the door again. The main level was littered with old lumber and broken machinery. Even squatters would find another place to sleep after looking at this shithole. He imagined it was once a thriving factory, but now it was just a relic from a time long past.

The lone door at the back led to the basement and his private domain. He unlocked the door, this one more heavily fortified, and flicked on the lights. Cayden led her down the narrow staircase, and she wrapped herself around his arm in fear of falling. When they got to the bottom, he tugged off her blindfold. Nothing in the basement would give away their location. And she wasn't going anywhere.

He pointed to the sofa, then proceeded to take off his jacket and toss it on the coffee table. All his equipment was covered in a thick layer of dust. He grabbed a rag and swiped it over his monitors, computers, and surveillance gear.

Cayden looked around the bachelor pad. Everything was as he left it. There was a mini fridge, bed, sofa, and every other comfort he needed for an extended stakeout. He leaned over the keyboard, booting up his systems.

"Where are we?"

He turned his head. "Far from home, little girl."

She narrowed her eyes, and he went back to his work. Maybe the Morenov family would pay for her return. He could turn an inconvenience into a payday. He'd need the added funds to get himself set up somewhere new. His basement apartment in the heart of the city had been home for years. It was in the middle of his stomping grounds and being forced out now that his identity was public didn't sit well with him.

"Why am I still alive? Hawk said you wanted me dead."

He sat in his office chair and twirled around to face her. Cayden leaned over, his elbows resting on his knees. "You're brave," he said. "But not too bright. You shouldn't be putting ideas in my head."

"Is it money you want?"

He smirked. "Sorry, princess, but you can't buy your way out of this one."

"Everyone wants something. Do you plan to keep me here forever?"

Cayden shrugged. "Maybe. That's really up to you and *Hawk*, isn't it?"

"You were worried about me going to the cops. I'm not a civilian. I've lived my life around crime," she said. "I know how to keep my mouth shut."

He reached around and hit a few keys to reveal the security in his apartment. After rewinding to the first intrusion, he hit play. Several large screens above him showed Hawk lounging on *his* sofa, petting *his* cat, then rummaging through *his* personal shit.

"It's too late for any of that, sweetheart. Thank your boy for that."

She watched the footage, her lips parted. Sophia cringed when Hawk punched a hole in his drywall.

"Thanks to Mr. Go-Getter, my identity is no longer a secret. That doesn't bode well for anyone in this business. If it wasn't for him, you'd be home by now."

"No, he bought me time. You weren't going to let me leave that hotel alive. I'm not stupid," she said. Sophia looked him right in the eye. "Is there any scenario where you don't kill me?"

He wasn't sure what to make of Vasily's little girl. She was fearless and kept trying to push his buttons. He had to remind himself this had never been about her. He'd entered the Morenov mansion set on revenge, on killing Vasily in retaliation for taking everything that ever mattered to him. He didn't give a shit about his men or his daughter.

She'd been in the wrong place at the wrong time.

Sophia was next in line to the Morenov Empire, so not his average witness. Her innocence was all an act he wasn't buying.

Now that his name was out there, he didn't really see the urgency in killing her. He was waiting things out, and expected this could end with a trade, both parties going their own way.

"He took my cat."

"What?"

Cayden stood up. "You better hope he doesn't hurt her. She's all the family I have."

Sophia actually kept quiet, which was nice for a change. He checked out his fridge, but there was nothing to eat. He'd have to get the place supplied in case this took longer than he hoped. At least his minibar was stocked. He knew for a fact he could live off booze and cigarettes for a damn long time.

He reached for a glass, but they were all dirty, so he drank straight from the bottle. "Want some?" Cayden held out the bottle.

"You're disgusting."

He sat on the coffee table directly in front of her, taking another swig, then licked his lips. "I know you're probably used to the very best." He waved the hand holding the bottle in the air. "And this is big time slumming for you. But you know what? I don't care about your fancy upbringing. Spoiled brats like you make me sick."

"I hate you," she spat. "You know nothing about me."

"Then tell me why I'm wrong."

"Money can't buy happiness. It can't buy love."

"Daddy didn't love you? He has men willing to die for you, so I doubt that's true."

Her jaw clenched. Cayden decided she was an amusement. Getting her feathers ruffled would be a welcome distraction while he waited this shit out.

She bolted to her feet and came at him with both fists, throwing her weight forward. He wasn't expecting it, and dropped his bottle of whisky, the glass shattering on the concrete floor. She pounded at his chest, arms flailing, all the while crying and trying to overpower him. He stood up, grabbed her around the waist and slung her over his shoulder. She kicked and struggled as he carried her across the room.

"You don't know me!" she shouted. "My father didn't love me. And I never wanted his money. You have no idea what I've been through!"

He dropped her down on his bed, shackling her hands at the sides of her face to keep her from striking him. Her eyes were red-rimmed, tears staining her fair skin. "You want to talk shit childhoods, I'm an expert. You had it all. Don't tell me you don't miss being queen of the castle."

"I never asked for any of it. I just wanted his love." She fought to free her hands, straining and getting more frustrated when she couldn't move. He kept her pinned until she lost her steam. Sophia started to calm down, trying to catch her breath. "I never got it. Thanks to you, I'll never get a chance to, either."

As soon as he eased his weight off her wrists, she tugged her hands free and twisted her body, knocking him to his side. She didn't know when to quit. They struggled briefly. He wrapped his arms around her to keep her immobile and had to use his foot to keep her from kicking. He could have snapped her neck or knocked her out with a single punch. Cayden wasn't sure why he kept humoring her.

"I guess you like being tied to a fucking toilet because it looks like you'll be sleeping on the bathroom floor again. The one here ain't as nice as the hotel's."

Their faces were inches apart, the volatile energy in the room fueling him. He could play this game better than her even on his worst day. She didn't know who she was fucking with.

"You took him from me," she cried, barely above a whisper.

Something changed.

Her strength shifted to vulnerability in the span of a second. She wasn't acting. Her tears were real. He could feel her pain, and she suddenly became more than just a wealthy captive. Cayden saw a new side to her, a broken side he could relate to.

"Behave yourself." He moved his foot and eased up on his bear hold, but he still had her pinned tight to his body. She wiggled her arms up until her forearms were pressed to his chest. She grabbed handfuls of his t-shirt, and her stomach lurched as deep sobs stole the last of her fire.

Sophia rested her forehead against him and cried, her body shuddering. "I can't do this anymore. I just can't." He leaned away, willing to give her some space. "No, don't leave me."

This chick confused the shit out of him.

"I'm the bad guy, remember?" He ran his hand through her black hair, noticing his shitty dye-job, her roots still a mix of black and blonde. One moment ready to kill, the next completely broken.

He didn't know what to make of Sophia Morenov.

****

Her father was gone. All his men, the ones normally in charge of protecting her, were gone.

Hawk was gone.

Sophia never felt so alone and vulnerable. Even when she was being whisked away after her father's murder scene, at least she'd had Hawk.

This was worse.

She was scared, tired, confused, and needed comfort … anywhere she could find it. Cayden was cruel and vicious, but men didn't turn cold if they'd had an easy life. Her father had stolen people Cayden loved, and it wasn't the first time her father had arranged hits on innocents. Part of her knew Vasily Morenov's lifestyle would come back to bite him in the ass. As invincible as her father appeared, no man could escape death.

What Cayden didn't realize was she wasn't like women from other crime families. Sophia wasn't an evil person, and she wasn't ready to order hits or sell her soul for money. All she ever wanted was love and freedom.

She was born into a lifestyle that never suited her. She always felt alone, never belonging, always searching for something more.

It hurt her when Cayden assumed she was a spoiled bitch. Sophia would have traded every last thing she owned for something as intangible as a real conversation, true love, or friendship with a person not paid to be nice to her.

"What happened to you, Cayden? What changes an innocent little boy into a criminal?"

She hated herself for feeling it, but she was falling for her captor. He was gorgeous, those narrowed blue eyes sharp and intelligent. She'd seen all his tattoos before, and just like with Hawk, they turned her on.

What happened if the bad guy could fall in love?

Could she change him, make him love her?

Sophia bit the inside of her lip. She was fucked up, getting wet for the man who'd murdered her own father. This was Stockholm syndrome at its finest, and she should know better. But she still didn't care.

"You're assuming I was ever innocent."

"People aren't born evil," she said.

She reached up to touch his face, craving to feel the dark stubble coming in, but he snatched her wrist before she could make contact. "My father was a big player in the criminal underworld. When my mother was murdered by one of his rivals, he went crazy, killed everyone he could before being taken down. No one remembered the baby."

His father was passionate, just like Cayden. Only he'd come out with a scar rather than a death certificate.

"That's why people in our world aren't supposed to have a happily ever after. When you love something, you become an easy target. I'm not even sure I know what love is."

"I never had a choice in life," he said. "I was only a few months old when the government stepped in. I ended up in the system, the ninth circle of hell, and you don't know what that shit can do to a kid. If I could cut the memories from my head, I wouldn't think twice."

God, she wanted to fix him, to heal him with her love. She'd always been a hopeless romantic. Sophia had tried to get through to Hawk, to show him how much she loved him, but he only ever pushed her away. Her fantasies never evolved much beyond her imagination.

Maybe she was destined to fall for all the wrong kinds of men, thanks to her father and the daddy issues he'd piled onto her.

"You're a man now," she whispered. "You can't live in the past forever."

"It shaped me into the bastard I am today. I can't change that."

She leaned closer to him. They were both still lying on the bed, her wrist still in his firm grip. She wished he'd kiss her. Was that insane? Sophia could already taste his lips, and she craved his domination. "Like when you kissed me in the elevator? Was that just an act?"

"It's all part of the job." He rolled off the bed, putting an end to the brief intimacy she felt growing between them.

He sat back in his office chair, the leather creaking as he spun round to face his screens. She watched him, angry that she craved his affection. Angry that he showed no interest.

Just like Hawk.

Sophia hated Cayden more than any person in the world—at least she should. She'd witnessed him kill her father, take everything from her with one bullet. The man didn't give two shits about her, either.

WITNESS PROTECTION

As soon as it was more convenient, she'd be dead.

Chapter Seven

How could a woman he barely knew manage to fuck with his head? His cock felt heavy in his jeans as he bolted from the bed. Cayden flew solo and wasn't the type to get seduced by any woman. One-night stands were as far as he committed, and even then, he rarely knew their names.

His captive was a mix of wildcat and scared kitten, one minute trying to attack him, the next seeking him for comfort. He was supposed to kill her or use her as a pawn, not dry her fucking tears.

Before he could think straight, his cell went off.

"I have a job for you."

Cayden wasn't exactly in a position to take on new hits, not with Ms. Fancy Pants in tow. "I'm laying low for a bit." He reached in his jacket pocket for his smokes and lit up.

"Oh right, Vasily's kid, eh?"

"How'd you know about that?"

Ricky was the underworld equivalent to a temp agency. He was one of the middle-men who hooked up people wanting someone dead with the people who specialized in getting it done. "Word gets around."

"Then you know why I'm unavailable."

"No, Cayden, you gotta do me this one. It's fucking easy money, I swear. It'll take you, like, two hours max," Ricky said. "I'm in a hard place."

He pinched the bridge of his nose. "Fine."

"Where you at, buddy?"

"Remember the old factory?"

"Be there shortly."

Cayden tossed his cell on the desk. He didn't need this right now, but if he pissed off Ricky, he'd never see a good assignment from him again. The sleazeball liked to hold a grudge.

He'd just taken a deep drag when something hit him in the head, making his vision swim. Sounds became muffled. His ears rang. He pulled himself together, gripping the edges of his desk, and whipped his head to the side. Sophia stood there with the base of his marble table lamp in her hands.

"Are you fucking kidding me?" He stood up, forcing her to walk backwards.

"I'm sorry," she said, still holding the lamp as if ready to hit a home run.

"Give it to me right now, goddammit."

She shook her head.

He snatched it from her hands before she knew what was happening.

Anger washed over him—hot, red, and blinding. It tainted his blood, made his heart race to a toxic beat. All the pain and hate and regret bubbled to the surface as it often did. His dark side wanted out, the one trying to escape since Frank's murder.

Cayden tossed the lamp on the sofa, continuing to stare her down and back her up. He wanted to strangle the fucking life out of her, but something inside him resisted. Not because of the money or the complications with the Barettis and Morenovs. No, it was something else.

Something foreign and intrusive.

She looked up at him with those big, brown, deceptively innocent eyes. How many times had his victims pissed themselves and begged for their lives? Sophia put on her diamond plating, but he saw right through it. She was a lost little girl, and just about every person he knew would eat her up and spit her out, no matter how tough she thought she was.

Part of him wanted to protect her from the world.

Protect her from himself.

"I thought you heard me coming. I didn't think I'd actually get a shot in," she said. Her chest heaved as she hit the wall behind her.

"Well, you did," he said, his voice controlled. "Now I can't trust you to have free rein around here."

"No, please. I won't do it again."

As soon as he turned his back, he'd bet his last dollar she'd try the same damn thing. "I should teach you a lesson, show you what happens when you pull shit like this."

Her lips parted, but no words escaped.

He fisted his hand into the hair at the base of her skull, making her neck crane back. She squinted from the pain but refused to make a sound. He lowered his head until only a breath away from her lips. "One minute you're ready to kiss me. The next you want me dead. Which is it, princess?"

She didn't answer. The sound of her heavy breathing dominated the room.

The buzzer sounded, loud and grating from the main doors of the factory. That bastard Ricky was quick. Cayden stared down at Sophia for another minute, making no move to answer the door despite the repeated buzzing. He ever so slowly released his hold of her hair. The tension in her shoulders eased, and she exhaled once the pressure was gone.

"I'll deal with you later. Sit and keep quiet."

Once she was on the sofa, he darted up the staircase to the main level and let Ricky inside. Business must have been good because the Italian's gut was twice the size.

Ricky followed behind him through the factory, each step punctuated from the mess of broken glass and scrap metal on the ground. "How's life been treating you,

Cayden?"

"Same shit, different day."

"I was sorry to hear about Frank and his family. That was messed up."

"Yeah."

He opened the door to the basement, half expecting Sophia to be ready to bolt, but the staircase was clear. She was sitting on the sofa where he'd left her. He ignored her and sat on his chair, rubbing the spot where she'd hit him.

"Aren't you going to introduce us?" asked Ricky.

"What's the code?" he asked.

Ricky gave him the code, and he entered it into his encrypted program. The details of the contract appeared on his screen. It was a quick find and eliminate. His favorite. And it was only half an hour away. He scanned through some of the details.

"Hey, gorgeous. My name's Big Rick."

Cayden turned in his chair. Ricky was only a few feet from the sofa. "Don't talk to her."

Ricky put up his arms at the elbows in mock surrender, taking a step back.

As he continued to read through the file, he frowned. "Why did you bother driving out here to give me the code? You could have used our secure line." He hadn't seen Ricky in the flesh for years. There was no need.

Ricky walked to the other side of the room near the stairs, motioning for Cayden to follow. "Listen, Cayden," he whispered. "I have a sweet deal. How'd you like to split three million dollars?"

He smirked. "What's the catch?"

"Here's the beauty of it. You don't have to do jack shit. Just give me the girl, then carry on your day."

The girl?

He froze.

That wasn't the answer he expected.

"What the fuck are you talking about?"

"Give me Vasily's girl, and I'll wire you your cut within twenty-four hours. You know I'm good for it," said Ricky.

Cayden turned and glanced at Sophia. She looked out of place, fidgeting with the decorative metal studs on the edge of the sofa. "Who the hell would pay that for her?"

"I'm not sharing my contact."

"Baretti?"

Ricky shook his head.

He would have been happy trading Sophia in exchange for his cat, Rosie. Now the ante had been upped. One point five million without lifting a finger. He'd be a fucking idiot not to take the deal.

"Sorry, Ricky. I'll pass. When this contract's finished, I'll give you a call."

Ricky grabbed his shirt in a tight fist. "I don't think you understand what's at stake here."

He looked down at Ricky's chubby fist, and the other man dropped his arm.

"Time to leave."

"This is a mistake, Cayden. Think about what you're doing here. Nobody's going to give you a higher price than that. She ain't going up in value if you sit on her."

He pointed to the staircase, but his defenses went up when he saw two sets of black boots descending the stairs.

A fucking set up.

"Come here, sweetheart," said Ricky, motioning for Sophia to come with a curled finger. "Don't be a hero," he said to Cayden.

He crossed his arms over his chest. "I assume my cut is out of the question now."

"You should have taken the deal, buddy."

Ricky's partners stood at the bottom of the stairs, their hands on the butts of their weapons. There was way too much tension in such a small space. He had to remind himself loyalty was a thing of the past, and everyone in his line of work worshiped the almighty dollar above all else.

Sophia walked across the room, all eyes on her. She stopped when she reached Cayden.

"Come on, now," said Ricky, holding out his hand.

"Three mill. *Dead or alive*?" asked Cayden.

Ricky's silence was his answer. She only had hours to live. He assumed it was one of Morenov's rivals putting up the bounty.

The fat fuck walked toward Sophia, irritation lashing in his eyes. She wrapped herself around Cayden's arm, holding tight, like a child seeking the protection of a parent.

But he'd taken that from her, hadn't he? She had no one to protect her anymore.

When Ricky reached for her, Cayden shook his head. "No touching."

"Don't be stupid. Give her to me."

Cayden didn't comply, so Ricky turned and nodded to his goons. They came for Sophia. These types of assholes were a dime a dozen. He began to see red, whisky-tainted blood pumping through his veins.

Just give her to them. Your problem will be gone, and you can move on with your life.

The first one grabbed Sophia, dragging her away. She screamed and kicked, digging in her heals while reaching back for Cayden. Odd how she'd seek out the man who'd killed her father. Maybe she saw him as the lesser of two evils. Either way, she wasn't his responsibility.

Once Hawk realized Ricky had her, the Barettis would refocus their attention, leaving Cayden off the radar once again.

"Nice doing business with you," said Ricky, following his men.

Cayden hadn't moved.

Sophia was a wildcat, squirming and flailing her body. The other man pulled back his hand to slap her. Cayden grabbed the Glock from the back of his jeans and put a bullet between his eyes before he could strike her.

His body crashed to the concrete like a falling oak.

Sophia screamed.

"Get her out of here," Ricky shouted to his last man standing, pulling out his handgun and aiming it at Cayden. "Stay back."

"Cayden!" she called as the guy hauled her up the stairs.

He shot the man in the calf, and he tumbled back, rolling down the stairs. Sophia fell on top of him. Cayden finished the piece of shit off with a head shot. Ricky moved quick, wrapping his arm around her neck, her back pressed to his chest. He kept his gun pointed at Cayden as he clumsily tried to get up the stairs backwards with Sophia as a human shield.

Sophia held Ricky's forearm with both hands to keep him from choking her. She clawed and struggled, gasping for breath.

"This bitch is already dead, so I plan to get paid. Since when did you grow a damn conscience, Cayden? You're getting weak in your old age."

"Let her go," he warned.

"Not happening." Ricky managed to get to the top of the stairs and into the factory, disappearing with Sophia.

Your problem's gone. Just turn around and forget this shit.

****

The man reeked of prosciutto and onions, and her stomach roiled. His elbow bent across her neck, nearly stealing all her breath. He was rough and callous, yanking and prodding her through the unfinished parking lot.

At first, she swore Cayden was going to save her, to protect her like Hawk always had.

But she was wrong.

She was being passed around from bad to worse, an easy victim now that her father's protective arm was no more. He'd kept her locked away, and said it was for her own safety.

Maybe he'd been right.

Now, on her own, it seemed everyone wanted her dead. There was nowhere to hide. She was tried and convicted by her name alone.

It wasn't fair.

But in the criminal underworld, justice was in the hands of the most lethal men. Survival of the most brutal.

He released his hold on her. "Maybe we'll be able to get in some *quality time* before I hand you over," Ricky said, his lips twisted in a sick grin. "You'd like that, wouldn't you?"

Sophia wasn't going to let this pig touch her. She'd die first.

When they got to his car, there was no sign of Cayden. Tears pricked her eyes, but she had no time for an emotional overload now. She had to be strong, to fight, to make sure she died a virgin and not some toy for this heartless thug.

He opened the passenger door and shoved her down into the seat, his hand lingering too long on her shoulder.

A shiver rolled up her back.

This was the end for her. Whoever she was being sold to wanted her dead. She thought of Hawk. Thought of the mother she never knew, the father she'd lost, and the life she never got to live. There were so many dreams that would forever be unfulfilled.

Ricky leaned closer and she tensed, but he jolted to a standstill with a throaty gasp, the silver tip of a blade appearing in the center of his chest. It was surreal. He stared at her with flat eyes, his life ebbing away as his shirt transformed from white to crimson.

She froze, too in shock to move or scream. So much blood. The same blood coating the marble floors in her home.

"You should have listened. I told you no touching." The dead body was cast aside, and Cayden reached his hand out for her.

Her father's murderer.

Her kidnapper.

Her savior.

She couldn't move. He hoisted her out of the seat. Her body felt like lead, and she was helpless in his arms as he carried her back to the factory. The scent of his woodsy cologne made her feel safe. She remembered Hawk carrying her out of her house on the day when everything changed.

Why did she feel the same security with Cayden? He didn't deserve her forgiveness. And she shouldn't feel such dark desires for a man she should detest.

But he'd come back for her. Why?

She could only assume he wanted the payday for

himself, not willing to share with anyone else. But she could pretend.

Pretend he loved her.

Pretend he'd do anything to protect her.

Sophia had a vivid imagination, and it was a delicious thought. With the amount of alone time she had growing up, a creative mind was vital to her sanity. It kept reality tolerable and kept the loneliness at bay.

He didn't set her down until they were back in the basement, his breathing not even labored after carrying her the whole way. Cayden sat her down on the sofa. She held out her arms in front of her, resting them on her knees. She stared at the bodies, then the splattering of blood against her pale skin. It reminded her of abstract art. Of death. Her mind fractured, that day coming back to haunt her again. Her body trembled involuntarily.

Cayden sat on the coffee table in front of her. "Shit." He took one of her arms and began wiping it with a damp rag. She watched the movement of each stroke, seeing the blood smear, then disappear. "You can't let it get to you," he said. "Being Vasily's daughter you should be used to all this."

She shook her head. "I'm not as strong as you think."

"You can sure put up a fight. Have you never seen blood before? I thought you were going to pass out."

Yes, she'd witnessed a lot growing up, even if her father tried to shield her from the worst of it. Some days nothing fazed her, and she was ready to take on the world. Days like today, she wanted to be sheltered, protected, and hidden from everything dark and dangerous.

Since witnessing her father's death, blood seemed to unhinge her.

"It reminds me of the day you killed my father."
She glanced up, meeting him eye for eye.

"You gonna remind me of that forever?"

He acted too casual about murder.

"That depends. Are you keeping me locked away forever?"

Cayden finished cleaning her arms. "A lot of people want you dead. I mean, a lot. There's a price on your head, and some pretty scary fuckers are determined to cash in."

"Like you?"

"This was never about money for me. This was me settling a debt, nothing more. All this other shit wasn't part of the plan."

"I heard what Ricky told you. Three million, dead or alive." She swallowed the lump in her throat. "Even you can't say no to that pay day."

"No? You don't know me very well."

He stood up and her eyes traveled up his body.

His hard body.

She licked her lips and looked away. "I'm hungry," she said, desperate to focus on anything but her twisted desires. "Do you have anything to eat here?"

"No," he said. "I can order a pizza. Do you like pizza?"

Sophia smiled. "Doesn't everyone?"

He sat on his office chair, spinning around to face her. "There's a place near me that has the best pizza. You'll have to try it one day."

"What's it called?"

"It's not a chain. Just a Mom-and-Pop shop." His brow furrowed, his mood shifting as if a page turned in his mind. "The man who mentored me growing up, his name was Frank Almeida. His family owned a bakery in my neighborhood. They were good people. Business was always a struggle, but it didn't get them down. Your father had them all killed. The entire family. *One, two, three, four, five…*"

Her mouth fell agape.

"That was just over a month ago. Now it's just me, but I guess it's always been just me. It was stupid to think I belonged anywhere." He ran a hand through the longer hair falling over his eyes. "I wanted to go back in time. To fix shit. To make sure they never died. I didn't know about the extortion payments. And I was too late to save them."

"I'm sorry." She wanted to scream that she wasn't her father. She wasn't a monster.

He focused on her, his blue eyes piercing. "I wouldn't be much better if I let Ricky sell you to your father's enemies, would I? I couldn't save them, but I could save you."

She swallowed hard.

"Do you feel better now? Did killing my father bring you peace?"

He smirked. "I dreamt of killing him. It's all I thought about day and night. All I did was plan that day. It was the only thing that helped me get through the grief. I honestly believed that bullet would bring me the best high in history. All it did was end my obsession, forcing me to mourn. Frank was the first person that made me believe I wasn't a waste of space."

"So we're alike, you and I. We both have no one," she said.

"And we both have a price on our heads."

"Who wants you dead?"

He leaned back in his chair, crossing his arms behind his head. "That would be your boyfriend Hawk, the one who broke into my apartment and stole my cat."

"If you let me go, I'll tell him not to track you.

I'll make sure he gives your cat back."

Cayden shook his head. "Maybe I'll keep you. I haven't decided yet."

"What does that mean?"

"No more chatting," he said. "I have three bodies to deal with, and I'm going to order a pizza."

Chapter Eight

They'd been holed up for two days.

Cayden found out that Ricky had been trying to cash in on an open contract for Sophia. Oscar Esperanza ran one of the largest drug cartels in their end of the country. He was a ruthless bastard, known for killing women and children as scare tactics to keep his men loyal and associates from screwing him over. The vacuum left by Vasily's death made everyone eager to fill in the void. Until the Morenov heir was dead, the three million was up for grabs.

"We can't stay here much longer," said Cayden.

Sophia was lying on his bed, stomach down. She'd been doodling on some scrap paper for the past hour. Her innocence was twisting his reality. "Why not?"

"Ricky wasn't even a big player. Others will figure out where we are. I say we leave Friday morning at the latest."

It was Wednesday evening, and he wanted to be gone before the weekend. Esperanza wanted Sophia dead, with countless killers looking to cash in on the big payday. Antonio Baretti and Hawk wanted Cayden. He was starting to feel like a trapped rat in his little hideout. It was only a matter of time until someone came knocking.

She sat up and crossed her legs, flipping her hair back. "What are you going to do with me, Cayden?"

When she said his name, it always hit a sore spot. Using first names was too personal. And the way she fucking said it…

"I'm not following."

They'd been playing house for the past couple days, and they were getting way too comfortable together for his liking. For a hitman keeping a captive, he'd get an

"F" rating.

"The people after me are willing to pay millions. If you don't want the money, why keep me around? As long as you have me, there'll be contracts on your head."

"Fucked up, isn't it?"

She sighed, dropping the papers beside her and standing up. "You must have a plan."

"Wouldn't you like to know."

"You got your revenge. So now you either kill the witness or set her free. Isn't that where we're at?"

His jaw tightened.

He hated being put on the spot, especially when he'd been trying not to think too hard on the subject. He couldn't kill Sophia.

What he wanted was to keep her.

He'd never had a family of his own, just the borrowed foster families. They had their own kids, their own agendas. Cayden had always been an inconvenience, a paycheck, a punching bag.

And worse.

He'd fantasized what life would be like if his parents were still alive, conjuring up make-believe worlds to dull the pain of reality. Those were childish games he'd grown out of. He'd been numb most of his adulthood.

Now, being alone with Sophia, he once again wondered what life would be like with a family. A family of his own. Women had never looked at him with love, just lust. The two were worlds apart. He was unlovable, but it didn't make the desire for it any less. A woman like Sophia was beyond him, a fucking mafia princess. And who was he? Nothing. A joke. The jester. He shouldn't even be looking in her direction. Not after what he'd been through. All his baggage and dirty little secrets would forever haunt him.

Then there was Hawk.

The hero.

Just hearing his name made Cayden's hackles rise. Sophia didn't deny they were an item. Vladimir made it clear that Hawk would do anything for Sophia, even die for her. Only a man in love would go that far.

So, he was between a rock and a hard place. He wouldn't sell Sophia to Esperanza. The only other option would be to return her to Hawk. Maybe trade for his cat and end all this bullshit. What he wanted was to keep Sophia for himself, to make her love him, but he wasn't a fool. He'd learned as a child that he couldn't make another person love him, no matter how lonely he was or how deeply he craved it.

It felt better when he didn't care.

Easier.

Simpler.

Cayden would wait out the next two days, and then he'd hand her over to her own people. He deserved to enjoy her company for a little longer. Her father had killed everyone he cared about, leaving him with nothing. He wanted his reward.

"You're too brave for your own good. You realize almost every road leads to you in an early grave, don't you? Unless, of course, Hawk comes and saves the day."

"If you wanted me dead, you wouldn't have turned down that three million. That's a small fortune."

He held out his arms. "I know I look like I crawled out of the gutter, but, sweetheart, I have more money than I can ever spend."

"Okay, so is this about your cat?"

He laughed out loud. She had no idea how fucked up he was in the head.

He kept up his walls, keeping impersonal. It felt

safer that way. She was the first female to make him hunger for more than sex. All the others were an irritation. Maybe it was because women usually pursued him, and he knew he could never have Vasily's daughter. "Sophia, why don't you worry about looking pretty, and let me worry about my next move."

Cayden walked past her and caught a glimpse of the papers on his bed. He picked them up, but she rushed up behind him trying to snatch them away. "Give me those," she said.

He held the papers out of her reach as she hopped up in a poor attempt to grab them, her hands all over his body. He was a good foot taller than she was. "Relax."

Cayden looked at the papers. She'd done a pencil drawing of him when he was working at his computer. It was incredible. She had a rare talent, and he was intrigued. "They're not yours," she huffed.

He sat down on the edge of the bed, getting a better look at her work. "Hey, you drew me without my consent." The shadowing, the detail, the skill … she was much more than the crime boss's daughter he'd expected. "You should be proud. It's really good. I didn't know you were an artist."

"I'm not. It's just a hobby. Well, I usually paint."

"You should be an artist."

She smiled at him, and it felt like a punch in his chest. "You really like it?" Sophia sat down beside him, her leg brushing his.

"It's like a photo. You have talent. I could never pull that shit off."

"Everyone's good at something. What are your hobbies?"

Cayden stared off into space, trying to come up with an answer. He came up blank. It was an eye-opening moment for him. "I don't have any."

"You must have something you like to do. Besides kidnapping girls, of course."

He scowled.

"What do you do for fun?" she asked.

He ran a hand through his hair. "Is fighting a hobby? When Frank was alive he coached me in boxing. Before that I just did it for money."

"Sure, if you enjoyed it."

Inner reflection wasn't something he'd ever spent time on. Life was survival.

Eat. Sleep. Kill.

He passed her the drawings, his hand unintentionally coming down to rest on her thigh. Her body jolted, and she looked up at him with those big brown eyes.

"And Sophia likes to paint," he whispered.

She nodded, the papers falling from her fingers like autumn leaves as she reached for the collar of his shirt. Her lips parted, but she had nothing more to say. She tugged him down, and for the first time in his life he was helpless to resist.

Sophia Morenov was too young, too innocent, too complicated.

He kissed her, if he could even call it a kiss. A light brush of the lips. A soul-deep connection. He barely moved, breathing her in, feeling uniquely vulnerable. God, he wanted to taste her, devour her, know every part of her body.

Cayden slowly pulled back. Her hand still clutched the collar of his shirt.

"Was that acting?" she asked, almost too quiet to hear.

"What do you think?"

She swallowed and moved her hand onto her lap. "It felt real, but I know it couldn't be real."

"Are you a good judge of character?"

"Not when it comes to you."

He took a section of her hair, now an odd caramel color as the dye began to wash away. Soon she'd be the blonde beauty once again, and he'd be a bad memory.

Like the box of cheap hair dye.

"Maybe it's because there's nothing inside me, nothing worth salvaging anyway. Be leery of men without hobbies." He winked and let go of the strand of hair.

"People change. I can teach you how to draw."

Damn she was fucking adorable. He began to regret kidnapping her in the first place.

"That's your thing, sweetheart." Cayden stood up and scrubbed his hands over his face. "Look, I'm not keeping you, okay. Friday morning I'll drop you off downtown and you can call up your boyfriend to pick you up."

Maybe in another life he could have had a woman like Sophia. But he'd done too much shit that kept him up at night.

"He's not my boyfriend."

"He's ready to die for you."

"Because he's loyal to my father. Hawk has some twisted sense of duty and feels obligated to protect me. I'm not sure why he cares."

Because Sophia was a light to their darkness. In only a few days, her appeal was obvious. Hawk must already be infected by her. Cayden needed to cut ties before his sickness was irreversible.

"That's good. You'll need a protector with the bounty on your head."

She dropped backwards, her body briefly jostling until the mattress settled. She draped her forearm over her eyes. "I wish I could go far from here. Far from everywhere. Someplace no one could hurt me. I never asked for this life, but I'm going to pay for my father's sins until I die. Which is soon, by the sounds of it."

He wanted to tell her that if she was *his*, he'd never let anything happen to her. If she was his, he'd have a reason for living.

Cayden kept his mouth shut.

****

"I have her location," said Hawk. He could hardly speak, his heart still racing from the new revelation.

"Where?" asked Vlad.

"Just outside the city. I'm getting my shit together and heading over."

Three days had passed.

Three days not knowing if Sophia was alive or dead.

One of his guys found Cayden's car by hacking a red-light camera, then traced the vehicle location. It was parked in the factory district less than an hour away.

Hawk was busy preparing his cache of weapons, and then he'd do what he did best and get Vasily's daughter back. He wasn't a praying man, but he asked God to make sure that bastard hadn't put a hand on her. Whether he had or not, he still had to die. Cayden had killed Vasily, the only man he'd ever respected. Then he had the balls to take his only daughter.

He must want something if he took her alive rather than leaving a body for Hawk to find back at the hotel. They'd been right under his nose the entire time.

"Give me the address. I'll meet you there. We can take him down together."

Hawk shoved a 9mm into his holster. "No, I can't risk him knowing we're coming. He could panic and kill her."

"You shouldn't go alone," said Vlad. "We have a

lot of men at our disposal."

The old man had been a fixture in the Morenov home for as long as he could remember. He'd helped Vasily train him. He was all Hawk had left besides Sophia. "As soon as she's safe, I'll call you. I promise, I won't fuck this up."

He put his cell away and slid the last handgun into the back of his black jeans. It was time to set things straight, to make amends. He'd paint the street with that fucker's blood.

The drive was quiet at this time of night. It gave him time to think and reflect. With the sun set, the lights of the city were a thin line in his rearview mirror, inky blackness all round him. Some days the darkness swallowed him, not giving him enough air to breathe. Killing helped him feed the beast, sate the evil growing inside him. Vasily raised him to hate, to break, to kill. It was his norm. The only glint of light in his world was Sophia—her innocence, her love of painting, her big, brown eyes. She kept him grounded. Reminded him to be human.

He couldn't lose her.

Then there was the day everything changed between them. That kiss had become his obsession. Her lips were soft, her little tongue teasing. She was fucking precious to him, the only woman he wanted—but couldn't have.

His sole job as her protector was to keep her safe, to carry on his duty even though Vasily was gone. Hawk's loyalty was stronger than death.

He stopped his car several blocks from his target. For the last mile, he drove in darkness. There were no lights on in the factory, but that didn't mean a thing. Cayden was a professional, so Hawk wasn't expecting a cake walk. He wasn't foolish enough to let down his guards until Sophia was safe in his arms. As he moved in closer, he spotted the car that had helped lead him here. He kept close to the building, his back scraping the brick as he moved to the entrance, his gun at his side. There was a video camera near the entrance, so he kept in the shadows. The only way this would work was with the element of surprise. No mistakes.

Hawk dropped his duffel bag, rooting through the contents to find his glass cutter. He moved painstakingly slowly, carving out the closest large panel and removing it with care. He peered inside, mentally plotting his path. There was only one door at the rear of the factory, so that was where he'd head.

He took a breath, leaving his bag outside as he slipped inside. His boots crunched on broken glass and metal shards. *"Fuck!"* he whispered aloud. Even the floor was booby-trapped. Every step was punctuated, making his journey through the old factory as noisy as a minefield.

He was more than halfway to the basement entrance when a car door slammed shut outside. A flashlight bobbed up and down beyond the dirty glass panels, heading towards the building.

A loud rapping echoed through the empty factory.

Footsteps pounded up the steps from the basement. What the fuck was going on? He rushed to the back of the factory, using the banging as a distraction for his steps. Only seconds later, Cayden appeared. He flicked a switch, a single lightbulb dangling from the vaulting ceiling giving a wash of light to the massive factory.

Sophia had to be downstairs.

He swung around once Cayden was near the main door, keeping his gun drawn as he descended the staircase. He never realized these old factories had basements, or maybe it was a bunker made specifically for hiding out. Everyone in this business was paranoid.

And for good reason.

The lights were brighter in the basement. It was nothing like what he expected. As soon as he reached the bottom, his sights were on *her*.

Sophia sat cross-legged on a sofa.

Alive.

His adrenaline crash made his vision swim. The relief of finding Sophia Morenov after days of worrying was surreal.

"Sophia."

She looked up at him, not moving, not speaking. He started to think she'd been drugged and didn't recognize him, but then she got up and ran over, throwing herself into his arms. He kissed the top of her head, holding her close. Breathing her in.

Hawk closed his eyes, savoring the high of having her back. The past few days he'd been a fucking mess, thinking the absolute worst.

"You found me."

"Of course, I found you, baby." He never wanted to let her go, but now they had to get out of the building alive. "Who's at the door?"

"Pizza."

He looked around the room. It was completely renovated, out of place in the basement of an abandoned factory. Pizza and takeout containers were piled on the coffee table. There was an elaborate, top of the line computer set up and a bed at the back, the blankets rumpled.

"Did he touch you, Sophia?"

"What? No."

He took her hand, leading her up the stairs behind him. "I'll kill him."

"Hawk, no!" She attempted to tug her hand back. "He didn't hurt me. I promised him you'd leave him alone."

"*I* never made that promise."

The fucker had brainwashed her. Cayden had killed her father, kidnapped her, and now had her showing him mercy? It didn't make sense. Not after how torn she'd been about the murders back at the hotel. She was young, impressionable, and not thinking straight.

Shots fired upstairs.

He let go of Sophia and grabbed a second handgun, holding both out straight as he walked up the stairs. Did Cayden kill the fucking delivery boy?

"Stay here, Sophia."

When he got to the main level, windows broke as more shots rained inside. He fired back blindly. Cayden was crouched down behind a machine, shooting at a different target at the front entrance. A body lay halfway inside the factory, blood pooling. Hawk made his way across the room. Then he saw who Cayden was shooting at—Vlad.

"Vlad, get the fuck out!" He was going to get himself killed. Hawk specifically told him to stay out of this. The bastard must have traced his car.

"Don't shoot," Sophia called out. "Don't hurt him, Hawk!"

He turned his head. She was following him, walking into the damn factory. "Get back, Sophia! Get the fuck back!" More windows shattered. Who had Vlad brought with him? A fucking army?

"Sophia, get down! Go downstairs!" Cayden shouted, then fired again at the entrance. Why did he care if his hostage was shot or not? After hearing Sophia, Hawk kept checking on her between aiming and shooting.

Vlad was behind the brick wall, occasionally firing inside.

A bullet whizzed by Hawk's head. He refocused, tucking his handguns away and pulling out his Benelli M4 that he had strapped to his back. "Call them off, Vlad!"

His old friend stepped into sight, then aimed in his direction, firing off several shots. Sophia screamed. When he turned his head, she was crouched down hugging herself. There was blood.

Vlad looked him right in the eyes and fired again.

Chapter Nine

Hawk rushed toward Sophia, scooping her up at his side and hauling her to the basement. Once downstairs, he patted her down. A bullet had grazed her arm, but she was fine otherwise.

"What's happening?"

"I don't know yet. I think Vlad's switched sides."

She shook her head. "That's not possible."

"Baby, anything's possible in this game. Stay here. I have to deal with this."

He ran back up the stairs, blasting the windows and entrance once on the main floor. Cayden was gone. Likely dead.

Shadows crept along the outside of the building. Whoever Vlad had brought with him meant business. It pissed him off that they had probably been part of Vasily's crew. He'd known Vladimir his entire life. He was the last man standing, and Hawk never expected him to sell out. If he needed money, Sophia would have gladly given it to him.

Hawk made his way to one of the back entrances, then rounded the building so he could get them from behind before they got inside. Hawk wasn't sure what the fuck was going on, but they weren't going to get to that basement if he had any part of it.

Sophia had been taken from him once, and it wouldn't happen again.

As he turned the corner, he practically slammed into Cayden Walsh. Vasily's murderer. They both backed up and drew their weapons, arms straight, only feet apart.

Neither of them moved.

"You have my cat."

Hawk shrugged one shoulder. "You have my ward."

"Maybe you're not the man for the job considering how easy it was for me to take her."

He had him there. Hawk had screwed up and was paying the price now.

"You kept her alive. So, why'd you take her?" he asked. "And who hired you to assassinate Vasily Morenov?"

"No one hired me," said Cayden. "That was all me. Vasily wasn't the man you thought he was."

He didn't have time to give him the third degree. If Sophia wasn't in danger, he'd enjoy destroying Cayden Walsh nice and slow. Make him feel the same pain he'd inflicted on him by taking Vasily and throwing his life into turmoil. He also had a laundry list of questions he wanted to ask, but now wasn't the time.

"I'm taking the girl."

"I know," said Cayden.

He narrowed his eyes. This wasn't what he expected from Sophia's kidnapper. "You won't get in my way?"

"I planned to return her in the morning. But I'm not so sure anymore. Those are your men in there trying to send her to hell, no?"

"I'd never hurt her."

"Neither would I," said Cayden.

There stared at one another. He had to get back to Sophia before Vlad's men.

"Back the fuck off."

They both reversed course, each aiming at each other's heads until on different corners of the building. Once out of sight, Hawk immediately rushed along the wall toward the entrance. Timing was everything. He could see Vlad almost at the basement door through the broken glass. He fired inside, but that only revealed his location to the firing squad.

111

Hawk dropped down to his back, reloaded his pistol and kept firing between his legs, hitting two right away. He recognized Jimmy, one of Vasily's hitmen, and shot him in the chest three times before changing clips. There were too many. He'd never be able to get to Sophia in time.

Panic crept into his heart at the thought of losing her. Failing her. Vlad wouldn't take her alive, and he damn well knew it.

He got back to his feet to peer inside the factory. Cayden was already back inside from the back entrance. Vlad took cover behind some machinery. As much as it killed him to do it, he had no choice.

Another bullet hit the dirt next to his boot. "Cayden! Take Sophia!"

It didn't matter if Hawk came out of this alive. She was all that mattered. For some reason, Vasily's killer had kept Sophia breathing, and right now Hawk didn't have a friend in the world.

He'd go down a martyr. Sacrifice himself for the family. For Sophia.

He took a few deep breaths, centering himself, then charged to the entrance with his shotgun, unloading the fucker on everyone in his way. A bullet grazed his thigh, almost making his lose footing, and another got him in his side. The darkness shrouded the wild exchange, the deafening noise making his ears ring.

Images flashed in his head—Sophia's lips, Vasily's dead body, and a blurry figure of his mother.

All became quiet.

He wasn't sure how many he'd killed or how much time had passed. Was he even still alive? Hawk brushed himself off, scanning the darkness. He limped forward, the gravel crunching beneath his boots. There were bodies everywhere. Some he recognized, others he didn't. Gunpowder clouded the air, irritated his senses. He pushed open the main door, and it swung briefly on its last metal hinge before falling inwards, creating a bold echo and cloud of dust.

A bullet pinged off the wall.

Vladimir was on the ground near the basement, clutching his stomach with one hand and haphazardly aiming his handgun with the other.

"Drop it," said Hawk.

He was in pain, tired, and done with the fucking day. Cayden was gone. Hawk wasn't in the mood for games or more gunshot wounds.

Vlad shot again, missing him by a few feet. Hawk pulled his 9mm from its holster and shot the old man right in the hand. He yelped, dropping the gun.

Hawk walked over, each step punctuated. He squatted down next to his old friend. "Why?"

"Three million."

"Fucking sell-out."

Vlad spat blood. "I'm over sixty. My boss is dead. What did you expect me to do?"

"Not kill his daughter, that's for damn sure. I thought I could trust you, but you're no different than all the others." Hawk's emotions bubbled to the surface, which only pissed him off more. Vasily had been like a father, and Vlad had been a constant fixture in his life, a man he trusted.

Now he had no one. Only himself.

Vlad gasped, hunching to the side and curling up his legs. He had a mortal wound right in the gut. Cayden had ensured this was his last stop.

"Hawk, I need to tell you something." His voice became more and more faint. "Your parents…" He began to sputter blood.

Hawk holstered his gun and grabbed Vlad by the

collar with both fists, lifting him partially off the ground. The old man groaned in protest. "What about my parents?"

A sick grin appeared on his face. "You think Vasily saved you? Raised you because he'd always wanted a son?" He let out a choked laugh. "I was there. We killed your parents because your father refused to work for us. Vasily was going to rape your mother first, but he heard you coming downstairs, so he put a bullet in her head."

Hawk froze.

"Vasily felt sorry for you. Thought it would be a novelty to train his own assassin from childhood. I told him to kill you, but he never did listen to my advice."

A frog built up in his throat, burning with emotion. His eyes watered, but he wouldn't blink and give this two-faced pig the satisfaction.

"All these years, we've kept it from you. I told him that if you ever found out you'd kill us all. He'd created a monster."

"Does Sophia know?"

He scoffed. "That little bitch has her head in the clouds. She actually believes her mother was killed by a rival when she was born."

In one motion, he whipped out his gun, pressed it to Vladimir's temple and pulled the trigger, emptying his entire clip into the piece of shit. Hawk dropped down and rolled to his back when it was done. He was covered in blood splatter, but too fucked to care. He exhaled, staring at the lone bulb swinging above him.

Everything was a lie.

He didn't know how to feel. What to think.

His pants pooled with blood, the sticky fluid travelling down his thigh.

Hawk had devoted his entire life to the family, to

Vasily Morenov. He fucking worshiped the man. His only wish was to be his real son, flesh and blood. He wanted to belong so bad that he never questioned a thing. Never asked about his real name, his birth family, nothing. He'd put one hundred percent faith in Vasily.

He'd kept his distance from Sophia out of respect. Duty.

If he'd known the sick truth, he would have told her he loved her. Everything would be different. He'd pushed her away, turned her down again and again.

Now she was in the arms of another man.

"Live by the gun, die by the gun," he muttered.

Hawk lifted his gun, holding it to his head.

What was the point anymore?

He pulled the trigger.

****

"No! Go back!" Sophia kept up the hysterics as they drove down the dark, deserted highway. Her face was red and stained with tears. She slapped the glass of the passenger window again and again.

"Stop it," Cayden warned. "He's the one who told me to take you away. He wants you safe."

"They'll kill him! You can't leave him there."

"He knows what he's doing."

She began to panic, hyperventilating, blood dripping down her arm. He never realized just how much she cared about Hawk.

No one had ever thrown a fit on *his* account.

Cayden reached into the center console with his right hand as he steered with the other. He grabbed a needle, pulled the cap off with his teeth, then plunged it in into Sophia's neck.

"Sorry, baby. It's for your own good."

Within seconds, she slumped to the side, her body heavy. He adjusted her into a comfortable position, then focused on driving.

There was no way Hawk was getting out of there alive. They'd been outgunned and outnumbered. That meant Sophia was his responsibility now. He'd never asked for this, but he'd be lying if he said he wanted no part of it.

Women never interested him. The whole commitment thing sickened him, so he didn't allow himself to get attached or emotionally involved. After living through as much dysfunction as he had, he wanted no part of family life.

Sophia, she was everything. She'd infiltrated his head, his thoughts, his desires. What was it about her that he couldn't shake? The fact he'd made her an orphan? Or something simpler, like the freckles across her nose or the fullness of her lips?

He needed to get them set up for the night. Even with Hawk down, Antonio Baretti would still be on the hunt for him. And the bounty on Sophia was alive and well.

No place was safe.

Cayden drove a couple hours outside of the city. He had a trailer on three acres. Another of his many hideouts. There was no lighting, and everything was overgrown, the weeds attempting to devour the silver bullet.

He cut the engine, the drone of crickets trying to soothe him, but that wasn't possible tonight. After getting what he needed from the trunk and unlocking the front door to the trailer, he came back and scooped up Sophia into his arms. He'd only given her half a vial, so she'd be coming out of her sleep within the hour. He settled her on the queen bed in the back bedroom and closed the door.

He crashed on the sofa and raked his fingers into

his hair as he leaned his head back. He'd lost so much in the past couple months—Frank and his family, his apartment, his cat, his factory hideout, and maybe his heart. This was bullshit. When would it end?

Cayden pulled out his cell phone and called Randy.

"Where the fuck have you been? I've been calling for days," said Randy before he could get in a word.

"I've been ghosting. You have no idea how much heat is on me."

"Oh, I have an idea. Half the damn city wants you and the girl dead," said Randy. "Where are you?"

"I'm not trying to be an asshole, but I wouldn't trust Mother Teresa right now. No one knows where I am, and that's how I want it to stay."

"What about the girl? She still alive."

"Yeah, I have her. I think her bodyguard is dead. Things got ugly fast."

"You know how much they'll pay for her now?"

He took a breath. "Three million."

"Did you get hit in the head? Turn her in and end this shit. Move to another country for a few years, if you have to. If her man is dead, there's no trade."

"I'm not turning her in. It would be a death sentence."

Silence.

"Where are you, Cayden?"

"I'm not turning her in," he repeated.

There was no way in hell he'd trust anyone at this point. Everyone was in it for themselves first. In his world, money was god.

"You make no sense. Explain to me why you're keeping her?"

"Maybe I like her. Is it so wrong if I keep her for myself?"

Randy laughed on the other end of the line. "Are you sixteen? This isn't a game. Shit, if you want a woman, I can get you twenty bitches twice as hot as her."

"You wouldn't understand. I don't expect you to, because I don't understand it myself. All I know is she's different. I won't trade her life for money."

"You think she'd be as generous if the shoe was on the other foot, Cayden? She's the daughter of Vasily Morenov. Whatever she's convinced you of is a lie. Trust me on this."

"This is the last time you'll hear from me for a while. Take care of yourself, Randy." He ended the call, squeezing the phone in his hand, feeling like the only man in the world.

He went outside and set up his perimeter tripwire and activated all his security measures. He hoped they wouldn't be necessary. This place was in the middle of nowhere, owned by one of his anonymous corporations, and he'd switched cars shortly after putting Sophia to sleep to be on the safe side. He finally settled inside and checked the security and trackers on his phone.

"Hawk!"

Cayden ran up the three steps and slammed the door shut behind him. He rushed to the bedroom to find Sophia thrashing about, having some kind of nightmare. He straddled her body, pinning her wrists to the sides of her head. "Calm the fuck down."

She opened her eyes, her chest rising and falling like she'd run a marathon. "Cayden," she gasped.

His nerves settled, and he lifted off her, sitting on the side of the bed. "Sometimes there are side effects with that shit. You'll be fine."

She touched her neck. "You poisoned me."

"It's not poison. It just calmed you down. I use it all the time," he said.

"Yeah, on people you plan to kill."

He got off the bed and left the room. She followed him, grabbing the walls as she wobbled slightly on her feet.

"You should rest."

"No, you need to apologize!"

He was not in the mood to humor her. And she was way too feisty right now. "Listen, princess, as far as I'm concerned, I paid back my debt in full."

"You think you can repay me for killing my dad? We're not talking about eating my slice of pizza here."

"So why am I helping you if I can never repay you? No matter what I do, you'll always hate me. Always blame me for taking your father's life."

The small trailer snapped with emotion. It was all coming out to air.

"Don't forget Hawk. You left him for dead and ran off like a coward."

He bolted forward, his hand to her throat. Something inside him stopped him from squeezing too hard. Cayden had killed men for so much less.

"This isn't even my fight. I could have left you at the factory to get slaughtered by your father's men. Or taken the bounty and fucked off. I've lost everything because of you. All because I can't kill you."

"Why not? You're a killer, aren't you?"

He turned around, massaging behind his neck. No way could he say the truth and expose his heart—she'd tear it to pieces. "I have a thing about killing little girls."

"Bullshit, Cayden. If you haven't noticed I'm not a child."

Oh, he'd noticed. She had everything he could want—soft rounded hips, perky tits, and long legs. He may be over a decade older than she was, but he didn't care about numbers as far as Sophia was concerned.

"What do you want me to say?"

"Tell me something real, Cayden. Something that won't make me hate you more than I do right now."

"Hawk's alive."

"You know that for a fact?"

"I don't play games."

She nodded. "Okay, that's a start."

"Let me see your arm."

He hoisted her up to sit on the kitchen table, holding her arm out to examine it. "Just a graze. You'll live." He grabbed gauze and medical tape from his first aid kit and patched her up.

"What now?" she asked, her anger subsiding.

Cayden tidied up the kit. "I have frozen pizzas in the freezer and a stove."

Her tension visibly faded, her shoulders slumping, her steam petering to nothing. She gave him a little smile. "Good answer."

A lot was at stake. All the *"what ifs"* were like an elephant in the room they chose to ignore for their own sanity. Sometimes you had to survive day to day or even minute by minute. She didn't ask more about Hawk, and he didn't worry about their next move.

This was a *minute by minute* kind of day.

They ate in comfortable silence. Then she looked for the bathroom.

"Out of order, well the toilet anyway," he said. "You'll have to use the outhouse."

"Outhouse? Are you being serious?"

"Too good for you?"

She scowled and left the trailer, the screen slapping back in place. There was no lighting outside, and she hadn't taken a flashlight. He would have offered, but she wanted to prove she was tough shit, so he left her alone.

He kept tabs on her. When she didn't return after ten minutes, he stepped outside the trailer and waited. He heard her footsteps. The glow from the windows would be her beacon in the darkness.

Cayden tossed a rock into the woods behind her.

"Watch out for the wolves!" he called out.

Sophia screamed and raced toward him, throwing herself into his arms. It felt way too good to be her safety net.

"I've got you."

She clutched his shirt, looking up at him. "I'm not used to the wild."

"Time to spread your wings."

He ran his palm over her hair. Cayden couldn't remember the last time he cared to comfort another human being. With Sophia, it came naturally.

"Will you teach me how to fly?" He became hyper aware of her hands on his body, their proximity, and the tone of her voice.

"How about we get a good night sleep first." He winked at her and pulled away.

Once inside, he went to the bedroom to change for the night, tossing his shirt into the hamper.

Sophia went to wash up in the bathroom. They needed to get some rest and recharge before they both burned out. A lot of shit had just gone down. Tomorrow was another day.

She came in when he was half dressed, only wearing a pair of grey jogging pants. Sophia leaned against the doorframe, combing her fingers through her hair. "Were there really wolves out there?"

He approached the door, towering over her. Cayden slid his hand under her hair and cupped the back of her neck. His urge for physical contact overwhelmed him. The fact she didn't push him away only compounded the desire. "There are a lot of scary things out there."

"Will you protect me?"

He stared down at her. "What if I'm the worst of them?"

"You're not," she said.

She was destroying him, making him want something unattainable. "Really?" He pinched her sides with both hands, making her squeal. Cayden made growly wolf sounds as she crawled on his bed to escape him, but he pulled her legs, bringing her closer. He tickled her until she laughed uncontrollably, barely able to breathe.

Laughter.

It was a beautiful sound.

Something he'd missed since losing Frank and his family. Life had gotten way too damn miserable.

"Cayden!"

He held off long enough for her to catch her breath, continued, then stopped again.

"No more," she panted, her palms up on his chest.

He was on all fours with her body beneath him. Her eyes roamed over his bare chest. She licked her lips.

"But you're not afraid of anything, are you?"

"Just tickling. It's my weakness."

He smirked, starting up again, just enough to make her giggle. His fingers lingered on the skin at her side. "Then behave or I can go all night long."

She wet her lips, the humor fading away.

"Can you really?" she whispered.

Fuck, she was playing with fire. Her hair was mostly blonde now, her dark eyes piercing in the dim room. "Guess you'll never know."

She frowned. "Why not? Because of my father?"

"Because you're too good for me."

Sophia reached up and cupped his cheek, then scraped her nails along his stubble. "Don't let anyone fool you. I'm just an ordinary girl."

"And you love Hawk."

"Can't I love two men?"

He scoffed. "You don't love me, Sophia. Like every other woman, you don't realize it, but you want to use me. I'm not worth keeping."

****

Her womb coiled tight. Cayden's strong arms supported his weight on either side of her head. He was ripped and covered in ink. Her mouth salivated, craving to trace her tongue over every dark tattoo. Waves of heat and need washed over her, but he kept shutting her down. His reluctance made her more desperate to win.

Right now, she didn't want to think about death, the future, or all the nightmares strung together that she called life. What she wanted was to forget it all.

To feel love.

To at least pretend it was love.

To know a man's body.

"Don't refuse me, Cayden. I don't think my heart could take it."

He did a half push-up, his biceps bulging as he slowly lowered over her without making physical contact. He took a deep breath at her neckline, exhaling in almost a growl.

"If you knew everything about me, I guarantee you wouldn't feel the same."

"Then tell me." She turned her head to the side and kissed his forearm. "It can't be worse than what I already know."

"It is."

She began to unbutton her shirt. It was one of his since they'd been staying at his place for days. His eyes darted to the white lace of her bra as the shirt opened. He used his thigh to part her legs, dropping his hips against hers.

Sophia cried out, his hard cock pressing unforgivingly against her aching pussy. It felt so damn good. And she wanted it all.

The stress of the day, the horrors she wanted to forget, everything transformed into a sexual tension that bound her tight. She needed this. Needed Cayden.

Even with the minimal lighting, his blue eyes stole her breath away as he looked down at her without humor. "Lucky for you, I'm not that much of a bastard. I'm not going to fuck you."

"You're cruel. Is it because I'm a virgin?"

He smiled, then licked his lips, making her stomach flutter. "Are you now?"

"Please, Cayden. I need you."

He sat up, kneeling between her parted legs. He ran his hands over her thighs, making skitters dance along her skin. "I like when you beg."

"*Please*," she repeated.

He shook his head. "Trust me, you'd regret it in the morning."

She squirmed. He had no idea how desperate she felt. Her attraction for Cayden had her hot and throbbing. She wanted him all over her, his cock inside her. Sophia reached between her legs, but he grabbed her wrist. "You're killing me," she said.

His rock-solid control turned her on. Why did he keep resisting? A hitman for hire shouldn't have a glowing code of ethics. "I'll take away the ache, but that's it."

Sophia had no clue what that entailed, but she nodded eagerly.

"Take your pants off."

STACEY ESPINO

She shimmied out of her yoga pants, leaving her in just her little lace panties.

"Lose those, too."

Sophia swallowed hard, her courage slowly slipping away. She'd never been naked like this in front of a man. He knelt on the floor near the edge of the bed and pulled her down so his head was between her legs.

"Cayden, don't hurt me."

"I'll never hurt you. Just relax. I'll do all the work."

He ran a finger along her slit, moist from her arousal. She gasped and arched up, his intimate touch new and thrilling. "I want you, Cayden."

"Hush now. I haven't started yet."

His touch was soft and gentle, so different than how he'd treated her when he'd first kidnapped her. She trusted him. She closed her eyes and melted back against the mattress.

When he licked her pussy with his tongue, she pushed up on her elbows and looked down at him. It felt dirty and addictive. He sucked her with those thick lips, exploring with his tongue. Every move was electric, sending spikes of pleasure rocketing through her body.

He caught her watching. "Don't like it?" he asked.

She didn't realize how labored her breathing was until she tried to speak. "I love it."

He kissed her inner thigh. Those broad shoulders keeping her spread wide open. "You have a pretty little pussy."

Every time he complimented her, her heart swelled a little more. He suckled on her clit, making her pant and grab the sheets. The pressure built and built until she thought she'd lose her mind. Cayden had a whole set of skills she was quickly learning to appreciate.

He was merciless.

His rough stubble scraped her sensitive inner thighs, but it felt perfect. He made these masculine sounds of approval that turned her on even more. Wild like a wolf.

Her body coiled tighter. He never stopped or gave her respite, even when she begged. She kept saying his name like a mantra, losing all inhibitions as he picked up the pace, devouring her pussy, his strong hands cupping her ass.

"Shit," she muttered.

Every muscle in her body stiffened as a heat she'd never known blossomed deep in her cunt, then detonated, taking her by surprise. Waves of heat and raw bliss crashed through her. She cried out, grinding against Cayden's face as she rode out her orgasm. It was incredible and satisfied the annoying ache.

Her body felt heavy and spent. She was completely boneless.

Cayden stood up, his joggers low on his hips. She could see the diagonal outline of his hard cock in his pants. He was huge. She still wanted him.

"You can take the bed." He turned to leave the bedroom.

"That's it?" she called out.

She only heard his voice. "Told you I wasn't a bastard."

Sophia punched the mattress in frustration. She wanted more. Wanted his love. Kisses. Body. Passion. Everything. Not just quick sexual relief.

It scared her to think that when this was over, he'd walk out of her life forever. They had nothing to connect them other than death, contracts, and revenge. The thought of never seeing Cayden again made her anxious.

She was falling in love with the enemy.

Chapter Ten

Five days in paradise.

Cayden didn't care about money and what it could buy. What he wanted was intangible. Unattainable. After skating through life, each dark patch thinning the ice, he'd been close to drowning.

Then Sophia and her sweet innocence pulled him to the surface.

Now he was lost.

She trusted him, sought him for comfort, made him feel like he mattered. He'd trade everything he had for another day with her. But good things never lasted. It was time to return his prize to the rightful owner.

He'd put a tracker on Hawk's car when he left the factory. It would allow him to find Hawk after the melee, because right now Cayden and Sophia were off the grid and untouchable. Not even Hawk and all his hackers would be able to find them here.

"What do you think?"

Sophia sat on a stool in front of a makeshift easel he'd made for her out of scrap wood. Her happiness had taken over his life. The past week had felt like a hundred years, and it was hard to imagine life without her. But every day would only make the break harder.

She'd almost finished her painting. A nature scene. He stood behind her, not focused on her art, but her body. She straddled the stool in a pair of his black boxer briefs and one of his white undershirts. It had been wickedly hot, and his A/C unit was on the blink. It had been torture watching her saunter around half naked. She didn't realize how much she affected him.

He'd tossed and turned the past several nights, remembering the taste of her pussy, the sound as she cried his name. He wanted to be a bastard.

"Nice," he said.

"I wish I had blue."

"Sorry, sweetheart, you're lucky I found that stuff in the shed."

"It's so hot," she said, touching up some realistic leaves on a tree with her paintbrush. He loved her passion and devotion to her art. He didn't have anything like that in his life. There were so many layers to Sophia Morenov, and he wished he could have discovered them all. But their time together was running short.

He gathered her hair, allowing the air to hit her shoulders. He trailed his fingers through her hair, down her neck, and along her arm.

She set the paintbrush down. "That feels good."

Cayden leaned down and kissed her shoulder. He shouldn't, but he did anyway. She turned her head, and after a brief pause, they kissed. Really kissed. She swiveled around, wrapping her arms around his neck, deepening the kiss. She was eager, as if waiting for this moment since arriving. He hadn't planned on this, had wanted to keep avoiding intimacy, but Sophia was his kryptonite.

She stood up, then climbed the stump so they were almost face to face. He wrapped his arms around her waist, keeping her close, loving the feel of her in his grasp. When he slid his tongue along the seam of her lips, she opened for him. He couldn't get enough of her, kissing her until the whole world went away.

Hungry.

Desperate.

This kiss split him down the center. He was falling for her hard.

He lifted her up under the shoulders and did a spin with her, before resting her back on the stump. She was blonde again, her hair fanning around her like a fucking angel.

Cayden loved her. With every fiber of his being.

He didn't even care if his heart got broken. All he had was today. He was going to enjoy their time while it lasted.

"You're so strong."

He moved his hands lower, cupping her ass and squeezing. Cayden kissed behind her ear, then down her neck. She tossed her head to the side, giving him better access. He'd never wanted anything more. Even his revenge paled in comparison.

If he fucked her, he'd never be able to let her go. Could she even love a man like him?

"Cayden…"

"What is it, baby?"

"Are you ever going to leave me?"

He pulled back and observed at her. Her pink lips were swollen from kissing. "Where am I going to go?"

"After. When it's time to go back to real life. Will you forget me?"

"I'll never forget you."

Her eyes glistened, and a tear rolled down her cheek, as if she knew what he was thinking. "But you'll go back to your life." She hugged him around the neck. Sophia whispered in his ear. "Please say you'll never leave me."

"You feel that way now. Feelings change. People change."

She shook her head.

He'd killed her father while she watched. He'd kidnapped her, planned to kill her, and had treated her like shit. Cayden didn't deserve her, and if she thought there was something between them it was just her grief playing tricks on her. They were in their own bubble of space and time. When they left this hideaway, things would change.

Cayden would kill Esperanza and every single fucker looking to hurt her, so then she'd be safe. She had the whole world ahead of her, and he'd give it to her. But she didn't want him.

Not really.

She smoothed her hand over his bare shoulder, her eyes following the movement. With a fingertip, she traced the patterns of his tattoos. "I want this body. I want it to be mine," she said.

Damn, how could she make his cock harder from just a few words?

"I want you to fuck me."

"Sophia, watch your damn mouth." He hoisted her up, and she wrapped her legs around his waist. He carried her to the trailer, but instead of entering, he pressed her against the cool metal exterior.

Control yourself, Cayden.

She gasped. "That's cold. It feels good." Sophia wasn't wearing a bra under his wife-beater, and her nipples pebbled. "How old are you?"

"Thirty-five."

"Do you know how old I am?"

"I know everything about you."

"Not everything."

He tilted his head. "What am I missing?"

"You know facts and figures. Not my thoughts. Not my heart."

Cayden wanted to know it all. He wanted to run away with her, fuck her day and night, and never let her go. But this was a fantasy. It was smarter for him to stay as detached as possible. It would save him a lot of grief in the end.

He'd checked up on the tracker he'd put on Hawk's car. It was active. He'd never stop until he had

Sophia back. Cayden knew it because, if she was his, he'd travel heaven and earth to find her.

He set her to her feet, trying to distance himself. She smiled, taking his hand, leading him towards the woods.

"Where we going?"

"I want to play a game," she said. "Truth or dare."

"I don't like that sound of that."

She straddled a fallen log and patted it, motioning for him to do the same. Facing each other, less than a foot separating them, she ran her hand along his jawline. She had no fear of him, and it was refreshing. "Truth or dare, Cayden?"

He exhaled. "Truth."

"Have you ever been in love before?"

"No."

She smirked, clearly liking his answer. "Your turn."

He didn't want to play this game. It could be dangerous. "Truth or dare."

"Dare."

"Show me your tits."

This appeared to shock her. Which was the point, so she'd give up this silly game. Her mouth parted, and she licked her lips. She tugged the undershirt up and clutched it in her hands.

Fuck, her tits were perfect. Soft and sloping out into tempting little peaks.

He ran the backs of his fingers along the outside of her breast, watching her expression and the change in her breathing before she pulled the shirt back down.

His cock turned hard as oak. Such a tease.

"Truth or dare," she said.

"Truth."

"You can't use the same one," she said.

"My choice. You can't make the rules."

"Fine." She bit her lip, thinking hard. "What was the happiest day of your life?"

He didn't need to think on this one.

"Today. Being here with you."

She ran her thumb along his lips, leaning closer, but he continued. "Truth or dare."

"Truth."

"Do you love Hawk?"

She froze, then hugged herself. "Don't ask me that."

"It's your game, Sophia. Simple question."

Her playfulness vanished, leaving her a feather on the wind.

"I love *you*, too," she whispered.

He stood up and returned to the trailer, letting the screen door slam shut behind him. He couldn't do this. It was bullshit. Why was he so fucking angry?

Cayden had perfected the art of staying impersonal, keeping up his walls, and numbing emotions. Social workers listed him as a sociopath, but they didn't know the truth. They knew what he wanted them to believe.

Why did he care so much about Sophia? His heart felt like it was black and crumbling. He hated feeling like this.

She followed him into the trailer. "Cayden."

He whirled on her, a finger in her face. "You don't love me. Understand? Never say that shit again."

"What's so wrong with that?"

"Where would I even start? You can't love two men, Sophia. And you sure as hell can't love me."

He needed to get away from her to clear his head. Cayden grabbed a pack of smokes from the cupboard, pulling one out and putting it between his lips. He became frustrated when he couldn't find a lighter, sifting through the drawers and slamming them shut.

"I'm sorry," she said. "Please don't be mad at me." She ran both of her hands up his back, kissing his shoulder blades. He closed his eyes briefly, addicted to her touch. "I do love you."

He pulled away. "You don't know what love is, little girl. Let me guess, you tell the same shit to every man so you can get your way."

"Stop it."

He didn't believe her.

Felt like she was laughing at him.

Conning him.

Especially if she claimed to love Hawk, too. He'd gone through thirty-five years without hearing those words.

"This arrangement isn't working," he said. "Tomorrow I'll bring you to Hawk."

"And what about you?"

"Send me an invite to the wedding." He went to the bedroom, needing to get away from her. Of course, she was on his tail.

"Why are you being an asshole?"

"When did I claim to be otherwise? I'm a fucking murderer. I'm not a good man."

"You are. This is my fault."

He threw up his hands and sat on the edge of the bed. Why didn't she give up on him? Everyone else did.

She stood between his legs and pulled his head to her chest. He wanted to resist, but he was tired right down to the marrow. He could feel the softness of her breasts against his cheek.

"You don't have to be the tough guy every minute. You're allowed to have feelings, Cayden. It doesn't make you weak."

He listened to the sound of her heart beating. It calmed the beast.

Cayden wanted her to choose him over Hawk, but he'd never say it out loud. Her rejection would destroy him. Loving her back meant he left himself vulnerable. He was scared to death to get too close. To show her just how fucking needy he was for her love.

The pain of losing Frank and his family was excruciating because he'd allowed himself to care. If he allowed himself to fall in love with Sophia, it would fucking kill him to lose her.

"Sophia, I killed your father. You don't think that'll come up again? You'll always resent me."

"I don't want to talk about that now."

"Because this place isn't real. It's a fantasy where we get to forget the world," he said. He wanted her to understand that her love was conditional.

It was the only brand he knew.

****

She ran her hands through his hair, forcing his head back so he could look up at her. The corners of his blue eyes crinkled. "Fine. Let's not talk about real life or love. What makes you comfortable, Cayden?"

"This. Holding you."

He could say anything he wanted, but she knew the truth. Despite the fact he'd killed her father, she'd fallen for him, every broken piece. She had to come to grips with it all, to mourn, to sort through all her emotions at some point. In the end, she'd have to get over it—the anger, the hate, the memories.

She had to get through to Cayden before their stay at the trailer was over, as otherwise she could lose him forever. She couldn't lose him. There was a darkness inside him that had to be unleashed before he could heal.

Sophia wasn't afraid.

"What else?" Sex had to be the answer. It could bond them. He kept avoiding the topic, only taking things so far during the past week before pulling away. Why was he being a gentleman? She wasn't refusing him. And he had nothing to lose.

Sophia pushed him down to his back, his feet still on the floor. She ran her hands down his chest, over his hard abs, and slipped her fingers under the edge of his shorts. "Sophia…"

"Don't move," she warned. She ran her fingertips over the outline of his erection, feeling it firm up more under her touch.

He snatched her wrist. "Cut it out, Sophia."

"Why? I want this to be mine," she said.

"You can't have everything you want."

She scowled. "Are you saving yourself for someone else?"

"That ship sailed a long time ago," he said. "Sex I can handle, but with you … with you it would be different."

Her heart pounded in her chest. Could he love her back? Was it possible to win him over, to pull him back into the light?

He sat back up. Her pussy throbbed every time she saw how ready he was for her, and how easily he could deny himself. The men her father hired were all pigs. Cayden was different.

She sat on his lap. "What about a kiss?" She ached for him. All of him, inside and out.

Cayden cupped the side of her face and kissed her, deliciously thorough. The way he kissed was pure ownership, a complete domination. He turned her on, making her think of all the dirty things he could teach her. She remembered his mouth against her pussy, and she squirmed on his lap.

"How many women have you been with?"

He nipped her lip. "Doesn't matter. They were nothing to me."

"And me?"

"You're the Morenov princess."

She pulled back. "I told you not to call me that."

He ran the pad of his thumb along her lower lip. "*My* princess."

Her lips were dry, her entire body heating up. God, she wanted to be his.

She gasped when an alarm sounded in the other room. Cayden was on his feet within seconds, rushing to shut the blinds. "Get down. Don't move."

"What's going on?"

"It's my tripwire." He opened the closet and pulled out an assault rifle. Cayden knew how to handle his weapons. "I'll take care of it. I won't let anything happen to you."

She was on the floor, stomach down, watching him rush to the door of the trailer. First, he'd kidnapped her; now he wanted to protect her. All she could think about was him getting hurt.

A few tense minutes later, she heard him call her.

She bound out of the trailer. "It was just a deer." He pointed to the white tail scampering off. It was beautiful. This entire week in the wilderness had been an experience in itself.

The smile on her lips faded when someone grabbed her from behind, pulling her backwards, a gun to her head.

"Cayden!"

He whirled around, immediately bringing his rifle up into a shooting stance. "Let her go, asshole."

"Back off. I don't care about you. I just want

Vasily's girl."

Cayden didn't look afraid. Was he afraid of anything? "How'd you find us here?"

The man holding her chuckled. "It wasn't easy, that's for damn sure. There were seventeen stolen cars within thirty clicks of the factory the day you took her. Some were older models with no GPS, others were dead leads or already stripped. Then I traced the last known location of this one." He nodded to the car they'd driven here in almost a week earlier. "And here I am. Patience pays off."

"You alone?"

"Don't try anything funny," said the man.

"I just want the girl."

He laughed. "I don't plan to split the bounty, if that's what you're thinking. Not with you or anyone else."

"Last chance. Let her go."

"Fuck you."

Sophia screamed when Cayden's gun fired, deafening in the natural calm. A bullet hit the man in the leg, his weight dipping, and then she felt the spray of blood as a head shot took him out. She stood rooted in place, the body sprawled out beside her on the ground.

So much blood.

Her trigger.

Her voice stopped working, and she began to shake.

Cayden carried her inside the trailer, her mind a blur. He took her into the small bathroom with the broken toilet. He kept cursing under his breath as he turned on the shower.

She felt like a rag doll as he stripped her completely naked and helped her under the water. Sophia looked down as the blood swirled down the drain. She was too dazed to focus.

"Sophia!"

He jostled her, and she looked him in the eyes, reality slowly seeping back in. It was the story of her life. She'd go into shutdown, her survival mechanism to spare herself the horrors. Without Hawk. Without Cayden. She would be lost.

"Am I shot?"

"You're fine. And clean." He wrapped a towel around her as she stepped out of the shower. "Get dressed. We have to leave here now. I'm not waiting until tomorrow."

"Where will we go?"

"I've tracked Hawk's car. It's time for you to go home."

She didn't have a home. Not anymore. Home was a feeling. She wanted Hawk and Cayden. Both pushed her away, supposedly for her own good.

It was an impossible dream to hope she could have both men.

Which meant she'd never be happy. Imagining life without Hawk, her rock, was indigestible. But she'd fallen in love with Cayden, despite what he'd done. She couldn't stomach the thought of never seeing him again.

Maybe it would have been better to have gotten caught in the crossfire.

Chapter Eleven

Hawk peered under the dressing on his side, grimacing at the sight of the wound. He'd stapled himself back together in a rush, so it wasn't going to be pretty when it healed. The bullet had gone cleanly through his side, but he'd cut off the tattoo that piece of shit had given him. He wanted no memory of Vasily. If only he could cut the memories from his head as easily.

He looked out the window of his hotel window, the sun starting to set.

"Where are you?" he murmured.

He'd told Cayden to take Sophia. It was the only way to save her. But now he couldn't track her down. To know if she was okay.

He trusted no one. Especially with such a high bounty on her head.

Hawk picked his drink up, the ice jingling in the glass.

He'd come too close to blowing his own brains out at the factory. Luckily, he'd emptied his clip into that piece of shit Vlad first. It was hard to come to grips with his entire life being a fucking lie. Nothing made sense. He didn't know what was real or fabricated.

The fact Vasily Morenov had killed his parents, nearly raping his mother, changed the entire game. Sophia was the daughter of his enemy. But he'd never blame her. She was nothing like that bastard.

And she was his for the taking.

If he could find her.

He sat back on the sofa with his drink, the decanter on the coffee table. The place was a disaster—thanks to his rages and refusing the cleaning service. He'd been having nightmares, waking up in cold sweats. Memories of his mother haunted him. Her sweet voice singing him to sleep, her homemade meals, her blurred smile. He had so few memories, probably to block out the trauma he'd endured at only ten years old.

He tried to remember his parents' faces but failed. Hawk didn't want to forget them. It was bad enough he'd never have a chance to see them again.

Everything was taken from him thanks to one man.

Vasily was a fucking monster.

Sophia had always believed it, but Hawk had sided with her father, believing he was faultless. Hawk had been told Vasily saved him. He'd always wanted to be his real son, to belong and make him proud, but there was no love, only strict discipline, training, and mandatory compliance.

Vasily ruled by fear.

It was all Hawk knew, and he never questioned the way the family was run. He'd been loyal to a fault, to the point he'd almost lost Sophia's respect.

He wanted to right the wrongs but wasn't sure who he was any more.

His identity, his focus, his past and future were all in upheaval. He'd have to investigate his parents' history when the pain wasn't so fresh. What he needed right now was Sophia's sweet innocence. If he could focus on helping her, on being her hero, he could ignore his own pain. He needed someone familiar.

The phone rang.

It was probably hotel security wondering what all the fucking banging was earlier. He had a lot of anger he needed to vent. Anything not bolted down had been destroyed. Luckily, this was a Morenov-owned hotel. "Yeah."

"Mr. Smith, you have a guest in the lobby. Did you want to come down or would you like me to send her up?"

"Who is it?"

"She says her name is Sophia."

His heart skipped a beat. He bolted upright in his seat. Just hearing her name brought him to full attention, despite the alcohol in his system. It could still be a trap. The lobby was bustling, so it was a good place to meet.

"I'll come down."

Hawk poured the rest of his drink down the drain, splashed some water on his face, and ran his hands through his hair. He was a fucking mess, but still couldn't wait to get his ass downstairs.

As soon as the elevator doors opened, he scanned the lobby for Sophia.

There she was.

She stood near the far wall, alone, her long, blonde hair all natural again. As he got closer, he saw her face was blotchy from crying.

Once she noticed him in front of her, she wrapped her arms around his waist and rested her head on his chest. He draped his arms over her. "Thank God I have you back. Tell me what's wrong, Sophia. Tell me what happened."

She peered up at him, fresh tears slipping from the corners of her eyes. "He's gone."

"Who's gone?"

"Cayden. He just dropped me off here with a room number. He wouldn't even come in."

"I thought he wanted his fucking cat."

She cried again, deep sobs as her tears soaked into his shirt. What had Cayden done to her? She should hate him. She *did* hate him at one point.

Hawk was finding it difficult to pull up the same murderous passion now that he knew what kind of man Vasily was. Vasily Morenov had taken all their families.

Made them all orphans.

"Let's go upstairs. I have a room." He kept his arm around her shoulder and led her to the elevator. It was surreal having her back. So much had happened. He'd nearly gotten her back last week, but then Vlad showed his true colors and he'd lost her again.

He couldn't let her out of his sight now. Hawk needed her as much as she needed him at this point.

Hawk ushered her inside his room and closed the door. He led Sophia to the sofa and sat her down, then moved to the open kitchen.

"Can I get you something? Water, pop, tea?"

"Hawk…"

She looked at him, her face tearstained, her lower lip trembling. He didn't want to fuck this up. His feelings for Sophia were a blur. He wanted to be her protector, the man her father expected him to be. But that asshole was a memory he wanted to wipe from his mind. He had no one to be loyal to at this point—except her.

Sophia had been through hell, and if he added his real feelings into the mix, it would break her. He had to be her rock. Had to put her first.

He reluctantly came and sat on the sofa. "Did he hurt you?"

"No. He was good to me. And he doesn't deserve to have a hit on his head. Please, call it off."

He nodded. "You're safe now. There's no reason for Antonio to go after him. I'll call him and tell him to stop looking."

"Thank you."

They were both quiet. He didn't know where to start.

"You've had a change of heart about him. About Cayden."

"My father killed people he loved. He's not a

143

monster."

He tilted his head, thinking, wondering. The way she spoke of Cayden now was a lot different than before. He wanted to know everything that had gone on between them but was too afraid to ask. He remembered the rumpled comforters in the basement of the factory.

"Are you still a virgin, Sophia?"

She swallowed hard, her lips parting. "Why are you asking me that?"

"Answer me."

"We didn't have sex, Hawk, so yes, I'm still a virgin. In fact, he was a perfect gentleman."

Every bone in his body felt like jelly for a moment as the huge weight eased off his shoulders. He exhaled, one hurdle crossed.

"Good. You've been through too much. You're probably not thinking right."

"I'm thinking fine," she said. "What happened with Vlad?"

He blew out a breath. "I killed him. He wasn't who I thought he was." He didn't expand on the information he found out about Vasily. Sophia had issues with her father, but he wouldn't reveal just how deep his sins reached.

"What about you, Hawk? Are you second guessing things?"

"You're worried about me killing you or turning you over to your father's enemies? Watch your damn mouth, Sophia. I'm here because I want to be."

"Because of your loyalty."

"No," he nearly shouted. "Because of you." His voice petered out to a whisper.

She scooted over to him, resting her head on his chest. He wrapped his arm around his shoulders. "I want this to end. I want life to be normal."

"We'll meet with a lawyer tomorrow. Get things sorted. Are you going to want to move back home once things are safe?"

Sophia shook her head. "I can't go back there. All the good memories are tainted with blood. I'll only remember that day."

"Then we'll arrange a sale. Get all the paperwork together."

"Thank you for helping me. I wouldn't know where to start."

Vasily had thought himself invincible. Immortal. He had no plans in place for after his death. Everything would revert to his only heir.

Being there for Sophia helped him to focus on something other than his own pain. The fact his entire life had been a lie, and the man he'd loved killed his family.

"Are you hungry?"

"No, we had food on the way over." She absently played with the collar of his shirt. Her scent was familiar, unique to her, even without the strawberry shampoo.

"Do you recognize this place?"

"Should I?"

"Your father owns it. Well, you own it now."

"I don't care. There are still a lot of people who want me dead. I'm not safe anywhere."

"Who told you that?"

"Someone already tried to kill me this afternoon. That's why Cayden brought me here. He says he's going to go after whoever put out my contract."

Cayden couldn't take on Oscar Esperanza on his own. He had a small army of men working for him, and the contract wasn't exclusive, meaning every hitman in the city wanted a piece of the three million. Then again, Cayden had managed to take out Vasily Morenov and his top men in his own home.

At least one other person seemed to care more about Sophia than the payout. Hawk should help Cayden, maybe team up and get this done, but he also couldn't trust anyone else to watch over Sophia. He couldn't leave her alone.

"Did you get hurt?"

"I'm fine. He killed the man and took his car. I don't know where Cayden's going to go. He says all the places he stays at are hot."

"I think he can handle himself. He's survived this long." He didn't want to hear about Cayden any more. Hawk was starting to get a complex. "You know what next week is?"

She took a minute before she knew what he was talking about. "Doesn't matter."

"You have to care. You'll be turning twenty-five."

Hawk got up and went to the bar.

"And my father would be planning one of my big birthday parties." She pulled up her legs, curling up on the sofa, then tucked her hair behind her ears. "I really don't want to think about it."

He hated seeing her sad. She looked so fucking lost.

"We'll do something special." He poured his drink.

"Why are you limping? You're hurt."

Hawk leaned against the bar and took a swig, looking at her as he lowered the glass. "I was shot. It's not the first time. Nothing serious."

"Where?"

"My leg. My side."

She jumped to her feet and rushed over to him. "Because of me." Her hands were on him, her little fingers fiddling with the buttons of his shirt. He set his glass down and stilled her hands.

"Sophia, I'd die for you. I wouldn't think twice."

She cupped his face.

"I love you, Hawk. I'll always love you."

He closed his eyes, taking a deep breath. Sophia alone was capable of toying with his emotions. "I love you, too."

"What kind of love?"

He slipped around her. "Let's not do this. It's late. I'm going to jump in the shower quick, and then you can have the bedroom."

What was he supposed to say?

He'd been in love with her for years, keeping his real feelings bottled up because her father would never approve of him pursing her. Now he wasn't sure which path to take. If he told her he was madly in love with her, there was no turning back. She needed a stable person in her life right now, and adding romance would only complicate things. She may not even be thinking straight, just looking for love because of her grief.

He tugged off his t-shirt in the bathroom, tossing it on the floor. Then he peeled away the bandage on his side. His wound had been healing for nearly a week, but still had a long way to go. Luckily it had been one of his smallest tattoos. He'd put some antibiotic ointment on after his shower and let it air out overnight.

Once in the shower, the warm water rushing over his body, he soaped up and thought of Sophia. He was a bastard for thinking about sex when she was in such turmoil. Hawk ran his hand over his hard length, stroking his cock, imagining Sophia's tight little virgin pussy. She was just outside in the living room, so vulnerable, so damn beautiful. He pumped his hand faster, bracing the other on the tiles. If he didn't relieve himself, he wouldn't be able to keep his cool around her. She was too tempting, always teasing, even if she didn't realize it.

She knocked on the bathroom door, startling him.

"Just a minute," he called out.

He kept jerking off, the pressure rising, his balls pulling up tight. Hawk groaned as he came, the relief instantaneous. He stayed under the water for a minute, his breath normalizing.

Hawk towel dried, then wrapped it around his waist.

He cracked open the bathroom door. "Sophia?"

She pushed her way inside, despite his body blocking the way. "Let me see," she said. She trapped him against the counter, her eyes on the gnarly wound with the unsightly staples. "Hawk…"

"It looks worse than it is, honestly."

She ran the tips of her fingers around the area. The room was humid and smelled like Irish Spring. "The tattoo my dad gave you. It was right here." Her eyes filled with tears. "You said it was special."

"It *was*." Past tense.

He moved around her to the bedroom, grabbing a fresh pair of boxers and slipping them on under the towel. He rummaged through the drawers for a pair of joggers, but she wouldn't leave him alone. She wasn't the only victim here. Her father had done a real fucking number on him, and he'd only just discovered it.

"That doesn't look like a gunshot wound. I've seen so many."

He shrugged, stepping into his joggers, trying his damnedest to avoid her. "Look, I was lucky to get out of there alive. Okay? Let's move on."

"You should see a doctor."

Hawk threw up his arms. "It's fine!"

She narrowed her eyes, clearing not falling for his

diversion. She'd come to him broken, and now she decided to be fearless?

He attempted to get past her to grab a shirt from his closet, but she pushed him in the chest. His body didn't budge, but he stopped. "Stop lying to me, Hawk. Something happened. You're different now."

"I'm the same. What about you, Sophia? Have you changed?"

His thoughts kept drifting to Cayden and the way she said his name. He'd always kept her sheltered—her father's orders. Maybe the freedom had been too much too soon.

Her fingers drifted down his chest to his abs. "I'm starting to think my father wasn't the man I thought he was."

"You were always upset with him," he reminded. "You never put him on a pedestal."

"I still had hope that he'd change, that he'd start loving me again. It's like something clicked when I stopped being a kid. He only tolerated me after that. After everything I've learned, maybe he really was a monster."

He kept still and quiet.

"What? You're not defending him?"

"Maybe you were right all along, Sophia."

****

What did that mean?

Sophia was tired of hearing Hawk sing her father's praises. She always believed it was the reason he never behaved out of line, not even an inappropriate look. If he'd stopped trying to feed her bullshit about her father, what had changed? Something must have happened at the factory, but what?

"Can you stop treating me like a child, Hawk, and really talk to me?"

He sat on the edge of the bed, leaning over to rest his elbows on his knees. "I found out something about my past that didn't sit well with me."

"*Your* past?"

"Vlad decided to confess his sins before he died. Before I killed him."

She swallowed hard, afraid of what he may say. Hawk had always been strong, fearless, never faltering. To see him broken shook her to the core.

Sophia sat next to him, resting her hand on his thigh.

"I shouldn't be telling you any of this. You've been through enough."

"I know what my father was. I'm not going to make excuses for him."

He bolted back to his feet, pacing back and forth. She couldn't help but admire his toned body and those strong arms covered in ink. His joggers fit deliciously over his hard ass.

He kept taking breaths, like getting pumped up for a run. Then he stopped and looked right at her. "Your father made me an orphan."

She frowned. "I don't understand. He took you in when you were ten."

"Because he murdered my mother and father. For some reason he had pity on me. That's why I'm alive." He ran a hand through his hair. "I gave him everything, my entire fucking life, my complete loyalty. I kept my distance from you out of respect for Vasily. But it was all a lie."

She was too shocked to reply. Sophia should be reassuring him, apologizing, saying something to comfort him. Her father had killed Cayden's loved ones, and now this. She wished her father was alive just so she could tell him to go to hell.

"Oh, Hawk—"

"You don't have to say anything, Sophia. It's not your fault. He kept you in the dark about everything. I know that."

She cautiously approached him. Never had she seen him so torn, so filled with emotion. He'd always been the level-headed one, the voice of reason, the man to turn her down again and again.

"He took that from you. It doesn't matter if it's not my fault, Hawk. I know how much family meant to you." She touched his arm, and he shocked her when he lowered to her level and hugged her, his head on her shoulder as he sought comfort.

She held him, her hands on his bare back. He didn't cry, but her father had hurt him, destroyed an integral part of who he was. His vulnerability only drew her closer. Hawk had been one of her father's most loyal men, trained by him personally since he was much too young to be involved in violence. She saw how Hawk worshipped her father. It had rubbed her wrong on countless occasions. To find out his devotion had been to a monster would be a crushing blow.

And she knew what it felt like to never know her mother.

"I'm so sorry," she whispered. She leaned back and cupped his face, his stubble pricking her fingers. "You're the one shot. You're the one dealing with this. All you've ever done is protect me. You don't deserve this, Hawk."

There was no chance for revenge. Hawk would have to live with this for the rest of his life. She thought of the scar and the tattoo he'd cherished. He'd cut it right off his body. That was something she wouldn't have been able to do. The past week must have been a nightmare for Hawk. His hotel room was testament to his pain. She wished she could have been there for him when he'd needed her.

"You're all I have," he said.

How many times had she said the same thing to Hawk? She'd felt like a burden to him since the assassination. To hear him say those words brought her closer to him. She felt less lonely. Less afraid of what was to come.

Chapter Twelve

Six days in the same hotel room.

It was her birthday. His little Sophia was turning twenty-five.

The past week had started out turbulent, but he'd managed to push down the pain of Vasily's betrayal. He never wanted to deal with it. It was Vasily who'd taught him to bury his emotions and stifle empathy in order to be the best hitman possible. Killers couldn't have second thoughts.

The nightmares were subsiding, but there had been a couple nights when Sophia had to wake him up. The betrayal burrowed deep, gutting him, making him question his own character.

At least he'd had the pleasure of killing Vlad, but Vasily had gotten off easy with that single bullet. Cayden had his revenge on the bastard, and now Hawk would never have the pleasure. He'd never get the answers he wanted.

Hawk had gone through the gamut—rage, betrayal, sadness, grief. He not only lost the family he'd never really known, blood relatives, a mother and father, but had Vasily ever loved or cared about him? Had he been just a tool to be used and shaped? Even after everything he knew, the little boy inside him craved Vasily's unconditional love. A fantasy created from a broken mind.

He'd never know the truth.

"Ten minutes, Sophia!" he called out from the living room.

He planned to take her to dinner, to give her the night of her life. With a price still on Sophia's head, it was dangerous going out in public, but he wouldn't keep her locked up like a damn prisoner on her birthday. Her father had done that to her all her life, and he'd been an accomplice.

If trouble came along, Hawk would be ready. He was always on alert, always prepared.

Sophia had been reluctant to celebrate, but he wouldn't hear it. They both needed a chance to unwind, to enjoy life rather than hiding from it.

All week he'd been trying to contact Antonio Baretti to get him to call off the hit on Cayden, but he couldn't get through. It didn't sit well with him.

He looked out the windows, into a world he had no connection to. Life had been *the family*, and now only Sophia was left.

"What do you think?"

Hawk turned around. Sophia wore a long black dress with a side slit that traveled all the way to her hip. The low neck revealed too much cleavage. She took some steps toward him, her heels clicking on the tiles.

Her long, blonde hair had been brushed smooth, flowing loose behind her.

"Well? Do you like it?"

"It's a little risqué," he said. "But you're all grown up, aren't you?"

She was stunning, the most beautiful woman in the world. He'd let her do some online ordering to get some essentials, including her birthday dress.

"You clean up nice yourself." She walked a circle around him. He'd put on one of his best suits, going all out for her birthday. Concealing weapons was always easier with a jacket. "Where you taking me, Hawk?"

"It's a secret. You okay with that?"

"I trust you." She adjusted his tie, her hands lingering on his chest. Every muscle in his body tensed. "One rule for tonight."

"What's that?" he asked.

"No sadness. No memories. This is our night. Just you and me."

He smoothed his hand over her hair. "Sounds good." Hawk took her hand and led her to the door. Today was a new beginning, the first day of the rest of their lives.

As they drove to the restaurant, one of the finest in the city, Sophia kept quiet.

"You okay?" he asked.

"This is a new car."

"Cayden tracked my last one, so I decided it was time for a change," he said.

"Don't say that name. Please."

He tensed. All week, he'd wanted to bring up the other man, but pushed the desire away. Today was her birthday, so he wasn't going to start any shit tonight. "Okay."

"I'm tired of living in a hotel," she said a while later. "We have to start thinking of the future."

"The house is for sale. Everything's in the works now. It won't be long."

She shifted in her seat to face him better. "Will we be together? I don't want to live alone."

"I'll never leave you alone," he said.

She wasn't a child, but she'd also been sheltered from the world. He couldn't imagine her living alone in a big house, fending for herself. The world was a dangerous place, especially for the only heir of Vasily Morenov. But was she looking for comfort or a companion? He wanted to be her everything, but he refused to push himself on her, to force her into a life she'd regret.

They pulled up to the restaurant, and he left the car with the valet. The lights and glamor cut the darkness of the evening as they walked up the grand steps to the restaurant.

"Mr. Tesino. Please follow me." The hostess led them to their private alcove in the restaurant. The very best for his Sophia. Her father would have done the same. Hawk would say that fucker was incapable of love, but even monsters managed to love their own.

Once seated at their table, he waved away the other staff. He wanted alone time with Sophia. She sat across from him at the small table, her dark eyes luminous in the candle light.

"Mr. Tesino?"

"I did some calls. That's my real surname, my parents' name. Turns out I have Italian blood, not Russian." He chuckled. *What a clusterfuck.*

"I like it. *Sophia Tesino*," she whispered, tasting the words.

"You're a Morenov."

"Until I'm married. I won't miss losing the name."

He fucking loved the sound of her having his name. Imagining her as his wife seemed to make all the wrongs of the world disappear. He'd keep his promise and keep tonight about them.

Hawk leaned over and pressed a finger to her lips. "Happy thoughts, baby."

She took his wrist and kissed his fingers. When she wrapped her lips around his thumb, he sat back in his seat, bracing the table with both hands, trying to will his hard-on away.

No such luck.

Sophia smiled. "We should move away from here. Far away. Maybe by the ocean. Or even the wilderness." She toyed with her napkin, folding and unfolding it. "Not a big house like ours, something cute and cozy. Something to call home."

"Sounds nice," he said.

He wasn't overly focused on her words. He was busy eyeing the fullness of her lips, and the soft swells of her breasts rising and falling with each breath. She was anything but a little girl in that dress.

"I have a present for you. I'll give it to you tonight."

"You never asked me what I wanted, though."

"You want something?"

Sophia was never one for material possessions. Her father always bought her the best, but it never impressed her. She put her weight on her forearms, getting as close to him as she could without lifting out of her seat. "I want *you*."

"You already have me, baby. That's not much of a wish."

"Hawk, I want you to kiss me, to touch me, to take my virginity. Tonight."

He looked to both sides, making sure they weren't overheard.

"Sophia, I won't do that."

She scowled. "My father's gone. Are you still refusing me out of loyalty, or is it something else? You're not attracted to me? Or do you love another woman?"

He was doing it again, playing his role as protector, the one Vasily groomed him for. But he had to push away that deep-seated impulse to deny himself. Things were different now.

"I don't want you to make a decision you'll regret."

"I love you, Hawk. I've fantasized about this for years. I know *exactly* what I want."

He shifted in his seat, his cock heavy in his slacks. He wasn't going to push her away any more.

There was no reason to. He could take care of her, love her, protect her. No other man was good enough.

He licked his lips. "To answer your questions. No, I don't love another woman. And, yes, I am attracted to you. You have no idea just how much."

Her lips tilted into a smile she tried to hide. "Will you give me what I want?"

He copied her position, leaning onto his forearms until they were only a breath away, their fingertips touching. "I wouldn't want to disappoint the birthday girl."

Her lips parted, and she let out a barely audible sigh. She hadn't expected him to comply. He wondered if she'd back out before the night was through.

"What will you do with me?" Her eyes were hooded, her demeanor transitioning. "Tell me, Hawk."

"First I'll make you take off that dress. Nice and slow. Bra and panties, too."

"You want me naked?"

He nodded. "And on the bed. Your legs spread open for me. I want to see that pretty virgin pussy. Make it mine."

"Yes," she murmured. "Tell me more."

"I'm going to make you come hard, baby. I'll eat your pussy until you're nice and wet, and then I'll fill you with my cock."

"*My* cock?"

"Yeah, baby. All yours.

The waitress approached, standing next to the table. "Are you ready to order?"

He had to remind himself that killing the waitress was not an option.

****

Sophia squirmed in her seat, her panties moist, her pussy tingling. They'd finally crossed that line from babysitter to something much more. No turning back. He'd conceded, and he agreed to give her exactly what she wanted.

Had her father had such a hold over him all these years?

Hearing him talk dirty, imagining all the wicked things he planned for her, made her entire body heat from the inside out. Her womb coiled tight, her clit throbbing, and she swore she'd spontaneously orgasm until the waitress showed up.

She took a breath, ordered, and then waited for Hawk to say something. Had she gone too far? Did he think less of her? This was so new for their relationship.

"You're mine, Sophia. Your father can't deny me anymore. Tell me you're mine."

"Yes, Hawk."

"I've been a fool, but I won't be anymore. I'll take care of you. And I'll never refuse you anything."

Her entire body seemed to sigh in relief. Such beautiful words.

No more begging.

No more wishing.

Hawk promised to be everything she'd ever wanted.

"I like the sound of that," she said. "I couldn't have asked for a better birthday gift. Ever since that day, I was lost."

"It's you and me. Never doubt my loyalty to you, Sophia."

She thought of Cayden and her happiness diluted. How could she love two men equally? What was wrong with her? She'd end up destroying them both if she mentioned her true fantasy.

Sophia kept her mouth shut.

They enjoyed their meal, and she didn't talk

much. Her mind was elsewhere, everywhere. She was excited to take the next step with Hawk, but she missed Cayden and wondered where he was.

Maybe she *was* a whore like her mother. She'd heard it enough from her father before he died. Why else would she have such deviant thoughts?

"Do you want dessert? How about a piece of cake for your birthday?" he asked.

"Only if it's takeout. I want to see your present." She stood up, careful of each step in her high heels. "I'll just visit the washroom before we go."

"Okay, I'll get the check." He winked at her, and her heart fluttered. Hawk was ridiculously handsome, and she loved him in a three-piece suit.

She weaved around tables toward the hallway to the washrooms. A lot of eyes were on her, but she was showing a lot of skin, so ignored the attention. She'd needed as much ammunition as possible to get Hawk to see her as a woman.

Tonight, everything would change.

Her excitement mixed with her increasing nerves, making her feel uneasy. She'd regroup and pull herself together in the washroom before leaving with Hawk. There was nothing to be afraid of. Hawk was her rock. She loved him, trusted him, and wanted him to dominate her body.

He'd never hurt her.

The bathroom was huge and empty. Her heels echoed as she walked along the row of sinks, admiring all the gold and ivory detailing. Hawk really did give her the very best for her birthday.

She leaned over the counter to touch up her lipstick.

The shadow of someone entering the washroom reflected in the mirror.

A man.

Sophia twirled around, bracing her hands on the counter behind her to keep from falling. He smirked, staring, pacing back and forth. She knew right away he was a hitman. And he was there to kill her.

Adrenaline burned her veins, but she refused to show the bastard fear.

"I think you're lost. This is the woman's washroom," she said.

Something emerged from his sleeve. A garrote. She'd seen some of her father's enemies take their last breath with one of those.

"I'll scream."

"It wouldn't be fun otherwise," he said.

He took a step forward, and she turned and grabbed a ceramic soap dish, almost sad that she was about to destroy it. Sophia whipped it at his head, then scrambled down the counter to grab another.

Her heart raced as he closed the distance between them. He was so much bigger than she was, but she'd go down fighting. She grabbed one of her stilettos off her foot and used the heel as a weapon, jabbing him in the shoulder as hard as she could.

I'm going to die on my birthday.

Her attack only served to agitate him, his brow furrowing as he threw her shoe and pulled her closer. She felt the cool metal wire brush her arm, and she whimpered, too tempted to beg for her life.

Then someone was behind him, a huge arm around his neck. He released his grip on her, clawing at Hawk's crisp white sleeve as he gasped for breath.

"Who hired you, asshole?"

She collapsed, using the counter to support her weight. Her relief made her dizzy.

"It's an open contract," he squeaked out.

"Three million's a lot of money. I get that," said Hawk. "But it becomes a problem when your target is my ward." In a quick move, he snapped the big guy's neck, then lowered him to the ground before dragging him away by the arms.

She hadn't moved.

He'd saved her. His strength, confidence, and skill only increased her desire. She was too used to life and death drama to let it ruin her night.

Hawk came back, brushing off his jacket like nothing happened. He looked in the mirror as he ran a hand through his hair.

"Are you okay?"

She nodded. "How'd he find me here?"

"Anywhere public is a gamble," he said, picking up her missing shoe. "We better get out of here."

She stopped him when he tried to usher her out.

"What's wrong?"

"You called me your ward again," she said.

"I'm not following."

She rested her hand on his chest. "I'm not your ward. You're not my father's hired babysitter, anymore."

"I'll always protect you. Nothing will change that."

"I want to be your woman, Hawk, not your ward."

He smiled, then took her hand in his, leading them to the washroom exit. Within minutes they were outside, waiting for the car. Hawk held her close to his side, a protective embrace. The nip in the air made the skin on her arms turn to gooseflesh. Or was it just having him next to her?

"Not my ward," he said. She looked up at him, thinking the conversation was over in the washroom. "This. Us. It'll take time for me to get used to."

"Nothing has to change," she said.

Tonight would be a good start because she planned to give her body over to him. She'd trust him not to hurt her, and she wouldn't refuse him anything. He thought of her as a child, and she planned to show him just how grown-up she could be.

Chapter Thirteen

Once they got to the hotel lobby, Hawk stopped at the front desk and ordered a piece of birthday cake to be delivered to the room. Money talked, and he was sure to describe exactly what he wanted.

"My feet hurt," she said when they emerged on their floor. "I'm not used to heels."

"Come on, jump up." He squatted down, urging her to climb on his back.

She giggled and wrapped her arms tight around his neck when he stood up. Her dress rode all the way up to her upper thighs. "I don't think I've ever had a piggyback before," she said.

"Hold on tight."

The hotel room was dark when they returned. Dark and quiet. He flicked on a light, but Sophia told him to turn it off. He set her down, and she walked over to the windows in her bare feet.

"I like the lights from the city at night. It's relaxing. Your eyes will adjust."

He came up behind her, running his hands along her sides, over the curves of her hips. She inhaled, leaning her head back on his chest.

"As long as I can see you," he said.

"Take my dress off, Hawk. Do everything you said you'd do."

Fuck, he wasn't ready for this. There was nothing he wanted more, but an internal battle kept raging despite the fact he'd made up his mind to claim her.

He peeled down the first strap of her dress, as slow as melting chocolate, leaving soft kisses on her bare shoulder. Her breath shuddered, but she didn't move. He slid the next one down, the top of her dress slipping to her waist. Hawk gathered her hair to one side, resting it in front of her as he kissed the back of her neck, rimming the shell of her ear with his tongue.

"My beautiful birthday girl," he whispered.

He unfastened her bra, letting it fall to the ground. The shadowed reflection of her bare breasts stared back at them from the glass. He snaked his arms around her, cupping her tits in his hands, the softness overflowing his fingers. Touching her felt deliciously forbidden.

Hawk growled, his erection pressed to her back. This was more than he deserved. He never thought this day would come.

She turned around in his arms, allowing the rest of her dress to fall heavily to the ground, leaving her in a whisper-thin pair of black lace panties.

"My turn," she said, unfastening his tie. When it was off, she put it around her own neck.

Sophia undid the buttons of his shirt, one at a time, painfully slow, then pushed the material over both shoulders. She ran her hands over his chest, down his stomach to his pants. He didn't stop her when she unbuckled his belt, pulling the leather clean from the loops. She palmed his cock over his slacks, and he snatched her wrist.

"What's wrong, Hawk?" she teased, those big dark eyes tearing down all his walls.

He couldn't keep hold of his control another second. Hawk cupped her face and kissed her hard on the mouth, turning and backing her up to the kitchen island. The soft lights from the city gave a wash of muted color to the walls. It was just the two of them. And she was all he needed.

He realized he could have lost her tonight.

Hawk hoisted her up onto the low counter, taking

up position between her legs. He tugged his dress shirt off, then grabbed her hips, sliding her to the edge of the cool granite.

"Are you hard for me, Hawk?"

"You'll find out soon enough," he said. He leaned over and painted a circle around her dusky pink areola with his tongue. She gasped, grabbing hold of his head. He sucked her tight little nipple into his mouth, flicking the firm bud until she whined for more. "You have perfect tits, Sophia."

"Touch me."

She writhed on the counter, so needy. He crouched down and spread her legs wider, swiping his tongue over the lace of her panties. She was wet, the scent of her arousal heady.

"Oh God, Hawk. Don't make me wait."

He had no plans on ripping her virginity from her. This only happened once, and he planned to enjoy every minute of it. He wanted to learn every curve, every freckle on her body and keep it to memory.

Hawk nuzzled her pussy, rubbing his face along the lace, kissing her sensitive inner thighs. "I'm going to eat you, baby."

"Yes, do it," she cried. Sophia leaned back on her elbows. Such a beautiful sight.

"Not yet."

He continued to explore her body, kissing along her legs, then over her stomach, making it quiver. She giggled, and it was the cutest sound. "I'm ticklish."

"I'll have to remember that for later." He winked. Then he cupped her breast and covered her nipple with his mouth, suckling her harder, rubbing his free hand over her panties simultaneously.

She braced a heel on the counter and arched up her hips, her breathing erratic. "More," she chanted.

"You want to scream louder?"

"Yes."

"You want my cock, baby girl? Want me filling this tight little pussy?" He pinched her clit, making her squeal.

"Hawk…"

She reached down to push her panties lower, wiggling, and anxious. He pulled her back up, holding her close, bare skin to skin. Hawk ran a finger around her eye, tracing her face. "You're so beautiful. My birthday girl." He kissed her on the lips once. "What do you miss, Sophia? Tell me one thing you miss since all this bullshit started."

"Painting." She ran her hand through his hair, and he leaned toward her touch. "But I wouldn't trade this for anything."

He had no plans of stealing her dreams. If he had to, he'd buy her a fucking studio. She was talented and inspired, and painting gave her life. It had been her passion since he could remember.

"I'll make all your dreams come true."

He scooped her into his arms and carried her to the bedroom, settling her on the unmade bed. She shuffled to the middle, and he stood in place.

"How many women have you had?"

"Does it matter?"

She shrugged. "You'll compare me to them."

"Then you have nothing to worry about. You're the only woman I want, Sophia."

Someone knocked at the entrance. He went to check, tucking a gun into the back of his slacks before opening the door. It was her birthday cake.

Hawk put his gun on the counter and brought the cake with him to the bedroom, setting the small tray on the edge of the bed. "Your birthday cake," he said.

"Thank you," she whispered, only focused on him.

He unzipped his pants, stepping out of them and tossing them onto a chair. She watched, staring at his boxers.

"Have you never seen a man naked before?"

She shook her head.

Innocent.

Pure.

Mine.

Hawk slipped off his boxers, his cock rock hard and virile, bobbing as he moved closer to the edge of the bed. He'd never been ashamed of his manhood. "You want to touch it? Come here. It's yours, remember?"

Sophia sat up and crawled to him, her body sexy as fuck. She knelt on the mattress, resting a hand on his chest. She hesitated, reaching out, but not touching.

He grabbed her hand, forcing her to grip him. "You can't hurt me."

She bit her lower lip, curiosity dancing in her eyes. With a light hold, she moved her fist up and down the length. He ground his teeth together, trying to hold onto his fracturing control. Pre-cum leaked from the tip of his cock.

"It's big," she said. "The skin is soft." When she bent over and kissed it, he pulled back, his heart jackhammering in his chest. "Did I hurt you?"

"I wasn't expecting that."

"I love you. All of you. Why wouldn't I kiss it?" She used a curled finger to beckon him closer. "Stop treating me like a child. I'm a woman, and I know what I want."

As soon as he stepped closer, she wrapped her fingers around the base of his shaft and covered his head with her hot, wet mouth. He shuddered, his eyes lolling

back in his head, every muscle flexing. He felt like a
beast, a physical transformation tearing through his body.
She worked his cock, sucking him, bobbing up and down
until he had to pull away in fear of coming down her
throat.

Tonight was supposed to be monumental. He'd
be claiming her virginity.

"Did you like it?"

"Too much," he said. "Now let's get these panties
off." She helped him pull them free from her body,
leaving her completely nude. And fucking perfect. "Hold
your legs open. Nice and wide. I want to see what's
mine."

She did as told without hesitation, making him
harder. Sophia held her knees, her pussy glistening. His
cock throbbed, heavy and aching.

"Hawk?"

"Stay just like that." He pumped his cock a
couple times. "Now touch yourself, baby."

She reached one hand between her legs, rolling
her clit under two fingers. In less than a minute, she
became agitated. "I want to feel you on top of me, Hawk.
I love you. I need you."

This was happening.

He grabbed both her legs, a little too hard,
holding her open. He dragged a finger over the top of her
birthday cake, collecting some icing. She panted,
following his movements. He spread the icing on each
side of her inner thighs, close to her pussy, then held out
his finger for her to lick the remainder. Watching those
sweet lips wrapped around him was nearly his undoing.

"Yummy," she said after licking his finger clean.

She gasped when he went down on her, eating her
out like a man on the edge. His plan for a slow, measured
exploration went out the window, and he feasted on her

sweet, young pussy.

****

Hawk looked like a panther on the prowl as he crawled over her, his huge shoulders bunching up as he lowered his face between her legs. She remembered Cayden, and knew she'd love Hawk's mouth on her pussy. Everything about it was deliciously naughty.

He wasn't as gentle as she expected. He was hungry, desperate, rough in a way that made her hornier. She liked this side of him. He lapped up and down with the flat of his tongue, driving her crazy. He licked away the icing, twirled his tongue around her clit, and teased her folds until she was writhing on the sheets.

"You're killing me, Hawk."

He flipped her over, forcing her shoulders down, her ass high in the air.

When he speared her ass with the tip of his tongue, she squealed, the firestorm of sensation taking her by surprise. He rimmed her asshole with his tongue before moving back to her pussy. The sloppy sounds he made, combined with his grunts and growls, had her desperate and wanton.

"So good," he mumbled, pressing her flat to the bed, stomach down. She felt a unique thrill and power being able to arouse the stoic Hawk. Finally, after all these years, he was hers. His body lowered over her, hot skin, hard muscle. His erection pressed against the back of her thighs.

He nipped her shoulder from behind, necking her, hitting every erogenous zone along the way. She couldn't take another minute of the beautiful torture.

"Please," she said.

He lifted enough that she could roll over underneath him. She parted her legs, wanting him heavy between them. "You sure about this? I don't want to hurt

STACEY ESPINO

you."

"I'm twenty-five, Hawk. We both want this. You should be the one."

She wrapped her arms around his neck, pulling him to her. It felt so intimate, skin to skin. He positioned his cock at her entrance, making her jolt. Every cell of her body felt like a livewire, and her pussy was wet and ready for him.

He pushed the thick mushroom head in an inch or so, and the instant fullness made her inhale sharply. Everything about Hawk was big and hard. She ran her hands over his back, feeling all the tense muscle as he slowly pushed inside her, taking away her virginity, making her his woman. The initial intrusion made her squint and grit her teeth in pain. It was an unusual discomfort mixed with pressure. The height of her arousal helped ease her through the worst of it.

Memories of him flashed in her mind. He'd always been there. And she'd loved him for as long as she could remember. They had a history together, and no one could take that away.

Hawk equaled security, strength, and safety.

And now he was hers.

"You okay?"

She was going to tell him he was big, and she'd never felt so full in her life, but she didn't want him to stop. "Yes."

Once he was inside her to the hilt, all those hard inches deep inside her, he exhaled, his breath on her neck. "You're tight. So fucking tight around my dick."

"Does it hurt you, Hawk?"

"No, but it's not easy going slow."

She swallowed her apprehension. "Then don't go slow. I'm yours now, Hawk. You can fuck me however you want to."

171

Her words unhinged him. He pulled almost out, then slid back in, slow and steady, over and over. The growing friction stole away any discomfort, and she quickly returned to that sweet zone. She tested her muscles around his cock, making him growl like an animal.

He picked up the pace, his body breaking out in a thin sheen of sweat. She wrapped her legs around his hips, holding his shoulders as he pistoned into her. Each pump of his hips brought her closer, the pressure building, the end in sight.

Hawk kissed her, fucked her and kissed her. "I love you," he whispered against her lips.

And that was all she needed.

Her core let go, her orgasm rattling her entire body as wave after wave of contractions squeezed Hawk's cock. She tensed, savoring every delicious sensation. He groaned, tightening his hold around her, fucking her harder until she felt him come inside her.

His body eased, his muscles relaxing.

Only the sound of their labored breathing could be heard in the bedroom. He rolled to his back, one arm draped over his eyes. She watched his large ribs rise and fall as he caught his breath. He fascinated her. All male and addictive.

She lightly touched the wound on his side. It had healed over but must still hurt. It was more than an injury. He thought he was removing a memory, but those staples and the scar that would remain would still remind him of the monster who stole his family.

Her father.

How could he love the daughter of a madman?

She felt a wave of guilt for all the harm her father had caused. So much death and pain. First Cayden, now Hawk. It would be wrong to mourn her father now, but she did. It was a small part, but a part she couldn't ignore.

If Hawk found out, he'd be disgusted. She'd have to keep her feelings bottled up.

"Come here, sweetheart." He tucked her into the crook of his arm. She felt warm and safe. The faint scent of his cologne surrounded her like a blanket.

"Thank you for the birthday present," she said, painting patterns over his chest with a finger.

He jolted up onto an elbow. "Your present." Hawk looked at his watch. "Almost midnight. It's still your birthday." He slipped off the bed, and she admired his hard ass as he walked over to the dresser. Even flaccid, his cock was impressive.

Hawk came back, bringing a small wrapped box with him.

She sat up and crossed her legs on the bed, taking it when he passed it to her. "What is it?"

"Open it."

She unwrapped the box and found a simple gold chain. Sophia set the box down and held up the chain, letting it dangle in the direction of the open door and the lights of the city. A small charm hung on the end with a gold "E".

Sophia frowned, trying to figure out what it signified. If Hawk bought her jewelry, she'd expect him to go all out. This necklace was very humble and unlike him.

Before she could ask about it, he spoke. "It was your mother's."

She clutched it in her fist, feeling the metal pinch her skin. Emotion bubbled in her throat.

"I don't understand."

"Your father kept it. I'm not sure why. I went back after the factory and cleaned out the safes. I thought you'd want to keep it."

"The "E"?"

"Her name was Elena."

Tears came out of nowhere. A name made the woman she'd never known feel real, not a fantasy. The brief times her father spoke of her were always angry and negative, but she refused to believe anything he said.

"I wish I could have known her. Everyone says I look like her."

"Then she must have been beautiful." Hawk kissed her temple. "And she would have been proud of the strong woman you've become."

"Not even memories. I have nothing but a necklace." She took a breath, steading herself. "Do you remember your mother?"

Then she recalled his nightmares earlier in the week. He'd mentioned his family, especially his mother.

"Blurry images, smells, tastes, and her singing to me."

She smiled. "Sounds heavenly."

They held each other, sitting on the edge of the bed.

Both broken.

Both survivors.

Chapter Fourteen

Cayden took a drag from his cigarette, then stretched his arm out the open driver's side window. He'd been sitting in his parked car for an hour, watching the goings and comings of the house partway down the block.

He'd be paying Oscar Esperanza a visit tonight.

Whether Cayden came out of this dead or alive didn't matter. But that motherfucker was going to burn in hell tonight for putting a hit on Sophia Morenov.

Once Oscar was pushing daisies, Sophia would be safe, and Cayden could rest in peace.

It was extra dark where he'd parked thanks the broken streetlights near him. He'd handled that yesterday as his plan took shape.

A light turned on upstairs in a house across the road. Someone walked in front of the window, and then darkness returned to the house a couple minutes later. His thoughts drifted to family again. A topic he avoided. He remembered Frank Almeida.

"Do you want to end up in jail? Another junkie no one remembers?"

"Who the fuck would remember me anyway? I have no history. I have nothing, no one."

Frank shook his head, his brow creasing. "No! You have me. My family is your family, Cayden. I won't watch you screw up your life." He squeezed his shoulder. A firm grip. "You're a good boy. Whether you see it or not, you have untapped potential. I won't sit back and watch you waste it."

"Why do you care?"

Cayden had been on a drinking binge, feeling

sorry for himself, his twisted past constantly haunting him. He'd only been a few years older than Sophia.

"God believes in second chances. I won't give up on you."

He took another deep inhale of his smoke, leaning his head back against the headrest. Where had God been his whole life? Had he forgotten about him, the little Irish bastard? Cayden was forgettable. Something to be used and discarded. The only good things he'd had in his life were gone.

First, Frank and his family.

Now, Sophia.

She'd have her happily ever after, but not with him. Her hero had her now, and he'd give her everything she wanted. It wouldn't take long for her to forget Cayden. Maybe she already had.

It didn't matter. Cayden was a nasty piece of shit, and she deserved the world.

In those brief weeks together, the Russian princess had stolen his heart, or fucking pissed on it, he wasn't sure. All he knew was he'd die for her.

Another car pulled up in Esperanza's driveway. More trouble. He palmed his duffel bag on the passenger seat. He had a shitload of firepower, and they weren't expecting him. What fool would kill the man putting up a three-million-dollar bounty? He'd be confident now, and Cayden was about to cut him down to size.

There was no point waiting any longer. He tossed his butt, and stepped out of the car, slinging the bag over his shoulder.

This was it. He almost looked forward to ending his time on this earth.

Sweet relief.

If he stuck around any longer, he'd end up numbing the pain with drugs and alcohol, becoming another waste of space. He had nothing to ground him, nothing he gave a shit about.

Maybe he'd get some points with the man upstairs for putting an end to two notorious kingpins.

Probably not.

He walked down the street, a Glock in his right hand. Cayden was good at one thing—killing. These motherfuckers didn't know what was coming.

Those words replayed in his head, like a mantra.

The most dangerous man in the world is the one with nothing to lose.

****

Sophia was twenty-five years old plus three days. He'd kept his hands to himself since her birthday so she could heal completely. She may have denied it, but he knew she was sore after losing her virginity. His thoughts were getting more and more filthy by the damn hour, and the wait time would be coming to an end very soon.

Hawk answered his phone. "Yeah."

"You wanted information on Esperanza?" asked Danny.

"Go on."

"Something big is going down at his place right now. I heard his men on their secure line. It's some crazy guy. One guy. He's got a fucking arsenal."

Cayden.

"Okay, thanks, Danny. Good work."

Fuck, that guy was going to get himself killed. Did Cayden have a death wish?

It wasn't Hawk's business, but it was. Morenov had killed both their families. They had that in common. And a lot more.

He knew Cayden was doing this for Sophia. She was an addiction. And he wasn't stupid to think nothing happened between the two of them when they were holed up together.

Regardless, he couldn't let Cayden do this on his own. Hawk's duty was to protect Sophia, to kill Esperanza and anyone else in his way. He wouldn't let Cayden take the pleasure of the kill from him again. And he wouldn't let Cayden die a martyr for Sophia to pine over.

She'd just taken her evening shower and was getting ready for bed.

"Baby, I have to go out for a bit."

"Where?"

"I need to settle some scores. Make things safe for you."

Sophia scowled. "And you'll leave me alone? Maybe I'll get kidnapped again."

She was testing him, but he couldn't play games with her now. Shit was going down as they spoke. "Don't be smart. Just stay put and I'll be back before you wake up."

Hawk opened his gun case on the kitchen counter, preparing everything he planned to bring along for this party. The more he thought about leaving Sophia alone, the more he second-guessed his decision. What if someone had followed them home from the restaurant the other day? A bounty hunter could be watching their room right now.

He didn't want an encore of their last hotel stay.

Shit, he'd have to bring her along.

When he returned to the room, she was already dressed. "Where do you think you're going?"

"I'm not going to be able to sleep wondering if you're dead or alive."

"Here. Take this." He held out a 9mm and pressed it to her palm. "But you're waiting in the car."

"What? I don't want a gun, Hawk. I don't even

know how to use them." She followed behind him. He grabbed his jacket off the back of the chair and tugged in on, covering his harnesses.

"This is top of the line. Has a silencer on it, too. Don't pull the trigger unless you're ready to kill. Otherwise, aim and have at it."

He took her hand as they walked down the hallway to the elevators. On the ride down, he went over the different variables in his head, zoning out. If things went their way, this could be the start of a beautiful new beginning.

"Hawk, you're scaring me."

He refocused, tilting her chin up. "I'm sorry," he said. "It's just that this is the day I've been waiting for. It's a chance to clear the contract on your head, to get out of hiding for good."

"What about the contract on Cayden?"

"Taken care of," he lied. He still couldn't get hold of Antonio. That shifty bastard was up to something.

He took the fastest route to the address.

Esperanza liked the finer things. The property took up half the block with a high, wrought-iron fence surrounding it. Hawk parked a block down the street and killed the engine, the silence settling in immediately.

"Okay, I'm going in. Stay here, keep down, and whatever you do don't leave the damn car. Understand?"

"Hawk, you can't go in there alone. It's crazy." She grabbed his sleeve. "Please, I can't lose you, too."

Tears glistened in her eyes. Only one thing would get her approval for him to get out of the car. "Cayden's already in there alone. I'm going to help him."

"What?"

"Two are better than one, no?"

She kept quiet as he left the car.

The streetlights were broken, giving him added

cover as he walked up the street. Tonight would decide their next move—more hiding or Sophia's dreams coming true.

He slipped in the iron gates, conveniently left ajar. The distant drone of the alarm system sent a chill up his spine. It reminded him of the night Vasily was murdered. No gunfire could mean everyone was dead, and he was too late. He pulled a balaclava over his face before entering the house, not wanting his image on their foyer security footage.

Hawk stepped over a body in the foyer. With his gun outstretched in front of him, he did a sweep of the main floor. All he found were bodies.

So many fucking corpses.

Blood everywhere.

The plaster walls were shot to shit, glass broken, and the massive chandelier a heap on the floor. What the hell went down here?

It looked worse than the massacre at Vasily's place.

"Don't move, motherfucker." The barrel of a gun pressed to his skull from behind.

Hawk acted on instinct. He ducked, spun around, and aimed his gun up at the bastard's face.

"Cayden?" He pulled the mask up to his forehead.

"Hawk? What the fuck are you doing here?"

"I came to help you."

Cayden lowered his weapon. "I don't need help."

"Where's Esperanza?"

He pointed his gun up the stairs.

"Dead?"

"Not yet," said Cayden.

Hawk stepped around the chandelier and raced up the stairs, broken glass crushing under his boots. Cayden was right behind him. No way was he losing the chance to give that fucker some payback for putting Sophia through hell. Half the lowlifes of the city were looking to cash in on her death thanks to Oscar and his hunger for power.

When he entered the master bedroom, Oscar was sitting on the ground against a wall, his hands tied behind his back, his mouth duct taped. He looked like he'd been through a fucking meat grinder.

"Holy shit."

Cayden joined him in the room, standing next to him. "No one fucks with Sophia."

Oscar whimpered.

Hawk walked back and forth, scratching his head with the muzzle of his gun as he addressed Oscar. "You couldn't leave well enough alone? Vasily was dead. You could have ruled the city, taken his place. But you went after his little girl like the sick bastard you are. Now what?" asked Hawk. "Now you get to die. All the money and power in the world can't save you from your fate now."

"You want to do this?" asked Cayden, talking as casually as discussing the weather.

"I'm just thinking about all the weeks of hell I went through because of him. I wanted to take my time, make him suffer. But it seems you've already taken care of that."

"You have no idea," said Cayden.

"Okay, then." Hawk aimed and fired. One head shot. Oscar's body slumped to the side.

He took a deep breath, knowing it was over and trying to digest it all. He'd take Sophia back to the hotel for at least another night until they planned their next move. It would take a while for word to get around about Oscar's death and the fact there was no one to pay out the three million.

"She's safe now," said Cayden.

"Well, she'll never be completely off the radar."

"That's why she has you, right?"

He watched as the other hitman left the room. Not another word. Hawk almost felt guilty for being the winner. Fuck, he felt like shit. He wasn't sure how it happened, but he knew Cayden loved Sophia. True love was a rarity in their world.

Hawk had done his research on Cayden Walsh. He never had an easy life.

Whatever. Not my problem.

He cautiously made his way out of the house and walked back to his vehicle. Cayden was getting into his own car, only a few away from his.

Just another day at the office.

Hawk opened the door and looked inside, then checked the backseat. Sophia was gone. He looked up and down the street and saw no sign of her.

You've got to be kidding me.

There was a pool of blood on the sidewalk. Panic flooded his veins.

As Cayden's car drove by him, he rushed to the street and slapped the roof, making him hit the brakes. He lowered the passenger window. "Car trouble?"

"Sophia's gone."

"What the fuck is that supposed to mean?"

Hawk took a shuddered breath, his reality spiraling out of control. "She was waiting in the car. She's gone. There's blood."

Cayden hopped out of the car, slamming the door shut. He came around the back of the vehicle, coming face to face with him. "Tell me you're fucking joking."

"I couldn't leave her alone at the hotel. You know how that worked out for me last time."

Cayden did a little spin, staring up at the stars. "I

entrusted her to you! You were supposed to keep her safe. Love her. Make her fucking happy." He turned around and punched Hawk in the face. Once, twice, three times.

He didn't move. Hawk deserved it, wanted the pain.

Cayden laughed out loud, a man on the edge. "Here I thought I wasn't good enough for her. Maybe it was the other way around. You're the one who doesn't deserve her!"

Hawk pulled out his cell. One of his informants may have heard something. He wouldn't stop until he had her back. He wouldn't entertain the idea should could already be dead.

"When I find her, I'm keeping her," said Cayden.

"Fuck you."

This time Hawk blocked him when he tried to strike him. He'd had enough. His mind had already switched to find and recover mode.

"Danny, you hear anything new? Anything about Sophia Morenov?"

"No, nothing. Just the bounty."

He dropped his arm, feeling defeated.

Cayden leaned against his car, bringing his own cell to his ear.

"I need information on Sophia Morenov, Randy. This is top priority shit."

After a couple minutes of talking and listening, he tucked his phone back into his pocket.

He looked pissed off.

"Well? Anything?"

"Word's gone out that there's going to be a wedding."

Hawk ran a hand through his hair, his face aching. "I don't give a shit. Anything about Sophia?"

"It's *her* wedding, asshole. She's marrying Antonio Baretti, Jr."

Chapter Fifteen

Cayden opened the door to his basement apartment, making sure it was safe before entering. It was good to be home. If he could even call it home any more. Now that he was off the radar, he didn't need to worry about hiding. He still wouldn't keep this place, too risky, but it was somewhere close to Antonio Baretti where they could lay low.

"Let me get this straight." Cayden tossed his keys on the coffee table. "You made a deal with Vasily's enemy to find Sophia?"

"I wasn't thinking. It was right after you'd stolen her from me."

"That happens a lot doesn't it?"

Hawk's fist clenched, but he kept his mouth shut. The tension between them was growing by the second. It was hard to be civil with Sophia MIA.

Cayden flicked on his computers, then went to the fridge. It was empty. Life had been in a toss-up for months.

"You realize he planned this the entire time, don't you?" asked Cayden.

Hawk sat on the sofa, leaning over his knees. He looked like shit.

"He played me. I knew I shouldn't have trusted him, but I just thought he was focused on killing you. He said he wanted to help out of respect for Vasily. I never for a minute thought he'd be after Sophia."

"Oscar wanted to kill her. Antonio's smarter. He's going to marry into the money and power. By force."

"Just shut the fuck up," said Hawk. "I can't think

about him touching her."

This was Hawk's fault. Cayden wouldn't have been so stupid.

"Maybe he's fucking her right now. That's on you, big boy."

Hawk leapt over the back of the couch, toppling it, taking him down like a wrecking ball. They were equal in size, both pissed off, both with nothing to lose.

And they loved the same woman.

They fought, punching and wrestling on the ground like crazed men. Furniture knocked over as they rolled on the floor. Cayden's boot went through the drywall. They didn't hold back, expelling all their pent-up energy in a blind rage.

Cayden dominated, choking him out, and then Hawk would take control, making him submit.

It came to a stalemate.

They sat against opposing walls, staring at each other, both breathless.

"We going to kill each other or save Sophia?" asked Cayden.

Hawk spat blood to the side.

"My informant says the wedding is this weekend. We have time to plan this out."

"Are we just getting her back or taking down the entire family?" asked Hawk.

"It's too big. The ripples would be endless. The only way to finish this is to marry her, destroying the Morenov Empire once and for all."

"It's all I want. We'll get her back, and I'll marry her."

Cayden stared at the other man, wanting to stab him in the heart, but knowing he had no chance at winning over Sophia.

Right now, the focus had to be getting her free,

and *then* they could worry about the aftermath. Should Cayden steal her away? Force her to love him? He exhaled, already feeling crushed.

He could still smell her, feel her, hear her voice.

How long until he forgot it all?

Until he had nothing left to hold on to?

Their breathing began to slow, the anger draining away. He had to admit the rumble had alleviated a lot of his buried stress. Hawk was a worthy opponent. Cayden had been fighting for decades, and usually came out on top.

"Who trained you?" asked Hawk.

"Myself."

"Your father had a reputation. Must be in your blood."

"No, I don't believe in blood. Loyalty is stronger. I had Frank Almeida. He opened his life to me, but Vasily ended that."

"And you ended Vasily."

Cayden tilted his head. "Still looking for your revenge?"

"No." Hawk adjusted his position, wincing briefly. "You were right about him. He killed my parents and pretended to be my savior. I have nothing left. Only a few blurry memories of my mother."

"And Sophia."

They met eyes again.

"You love her," said Hawk, a statement, not a question.

Cayden hoisted himself up to his feet, using the wall for leverage. He wouldn't admit his feelings to anyone. "Don't worry, she has her hero. She doesn't love me."

"You're wrong."

"And that wouldn't bother you? I thought you

wanted to marry her."

"She's complicated," said Hawk.

You're telling me.

He didn't ask for clarification, but a small flame came to life in his heart. Hope. He remembered their time together at the trailer. It had felt like love, and he'd never wanted it to end. If he had to choose, he'd forget the entire world and stay in their makeshift paradise forever.

Cayden shuffled his way to the kitchen, feeling like he'd been hit by a truck. He grabbed a smoke and lit up, leaning against the counter. "We have to eat. Want me to order pizza?"

Hawk was still sitting on the floor.

"Pizza? That our only option?"

"Sorry, no fine dining around here, Romeo. Pizza and wings are about it."

"Whatever, I'm too sore to care."

Cayden laughed. He couldn't help it. Their situation was so fucked up that it was comical. Two grown men, killing each other because they both loved the same woman, and forced to work together to save her.

At least he could laugh at his own life.

Hawk chuckled, dropping to his back, one knee bent up. "I wish I could have been there to see Oscar get his comeuppance. I've been dreaming about it for weeks."

"Don't worry, I pulled out all the stops."

"Well, thanks for giving me the kill," said Hawk. "I only wish I had the chance to have my revenge on Vasily. It should have been me."

"You were so loyal to him. You never questioned how you got in the family?"

"Never. It was blind devotion. Vasily gave me

my name—bird of prey. He trained me into the perfect killer."

He took a drag, sitting on a kitchen chair.

"Did he ever hurt Sophia?"

"He loved her. In his own fucked up way. He could never get over the fact her mother was a whore. It became a fixation."

"I couldn't find much on her mother," said Cayden.

"She worked at one of his whore-houses. One of the young Russians he'd smuggled over. She tried to hold the paternity over his head when she was pregnant. As soon as she gave birth, Vasily killed her, and tested the baby. Sophia was his."

"He killed her for nothing?"

"No, he would have anyway." Hawk came over and sat across the table from him. "Like I said, I never questioned the shit he did."

"Sophia know about it?"

Hawk shook his head. "I never had the heart to tell her the truth. It would destroy her. Even after everything I learned about my family, I still don't want her to hate her own father. The man's dead, and he did love her."

Cayden respected Hawk for putting Sophia first. Memories made a man. He knew that firsthand. He only wished he had more good ones to reflect on.

Sophia wanted to hate her father, but he saw the hurt in her eyes. All she'd wanted from Vasily was love, unconditional love.

****

Rather than waiting for food delivery, they decided to walk to Bruno's Pizzeria to pick up the pizza. It wasn't too far of a walk. The area was a cesspool, the kind of place good families warned their kids to stay far away from. They passed a couple guys doing a drug deal on the corner.

"Nice neighborhood," Hawk said.

"Am I supposed to be insulted?"

He shrugged. Hawk was too damn tired to fight anymore.

"You get used to it. I've lived around here most of my life," said Cayden "Even the cops ignore it for the most part."

Vasily may have been a bastard, but he only provided the best. Hawk was used to the highest standards from food and clothes and everything in between. "But you can probably live anywhere you want. I know how much contracts pay."

The Morenov family dabbled in just about everything—drugs, women, contracts, extortion. All Hawk knew was crime and sin. He was immune to the violence.

"I guess this neighborhood is the closest thing I have to a family. I mean, they're not the greatest roots, but they're all I have."

He thought his life had been more, but it was just as empty now. Hawk had nothing left.

"Never thought of leaving the life behind, maybe getting married and having some kids?"

Cayden scoffed.

The pizzeria came into view. He remembered it from the night he went in search of Sophia. "This is how I found you," he said.

"What are you talking about?"

"There was a pizza box in the back of your car when you kidnapped Vladimir. I followed the crumbs right to your door."

Cayden smirked. "You're good at tracking." He was quiet for a minute. "I should have killed that fucker.

That's what I get for having mercy."

"You're right. There's no place for mercy in this line of work. Vasily always emphasized the point."

He pushed open the glass door, and they entered the familiar pizza place. Hawk took a seat at an open table while Cayden went to order at the counter. The place smelled like a mix of food and cigarette smoke. He felt dirty just sitting there.

"Won't be long," said Cayden, sitting across from him.

Hawk had been holding onto a lot of questions. Something had changed between Sophia and Cayden after their last stint together. His imagination had been driving him crazy.

They sat in awkward silence for a while, and Cayden pulled out a cigarette and eased back in his chair. He started watching the boxing match on the small wall-mounted television.

"Where'd you take Sophia the week you were hiding her out?"

"One of my properties," he said absently. "Somewhere I lay low when things are too hot."

He nodded. "What did she think of it? I know she's used to a certain quality of life."

Cayden took another drag. "I never would have guessed she was a mafia princess. She didn't mind roughing it. Besides the lack of A/C, I think she actually liked it."

Hawk cracked his knuckles, heat creeping up his collar.

"She seemed attached to you after that week. Odd to fall for the enemy."

Cayden looked him in the eyes. He leaned forward and used the ashtray. "It went both ways. And I was saving her, if you've forgotten."

"What the fuck happened between the two of you?" he said between grated teeth, trying to rein in his volatile passion and not attract attention from the other patrons.

The other man only chuckled. "Relax, Romeo. I didn't fuck her, if that's what you're getting at."

"Then why does she love you? I know she does, so don't bullshit me," said Hawk.

He shrugged. "She loves you, too. Fickle little thing."

"I'd die for her. She's all I have."

"Then we have something else in common," said Cayden.

They both leaned away from each other, not saying a word. The teen behind the counter brought them the pizza box. Cayden paid, and they walked back to the apartment.

"Oh yeah, a junkie gave me your address. You should think twice who you trust with your personal information."

Cayden growled. "Amelia. We went to school together. Things didn't turn out so well for her."

They arrived back at the apartment and ate in silence.

Although he was used to fine dining, he had to admit the pizza was good. Maybe he was just too hungry to care.

Why did he feel so comfortable around Cayden? Even with the rivalry between them, he felt at ease around the other man. Hawk had never had close friendships, forever taught to guard his emotions. Trust created weakness. He didn't know how to be normal. Wasn't sure where to draw the line in social situations.

Cayden got up and poured himself a glass of water, then sat on the couch. He began to disassemble his guns.

"I just realized what's missing around here. Where the fuck is my cat?"

"She's safe."

Cayden smirked.

Hawk had no intention of killing the guy's cat. She was being boarded at a veterinarian's office downtown. He thought it would be good to have the cat for leverage, plus he worried about her being abandoned in the apartment.

"So, when did you first learn to shoot?" Cayden asked, not looking up from his task.

Hawk had never really reflected on it. He thought back to his childhood. He'd only been in Vasily's home for a few months before a gun had been thrust in his hands. The hitmen laughed at the child soldier, but he earned their respect with his natural skills with weapons.

"Ten years old. Vasily wanted me trained in everything. Guns are as much as part of me as anything else," he said. "What about you?"

"One of the foster fathers I stayed with was a hunter, so my first experience as a kid was with a rifle. Long fucking hours waiting in a blind. It wasn't until I was a teen that I really started experimenting."

Hawk sat on a chair in the living area, getting comfortable. This was nice. And fucked up.

"I had nothing to do with what went down at the bakery. I just wanted you to know that."

Cayden briefly glanced up at him, nodding once.

"I was the one to find them."

"I'm sorry," Hawk said. He meant it.

Cayden's jaw twitched. "It was a bloodbath. What I don't understand is why not just kill him? Why torture and slaughter a helpless man, his wife, and their three kids? He didn't even own a gun. He was a fucking baker."

"Vasily was a sick bastard. Before I killed Vladimir, he told me some of the details of my parents' murder. I had no idea. If I'd known, things would have been different."

"The only good thing that came out of him was his daughter."

He agreed one hundred percent.

Hawk watched as Cayden continued cleaning his guns, using oils and different techniques. They could probably teach each other a lot.

"Did you plan on killing Sophia?"

Cayden scoffed. "That was the plan."

"What changed?"

He leaned back, losing interest in his work. "She wasn't what I expected."

Sophia was fire and innocence intertwined. Hawk didn't need an explanation.

"What I don't understand is how you can be ready to die for her, but you don't want her for yourself? What's your reasoning?"

Cayden licked his lips, appearing to want to crawl out of his own skin. "She deserves better, okay?"

"And you think I'm a good catch?"

His brow furrowed. "I wouldn't go that far. Don't you have a history together? How long have you known her?"

"All my life. She was my ward since she turned eighteen. Until I found out what Vasily did to my family, I was very good at denying myself." Hawk clasped his fingers together. "You have any childhood sweethearts?"

Cayden shook his head. "I never get attached. And most of my childhood is blacked out."

"I've been in this business forever. Seen all kinds of people, from all walks of life. When it comes to childhoods, they can shape a person. No matter how much you think you're in control as an adult. Being beaten can make you strong, sometimes cruel, and the sexual abuse can really fuck with a person's head, mess them up beyond repair."

"And you're telling me this, why?"

"I can see it written all over you," said Hawk. "Why else am I still breathing? You're afraid of commitment because of whatever you went through."

Cayden kept quiet. He bristled, appearing uniquely threatened that Hawk managed to peel away his layers. He wasn't trying to be an asshole.

"You have a fancy degree, too? Am I an open book now? No way do I plan to admit the horrors I've lived through in foster care. Stick to contracts because you're a terrible shrink."

"Say you don't love her, and I'll leave you alone."

"Love isn't the question. It's about what Sophia deserves. I have nothing to offer."

Hawk leaned back in his chair. He could see himself in Cayden. Feel his pain. "You're cutting yourself short. Sophia's a smart woman. She wouldn't be drawn to an evil man."

Cayden blocked him out.

Hawk wasn't going to push him. What was the point? After Sophia was free, they'd probably never see him again.

They crashed for the night. After everything they'd been through, a good night of sleep was essential.

Hawk didn't wake up until the morning light hit him in the face from the narrow basement windows. He sat up on the sofa, feeling sore everywhere. His hand immediately went for his 9mm by his side. Everything was in place.

He looked toward the bedroom.

Cayden wasn't in the bed.

Hawk made his way toward the bedroom but heard the static of the shower. Something caught his eye. A piece of paper poked out the top of Cayden's jacket pocket. He pulled out the folded piece of paper, and it turned out to be a pencil drawing of Cayden. He stared at all the detail, and he knew right away it was drawn by Sophia.

She'd painted Hawk's portrait a while back.

Sophia said she loved him, but she loved Cayden, too. He'd hoped he was wrong, and tried to ignore it, but it was clear.

How could he ask her to forget about a man she'd fallen in love with?

He'd never give her up. Hawk had claimed her, and he wanted to marry her. He'd do anything for Sophia—but what if she wanted Cayden more? Could he walk away?

Fuck, he knew he couldn't.

As soon as the water stopped, he folded the paper and slipped it back in the jacket pocket and pushed away his emotions. He was getting a complex, worried about losing Sophia, but also feeling sorry for another man. Hawk wished he still hated Cayden with the same passion. It would make things so much easier.

He went to the kitchen.

It was nasty. Dishes in the sink, cheap laminate counters, and peeling paint on the cupboards. Nothing like he was used to in the Morenov mansion.

How could Cayden live like this? Hawk was used to everything money could buy.

Cayden came in the room, rubbing a towel over his head.

"You have coffee in here?" asked Hawk.

"In the cupboard."

Hawk opened and closed the doors, finding the instant coffee container. "This shit?"

"Hey, I'm not forcing it down your throat."

Hawk grimaced. "I'm going to jump in the shower."

"I think I used all the hot water but help yourself."

He couldn't wait to get settled, to have a fucking address, dry-cleaned clothes, and plush towels. Hawk wanted the happily ever after with Sophia. And he wanted to hate Cayden.

Nothing was going according to plan.

Hawk looked at himself in the bathroom mirror, touching his cheek with a finger. The shadow of a bruise already appeared on his cheek. He'd initiated the fight, but it was because of his own guilt. Cayden had gone above and beyond keeping Sophia safe. Everyone else was out to destroy her. It was a big world, and Hawk would have his hands full once it was just him taking care of her.

His wounds were healing up well, and besides the new bruises, he was almost as good as new.

When he came back into the kitchen after washing and dressing, there were takeout coffee and pastries on the table. He raised an eyebrow at the offering.

"I did a quick coffee run. Wouldn't want you to go slumming."

Hawk took a seat, taken down a few pegs. "You have money, don't you?"

"Sure. Killing pays well."

"Then why live like this?"

Cayden exhaled, pushing his hair back. "I thought I made it clear yesterday. Look, not everyone lives the way you do. This neighborhood, it's not unique. Most people are struggling from paycheck to paycheck. You say Sophia was sheltered? Well, hate him or not, Vasily raised you with a silver spoon in your mouth."

Hawk scoffed. "Vasily was a beast. I can't tell you how many times he beat me, how many fucked up things he forced me to do before I even had hair on my balls. And I didn't live in the house with the family. I lived in the staff's wing, always reminded that I was a charity case."

"Okay, so he was harsh. You still had the best of everything."

"And you have money, so why live like a damn vagrant?"

"I don't care about fancy suits or overpriced coffee. I had nothing growing up, and if I change that now I'm selling out."

"How? You're just moving up in the world. People grow. People change. You should be proud to rise in the ranks."

"I don't want to become dependent. Look at you, right now. You miss all your posh shit. Me, I can survive anywhere. Take it all away, and I'm no worse off."

"How about I take away your smokes? You're still a slave, one way or another."

Cayden cursed under his breath and snuffed out his smoke in an overflowing ashtray. "This is just a choice. Not an addiction. I could give it up if I had to. I'd do it for—"

He stopped himself, but Hawk could fill in the blanks. He'd do it for *Sophia*. How could such a slip of a woman get under both their skins? Hawk could have any woman he wanted, and by the looks of it, so could Cayden.

It was hard to hate a man who loved what he

loved. It didn't make sense when he'd also kill to keep her. He had no one to turn to for advice. Even Vlad was gone. How would he know if his thoughts were normal or dark, healthy or twisted?

"Is that why you pushed Sophia away? Scared to lose her?"

Cayden narrowed his eyes. "What's up your ass? I gave you the girl, so stop rubbing it in my face. Move on and keep her off-topic."

"I wasn't trying to be a prick. Just trying to understand."

"Well, keep that social worker bullshit to yourself. The only reason you're here is so we can team up and get Sophia back."

"Okay, fine," said Hawk. He took one of the coffees and sipped on it. "My guy sent me the specs of Antonio's house." He dropped his cell on the table with the display open.

"*If* she's there."

"She's there. One of the maids sells us information. Sophia's being kept in one of the guest rooms. There're two guards outside the room," said Hawk.

"Locked away in an ivory tower. She's really playing the fairy tale card," said Cayden. "You get to be her knight in shining armor."

"She gets two heroes."

"Spoiled little princess. She always get what she wants?" asked Cayden.

"Pretty much."

Cayden sat on his computer chair and the monitors came to life. "I'll pull up everything I can. We'll have to wait for nightfall."

"Why? That's when they'll expect something. Daylight could give us an edge."

"I always work in the dark," said Cayden.

"Then I'll go myself."

"Don't be stupid. Two of us have a better chance. Remember, we're not there to wipe out the family, just get Sophia out in one piece."

"You saw the blood," said Hawk.

"And he can't marry a corpse. We have to use our heads."

Cayden was right. Rushing in with guns blazing wasn't the answer.

They went over everything they had from the layouts of the house and property to how many men they could be dealing with. The security system, the firepower, the cops, and their escape route. They went through Cayden's stockpile of ammo, organized their weapons side by side in silence, and packed up a small arsenal. Hand grenades for good measure.

It was war, and they didn't plan to lose.

Chapter Sixteen

"I hear you're refusing to eat." Antonio closed the bedroom door behind him, and she inwardly tensed. She knew better than to show weakness. These types of men thrived on instilling fear. And she had experience in dealing with them.

Sophia crossed her arms over her chest. "You're keeping me prisoner. I'm not going to eat."

Antonio Jr. walked back and forth, his hands clasped behind him. She remembered him from a few fundraisers her father made her attend years ago. "You know, my father thinks this is a match made in heaven. He believes there was some kind of divine intervention that brought us together to unite our houses. I understand his vision. Sounds perfect on paper."

"What's the truth?"

"You're smarter than that." He smirked. "I guess we should keep the ruse going at least a month after the wedding. It would be too suspicious if you got knocked off in the first couple weeks. I think a suicide note explaining how you couldn't deal with losing your father would be a nice touch. What do think?"

"Fuck you."

"You're lucky this weekend is important, or I'd have that pretty little face black and blue. You killed one of my favorite drivers, too."

Hawk had told her to pull the trigger if she needed to use her gun. She did. As soon as the group of men rushed her in the parked car, she'd unloaded the clip on them. It wasn't enough. The other men shoved her into the back of a van, put a cloth bag over her head, and brought her here.

She didn't even know if Hawk and Cayden were alive.

"I wish my father was here just so he could torture you, nice and slow. Maybe I'd watch."

"But he's dead, isn't he? It's just you, and soon the Morenov Empire will be gone for good."

"I won't marry you, so whatever you're planning is going to backfire."

He chuckled, a wicked, sleezy sound. "Test me, little bitch. I live for this shit, so be my guest."

She swallowed hard.

"I'm not afraid to die, asshole."

"Good, because it won't be long now," he said.

When he left the room, she exhaled, feeling weak and very, very alone. She looked down at the lawns far below and wondered if she could jump without breaking her legs.

If Hawk survived the raid on Oscar's house, how on earth would he figure out where she was? Antonio was supposed to be helping him. The contract on Cayden's head was called off, but apparently the Baretti family had their own wicked plans all along.

She just wanted to be a normal girl—with dreams, freedom, and *two* hitmen.

Sophia paced as she wrung her hands together. She'd only gotten a few hours' sleep last night, and she was surprised she managed that much. It was much better being Cayden's captive.

Her wedding day was fast approaching. More than an arranged marriage, but a forced sham of a wedding. She wouldn't do it. When she married, it would be for love.

She leaned against the wall and closed her eyes, envisioning what love looked like. She saw Cayden and Hawk. But how could she have one without the other?

The thought kept nagging her to the point of obsession. Why did love have to be so complicated?

Hawk had committed to her, given her everything. Cayden pushed her away, but the connection they had was real, pure, perfect. She wanted to heal him, show him that family could be a good thing. God, they all needed a redo from their fucked-up lives.

Sophia wasn't sure how many hours passed, but she jerked when the door opened again. She'd collected a few items to use as weapons and had them hidden around the room. It was another maid bringing her food. Her stomach rumbled when she smelled the offering, but she wouldn't give Antonio Jr. the satisfaction.

"Ms. Morenov, your food." The woman set the tray on the top of the dresser.

Sophia ignored her.

"I have a message for you," she whispered.

This caught her attention, and Sophia turned to look at the woman. She was Russian. Sophia could detect the accent. "What is it?"

She put a finger to her lips to signal her to be silent. "They're coming for you."

Tears instantly came to her eyes, and she slid down the wall and hugged her knees, crying as silently as she could. The woman left the room but had given her a gift. She didn't realize how much she needed that message. Lack of sleep, food, and safety … none of it compared to going on without hope.

She wasn't forgotten.

They. She hoped that meant Hawk and Cayden. Despite the danger and her breakdown, she felt something sensual travel through her body imagining them together.

Both saving her.

Both claiming her.

What if they made her choose? How the hell would she do it? It would destroy her. Destroy one of them.

No, Cayden would run before that happened. She clenched her fists together, anger taking over her desires. She wanted something she couldn't have.

It would be so simple if she hated Cayden. If the bad guy stayed the bad guy.

She'd end up hurting both the men she loved because of her twisted desires. And she hated herself because of it.

But was it so wrong?

Was she a monster like her father?

A whore like her mother?

She lay down on the floor, remembering her father, her childhood, her first kisses, and losing her heart twice. Part of her wished she could wake up in her own bed, nothing changed. But that wasn't the answer. Her life had seen sad and lonely, and despite some of the most trying events of her life in the past few weeks, she'd also experienced her most memorable.

****

Cayden wasn't a fan of doing his work in the light of day. Too visible. Too many witnesses. Dark deeds were meant to be committed after midnight. He came alive at night, felt at home with the outcasts.

But waiting wasn't an option. And Hawk was on his back to go forward with Sophia's rescue. Lover boy was thirsting to be the hero.

The entire Morenov revenge assassination had been about Vasily. An eye for an eye. Cayden had nothing personal against Sophia or Hawk. But once his feelings for Sophia changed into something much more complicated than murder, his resentment for Hawk grew each day.

By the time he saw Hawk in the flesh yesterday, his only wish was to wipe him off the face of the earth. The only reason he refrained was for *her*. Sophia loved Hawk, and he could give her the stable future she deserved. Cayden didn't know anything about family or women.

He'd fuck everything up.

But he wouldn't deny the temptation, the lure to just give in and make her his. It kept creeping into his thoughts, especially after dropping her off at the hotel after spending a week with her at the trailer. It had been one of the best weeks of his life.

She'd already ruined him for others.

He'd never loved a woman before Sophia.

But she'd choose Hawk. She said herself that she loved the other hitman. He'd avoid the disappointment and steer clear of the Russian princess.

"Ready?" asked Hawk.

Cayden patted himself down and grabbed his keys. "Yeah. I'm starving."

They took his car to an area diner to fuel up.

Last night they'd done a lot of talking, but the past couple hours they'd kept to themselves. Hawk used the pull up bars in the doorway of his bedroom, cranking out reps like a beast. They both had their own coping mechanisms.

"This place?" asked Hawk.

"We've been through this," said Cayden. "You're in a different world now. Nothing will be up to your standards. Play along for another day."

Normally he couldn't stand pretty boys. Hawk was an odd contradiction. A brutal killer wearing a Rolex and trained in the social graces. Cayden couldn't give a fuck about brand names, high priced trinkets, or kissing ass.

Sophia was part of that world of privilege.

Nausea hit him like a punch to the gut, so he stopped thinking about the happy couple. They were too perfect together. It wasn't resentment he felt, but raw jealousy.

He wished he could be a better man, be what she needed—like Hawk.

They took a booth, and he grabbed a laminated menu from the end of the table, even though he already knew what he was ordering.

"Did you know Sophia hates coffee?" asked Hawk.

Cayden glared at him over the top of his menu.

"And she hates cigarette smoke."

He tensed. "I thought I told you I could quit if I wanted to. I'm not a slave."

Hawk toyed with the sugar packets. "So, you *do* love her. You're ready to change to be what she wants."

Cayden slapped his hand on the table. The people at a neighboring booth looked their way. "Again, she's supposed to be off-topic. Stop playing games."

"How can she be off-topic? You care, or why would you be doing this? She's not your fucking problem. You can walk and forget about everything."

"And you can handle this rescue yourself?"

Hawk stared at him. "If I have to, sure. I'd go to hell for her."

So would I.

The tension grew thick, and it was because of the woman between them. The waitress came up and took their orders. He welcomed the distraction. She flirted with both of them, plumping up her cleavage and trying to be cute. Unlike most men, he didn't think with his dick, and was rarely impressed.

When she left, he leaned over on his forearms.

"She likes you, Hawk. You should give her your number. I'll bet she puts out on the first date."

"You're funny."

Cayden leaned back and shrugged.

"I think she's more your type. Like you said, this is your neighborhood. Perfect fit."

"Fuck that. My dick is clean. Just because I live here doesn't mean I'm ready to go dumpster diving. I happen to be very particular when it comes to women."

"So am I. There's only one for me."

He took a breath, trying to behave like a normal human being and push down the monster growing inside. "I know. *Sophia.* You enjoy mentioning it."

They faced off, having some kind of staring contest fit for grade school.

"It was her birthday last week." Hawk smirked, an evil fucking smirk.

Cayden leapt up, one knee on the table as he reached for Hawk's throat. Cutlery fell to the ground, and people gasped and screamed. As fast as his rage took over, it faded, and he sat back down realizing he'd made a scene.

Calm the fuck down, Cayden. You're walking away once she's free.

The waitress came up to them, keeping farther back this time. "My manager says you should probably leave."

"Yeah, we're not fucking leaving. I was defending your honor, sweetheart," said Cayden. My buddy told me he wanted your lips wrapped around his cock."

She blushed.

"My apologies," said Hawk, giving him a sideways scowl.

They ordered.

They ate in silence.

****

The closer they got to rescuing Sophia, the more her love for Cayden tormented Hawk. Why couldn't he hate the other man? Why hadn't he put a bullet in his head?

In a way they were alike, too alike.

They connected on a level he rarely reached with other men. This was only a couple days in the making.

And he knew more about Cayden, knew he'd been through a lot of hardcore shit. He felt guilty because if it wasn't for his past, he'd probably put up a decent fight for Sophia. But he was damaged to the point he wouldn't challenge him, and good enough that he wanted her happy.

Why didn't he feel relieved that Cayden would be out of the picture at the final scene? He shouldn't be reflecting on a stranger's feelings.

Hawk was already going soft without Vasily's influence.

"You will only speak Russian in front of me," Vasily said. *"If I hear one word of English, you'll get the belt."* He held up the thick leather loop as a reminder.

He'd only been eleven, not yet fluent in the new language.

He learned fast.

"You're going on a neighborhood run with Vladimir tonight. You need to learn how we run business in this house. You need to become a man."

Runs consisted of beatings and breaking bones. Forcing poor shop owners to pay money they didn't have. If he didn't do what Vlad said, he had to take their punishment in return. There had been numerous times he willingly took the beating for an old man or a woman who reminded him of his mother.

He had no choice. His life was fear. Control.
Morenov demanded unwavering loyalty.

They drove out to Antonio Baretti's mansion, parking a couple blocks away. They'd talked over their plan all night, going over the details again at the diner. The property was vast, no close neighbors.

"Okay, keep your head down. I don't want them recognizing us before we even get in the front doors," said Hawk.

They dressed as city hydro workers, occasionally marking up the sidewalk with orange spray paint as they neared the house. One man sat on the porch, and he could see the barrel of a rifle hidden under the chair legs. If this was late at night, there would be a lot more heat at the front of the house with a hostage being kept inside.

"Top floor," said Hawk. "Whoever gets there first, gets Sophia out. No mistakes."

They'd gone over the layout of the house and their plans over and over. He knew the house like the back of his hand.

"Let's do this," said Cayden.

He took a breath as they approached the guard on the porch. "Afternoon," said Hawk. "Do you know where your meter is located?"

Cayden leaned close and knocked him out with one short, hard punch to the face, not giving him time to answer. They arranged his body so it looked like he was asleep.

Once they entered the grand foyer, they fanned out, dropping off their fake uniform jackets to reveal the arsenals strapped to their bodies. They used their silencers and knives to take out the men on the main floor, hoping to get in and out with as little drama as possible.

There were only two of them, so shit could get

ugly quick if they weren't on their game every second.

Cayden pointed to the library as he ascended the staircase, his Glock in his outstretched arm. Hawk pushed open the double doors and did a quick sweep, not finding anyone. He went to join Cayden on the staircase.

This was way too easy.

There were three stories, so they had to get up another flight of narrower stairs after this. They'd just set foot on the second level when some bitch downstairs screamed, probably finding one of the bodies. All hell broke loose.

Doors opened and closed, and Baretti's men came at them from both directions. Hawk pulled out a second handgun, Cayden at his back covering the other direction. The gunfire rang in his ears, deafening, drywall flying at him from every direction. They inched their way toward the second staircase, taking cover in the stairwell.

Men shouted in Italian, rushing up the main stairs. The muffled sounds on their radios sounded with instructions to kill the intruders. Vasily demanded he become fluent in numerous languages. It did come in handy.

"Fuck!" Cayden gritted out.

He was down. Shot in the leg. Hawk was halfway up the second staircase.

"Just go. Get Sophia."

Hawk took a couple steps, but his conscience wouldn't let him go farther. He rushed back down, hoisting Cayden up onto his good leg, and supporting much of his weight as they walked up the last staircase together.

They were waiting for them on the third floor. Hawk leaned Cayden against the wall so he could ensure no more men came upstairs. Then he pulled out his big gun, the shotgun he had strapped to his back. He blasted his way through the guards, their bodies flying back from the impact.

The heavily guarded door had to be where they were keeping her. He leaned back and kicked the door open with one blow. Wood slinters rained down.

"Hawk!"

Sophia rushed over to him, but he used a hand to halt her. "Wait."

He took down another man rushing him from the long hallway, then motioned for her to take his hand. It felt like that night all over again. Vasily's assassination. Only things were so different now.

Where was Antonio Jr.?

He wouldn't give up his prize easily. If they got out of here alive, they'd need to go into hiding until they killed that prick.

They made their way back toward the staircase, Sophia clinging to him. He didn't have time to savor having her back. Not until they were out of danger.

"Cayden!" She squatted down when she found him sitting on the top stairs, a pool of blood under his thigh. His face was blanching of color.

"Sophia, stay close to me." He pulled his belt off his pants and bent down to create a tourniquet around Cayden's thigh. Then he forced Cayden to his feet, and helped him down the stairs, both aiming their guns in every new direction.

"Guess you were right about the daylight," said Cayden.

It could have been a hell of a lot worse.

"Hey, tell me that once we're out of here in once piece."

Chapter Seventeen

"Throw a grenade," said Hawk.

Cayden reached into one of the pockets on his harness and tossed it into the foyer once they were outside.

Sophia was terrified and relieved. When she'd heard gunshots, she knew something was going down. She'd kept far from the bedroom door just in case. Thank God it was them.

They were on the front lawns, in the daylight. Cayden was shot and unable to walk properly. Hawk kept his eyes peeled on everything, his breathing heavy.

The grenade went off, the earth quaking beneath her feet.

Chaos.

Confusion.

"Where's the car?" she asked.

"A couple blocks away," said Hawk. "Come on. Keep close."

Cayden grunted as they picked up the pace. "Leave me here. You won't make it to the car in time. Neighbors could have called the cops by now."

Hawk stopped, and she thought he'd leave Cayden behind. She was about to protest, but he surprised her, bending down and hoisting Cayden over one of his shoulders. Hawk's strength shocked her because the other man was just as heavy with muscle.

They jogged up the street, continually checking behind them.

Hawk pulled out his cellphone without missing a beat. "I need a doctor. A surgeon. Gunshot to the thigh. I'll pick them up in seven minutes at the corner by the old church."

Her heart raced, adrenaline pumping wildly through her veins.

When they reached the car, Hawk hauled Cayden into the backseat and tossed a shotgun onto his lap. "Get in, Sophia."

She jumped in the passenger seat, and Hawk immediately did a U-turn on the road and sped away.

No one said a word until they were a good five minutes down the highway.

"Will they follow?" she asked.

"Antonio won't give up so easily. Do you know where he is?" asked Hawk.

"He's gone most of the time. They're busy planning our wedding."

"Did he touch you?" asked Cayden.

She twisted around in her seat. "Oh God, we have to get you to a hospital."

"Did he touch you?"

"No, he kept me trapped in a room," she said. Sophia grabbed Hawk's sleeve. "He doesn't look good. We have to get him help."

"I'll handle everything. Let me think." They exited the highway. An elderly man with a black bag waited on the corner. Hawk pulled up next to him. "Get in."

The doctor started examining Cayden as they drove to the other end of the city, the rush hour traffic leaving the business district as they came in. "I'll park in the underground because we can't bring him in the front doors bleeding all over the damn place," said Hawk.

"Will he be okay?"

Hawk ignored her, driving down the dark, winding underground parking garage of a high-rise hotel.

"Does my father own this one?"

"No."

In their world, there was an entire underground of professionals. Doctors, teachers, lawyers, and even cops had been on her father's payroll. She was thankful Hawk was getting help. It was surreal seeing Cayden again. She thought she'd lost him forever when he'd dropped her off last time.

Her heart felt at peace being close to both men. If only it could last forever.

Hawk helped Cayden to the elevators, then left them there to rent a room in the lobby.

"Does it hurt?" she asked.

Sophia pressed her forearms to Cayden's chest, grabbing handfuls of his shirt.

"Not so much anymore."

Cayden's voice sounded weak, his pallor getting worse. He started to close his eyes. "Cayden, stay with me," she shouted. "Hawk will be back soon."

She cupped Cayden's cheek.

"He loves you," Cayden said. "He's a good man. He'll take care of you."

"Cayden, don't say that." He was talking like he was already gone, either a dead man or running away again. She wouldn't allow him to leave her. Tears streamed down her cheeks.

"Don't cry, baby."

"I love you, Cayden. I can't lose you."

When he started to collapse, Hawk was there to support him, dragging him into the elevator. "Nineteenth floor."

The doctor had cut off his pant leg in the car, and the bleeding had stopped. "He's in luck. The bullet didn't hit the femoral artery," said the doctor. "But he needs blood."

She sighed in relief, continually jostling Cayden

so he wouldn't go to sleep.

As soon as they got inside their suite, Hawk dropped Cayden on the sofa. "Take care of him, doc. I'll get some boiling water."

Sophia unbuckled and unzipped Cayden's black jeans, tugging the remaining material down past his hips. He was a dead weight, making it difficult. When she pulled her hands back, they were coated in blood. She held them in front of her face, staring at the crimson fluid, going into shock.

"Sophia! For God's sake. Go sit down." Hawk tore the jeans off the rest of the way and dropped some towels on the floor.

The doctor went right to work, opening his black bag on the coffee table. Hawk poured a bottle of booze over the wound and Cayden passed out.

"Do you know what you're doing?" she asked.

"He's one of the best, Sophia. Dr. Zelwik used to work for your father."

She watched, unable to look away, and angry that the sight of blood still affected her after all this time. An IV had been set up, and the doctor began a blood infusion between the two men. Hawk was O negative. She remembered her father mentioning it may come in handy for her.

Sophia stayed glued to the wall until it was done.

The doctor stitched up the side of Cayden's leg a while later. It was a small hole for all the blood she'd seen. "He'll be fine. Missed the bone. Mostly blood loss. Just let him sleep it off tonight. Tomorrow, he should be up and walking. I'll leave pain killers."

He set a bottle of narcotics on the table.

The doctor left the suite.

"He won't take them. Cayden has a thing about drugs, prescription or otherwise. He's a stubborn bastard," said Hawk.

"How do you know that?" she asked.

"We've had a couple days to reminisce while planning your rescue," he said. "I guess bringing you along the other night wasn't the best idea. I was afraid to leave you alone at the hotel."

"It brought the two of you together. I like the sound of that."

"Why?"

She shrugged, keeping her mouth shut. Sophia had to remind herself her feelings were abnormal. Good women fell in love with one man, not two.

Hawk pulled down his sleeve, just a Band-Aid on his arm. He stood up and approached her. There was fire in his eyes.

"You should rest. The doctor said you could get dizzy if you do too much too soon."

"Don't change the subject."

She wanted to back away from him, but she was already pinned against the wall. "What are you doing?" she asked, her voice barely forming a whisper.

Hawk tilted her chin up. "You love him. The man who killed your father."

Sophia kept quiet. Her body tensed, her fears seeping to the surface. Loving two meant losing both.

"Never lie to me, Sophia. Do you love him?"

She shrugged. "Maybe I don't know what love is."

"Do you love *me*?"

This time she looked him in the eyes.

"I don't want to hurt either of you, Hawk. I'm broken. Messed up in the head. I wish I was normal, but my life has always been far from it."

He inhaled, his chest expanding, his features set. Hawk began to pace in front of her, one hand squeezing behind his neck. "I'm ready to commit to you for the rest of my life. You have no idea how much I love you."

"Please don't hate me."

"I just want to understand," he said.

She shook her head. There was nothing to explain. He already knew the truth. It made her stomach knot, nausea washing over her in waves. She felt like a monster.

"Tell me what to do," she said.

Sophia held his shirt, needing to feel his affection, and desperate for a voice of reason.

He said nothing but leaned down to kiss her. She closed her eyes and savored the feel of his lips. The domination. His acceptance settled her nerves, her entire body feeling spineless and wanton.

"First things first. We need ice."

Hawk grabbed the ice bucket from the top of the bar and then took her hand as they left the suite. Cayden was still passed out on the couch, his color already improving.

They walked down the hall, and Hawk held a door open for her to enter. The tiles were cool on her bare feet compared to the carpet in the hall. The large ice machine took up the corner, but rather than filling the bucket, Hawk set it on the ground, his eyes focused on her. He pulled a wooden wedge from his pocket and shoved it under the door, sealing them in the small room.

Her heart began to race in anticipation.

"I've been holding back since your birthday. All I've been thinking about is fucking you again. Especially after losing you again. I think you've had enough time to recover, no?"

She nodded.

"Good girl." Sophia loved when he said that to her. It made her want to please him even more.

"Take off your clothes for me. I want to see you naked."

Sophia wasn't ashamed of her body. And she wanted Hawk, all of him, forever. She removed her shirt and pants, then unfastened her bra, and wiggled out of her panties. The room was chilly, and her nipples pebbled into tight little buds. Gooseflesh broke out on her arms. The exhilaration of standing there in the nude heated her from the inside out.

He nodded in approval, his jaw clenching. Hawk reached into the ice machine and pulled out a piece of ice, then approached her. "Is you pussy hot?"

Oh God, she was aching for him. She nodded, not trusting her voice.

He reached down and cupped her pussy with his free palm, making her yelp she was so sensitive. Hawk growled. He rubbed the ice over her clit, then up and down her folds. She braced a hand on his shoulder. New, intense sensations came to life, her breath catching in her throat.

"Take it, baby." He pushed the ice up her cunt, and the erotic invasion took her by surprise. The coldness brought made her nerves fire with need. She shuddered, her eyes fluttering shut. "Think you can handle more?"

"Okay…"

"Hold this one in."

He shoved another cube up her pussy, water leaking down her inner thighs as the ice melted. She gasped from the intensity. Hawk cupped her ass with both hands, squeezing hard. His fingers lingered close to her asshole. "I wonder if you'd even be able to handle getting double fucked. What do you think, baby? Will two cocks fit inside this little body?"

Then he lowered his big frame and sucked her nipple into his mouth. She tossed her head back and combed her fingers into his hair. Her pussy pulsed, and the only thing that would sate her was his hard cock.

She thought about his words. Was he considering sharing her with Cayden or just screwing with her head? It sounded dirty. Tempting. Perfect. But she wouldn't read too much into it. After being kidnapped by Antonio Jr., she was just relieved to be free and in the arms of the man she loved—safe and protected.

"Come here, sweetheart." He easily hoisted her up by the thighs, her back against the wall. She wrapped her arms around his neck, and legs around his waist, as he reached one hand down between them. She heard his zipper before he released his cock. "You're my whole world."

He ran the tip of his cock up and down over her clit, slippery and wet, then pushed inside her. "Hawk…"

"You're so fucking tight." He sank in deep, inch after thick inch, filling her to overflowing. "So sweet and perfect. All mine."

Hawk didn't hold back. He said he'd been pent-up, and it showed. This wasn't a slow exploration. It was sex. Fucking. Nothing fancy, but exactly what they both needed. The man pumped his hips at a furious pace, the friction and pressure against her clit had her hurtling toward a beautiful peak. She panted, and gasped with each up-thrust, her tits jostling. The sounds of hard, wet sex filled the small space. Hawk was well-endowed, so no cell inside her was left untouched.

She wondered is someone would come looking for ice and find them. The possibility of being caught spiked her arousal.

"I'm going to come," she said between breaths.

"Such a good girl, Sophia. Come for me." He continued to hold her, filling her with cock over and over until her body began to blossom.

"Yes!" she squealed, clawing at his shirt. And she came in a burst of heat, raw pleasure spreading like a wildfire. The sensations coursed through her womb, travelling all the way to her extremities. Wave after beautiful wave made her pussy clench. Hawk slowed down after coming inside her. He held her in place against the wall as their breathing calmed.

"I guess I better fill my ice bucket," he said. Hawk kissed her temple, lowering her to her feet so she could get dressed. A mix of water and cum leaked down her thighs. She used the paper towel dispenser and cleaned herself up.

She wondered if they were going to talk about the elephant in the room. Would he tell her what to do? Demand she forget Cayden? She wasn't sure what she'd do in that situation. Sophia didn't dare bring up the topic again, too afraid of where it could lead.

Although she hadn't lied to either man about loving the other, she also couldn't make a choice.

****

Cayden woke up with a start, the morning light hitting him in the eyes. He sat up and looked around, the night before mostly a blur. He was laid up on the sofa in some fancy hotel. Alone.

He looked down at his leg, attempting to move it. It was sore, but he'd live. Another scar for his collection.

He got to his feet, trying not to limp as he walked over to the closed bedroom door. He peered inside only to find Hawk and Sophia asleep together on the king-sized bed. His heart clenched looking at them, an outsider beyond the glass. He closed the door and went in search of his cell phone. It was on the coffee table with his harness and guns.

His heart was still racing. He had to get out of there. It was one thing to step aside for her best interest.

It was another to bear witness.

"Hey, Randy. What have you been up to?"

"I haven't heard from you in days, Cayden. You have your phone off?"

"Long story."

"There's no more bounty on the girl," he said. "You've lost your fucking window. I told you to cash out while you could."

He exhaled, feeling a wash of relief trickle through his body. No more contract hanging over Sophia. She'd be much safer now.

"I'm not worried about it, so neither should you be."

"You still have her?"

"No, I gave her back to her own people. I'm done. I feel like shit, look like shit, and I just want to get the fuck out of here. Can you arrange for my bike and some clothes?"

It must have been the tone of his voice, but Randy didn't argue. Sounded almost sympathetic. Did he realize Cayden's heartstrings were ripped to shreds, his sanity only a couple words away from fracturing into insanity?

He gave his friend the address and room number of the hotel. He couldn't exactly leave in his boxers.

The urge for a smoke took him by storm, especially with his emotions at an all-time high. Why should he bother to quit now? He had no reason to better himself. Not a fucking thing.

He started up the coffeemaker. It was something.

Cayden walked around the room, squinting with each step, but refusing to listen to the pain telling him to sit his ass down. What did he think would happen? That he'd save Sophia and she'd run into his arms like a fairy tale? Tell him she picked him over everyone else in the world? He'd never been anyone's number one, and that deep seated need to be wanted grew tenfold since he fell in love with the little mafia princess.

He'd have to hit the road, forget about her—this time for good. Maybe he'd move across the country where he had no chance of running into her or Hawk.

Or maybe he'd eat a bullet.

He began packing up his shit, tugging on his holsters as he waited for Randy to show up.

"What are you doing?"

He turned around to find Sophia standing there in an oversized t-shirt that barely reached her thighs. "Getting out of here. We're both free. No contracts on our heads."

"You can't just leave. Where will you go?"

Her concern only angered him at this point.

"Don't worry about it, little girl." He winked at her just to piss her off.

"Stop it," she said. Sophia approached him. "You're hurt. You have to lie down."

"I've been through worse."

"I don't care."

She reached for him, but he grabbed her arm to keep her back. "I know I don't come across as much, but believe it or not, I have feelings. Stop screwing with me, Sophia. You and Hawk can have your happy ever after now. Leave me the fuck out of it."

Tears filled her eyes. "I don't know what to do."

"I'll make it easy for you. Turn around and go back to the bedroom. I'll be gone next time you come out."

"No!" She grabbed his harnesses, pulling herself closer. He tried to push her away, but she screamed and latched on with both fists.

"What the hell's going on?" Hawk came out in his boxers, tugging Sophia off him and spinning her around. "Tell me, Sophia."

She shook her head and shrugged him off, walking to the windows. Her arms were wrapped around herself, her body shuddering as she silently continued crying.

Hawk looked at him. They both stood in place, no words, nothing but eye contact. He wanted to hate the other man, but he came up short. It was better for him to leave without a fight.

"I'll be out of your hair in twenty minutes. Just waiting on my ride."

Hawk nodded once.

"Sure you're up to it? You've been through a lot," said Hawk.

Cayden scoffed. "And you care?"

"I gave you my fucking blood. Take that however you want."

They both shut up again, but the emotions were strong in the room.

Cayden hadn't even realized Hawk had given him a transfusion. He'd been too out of it last night. Hawk's blood flowed through his veins. No one in their world would go to such a length. Hitmen were selfish, heartless, and greedy. Hawk wasn't like that.

"You guys should lay low for a while. Antonio Jr. will be looking for you. Get married, have a bunch of kids. He'll move on," said Cayden.

Where was Randy? He needed to get out of the suite. It would have been better if neither of them had woken up before he left.

Sophia turned around, her face blotchy from crying. She approached them. "I screwed up, okay? You guys shouldn't hate each other. *I'm* the one you should hate. I'm the one pitting the two of you against each other, but I swear it was never my intention."

Hawk bristled. "You want to be with Cayden, is that it? Just say it."

"I want something I can't have. Maybe it's better for me to leave on my own, to forget both of you. I'm a big girl. I'll figure things out."

"Are you kidding me?" said Hawk. "You're my responsibility."

"No, actually I'm not. My father's dead. And you know what kind of a monster he was, anyway. Maybe I'm no different. What I want is sick. You both deserve better."

"What do you want that's so terrible?" asked Hawk.

She looked at him. "You know what I want."

Why was Cayden out of the loop?

"How can I give you that? You really expect me to share you?"

"Whoa, hold on here," said Cayden. "Share what exactly?"

Someone knocked on the door. It had to be Randy. This was all over now. He'd hop on his bike and keep riding. The alternative appeared to be sharing Sophia with another man in some twisted threesome. He'd never played nicely, and certainly wasn't good at sharing.

As he thought about it, he realized it may be better than living without her, of feeling sorry for himself forever. Once he walked out that door, it would be over, and he wasn't sure how he'd handle that overwhelming feeling of want and loneliness.

He went to let Randy in.

"Cayden, no. Please don't leave like this," she said.

"Stop playing games, Sophia. You can't have everything you want."

"You've told me that before," she said. "I refuse to believe it."

Chapter Eighteen

Hawk stood on the sidelines, not knowing what step to take. He couldn't lose Sophia, but also couldn't make her happy if he cut Cayden out of her life. None of this would have happened if he'd claimed Sophia when they first kissed. Now everything was fucked up, and he had to make a choice. Accept Cayden into the fold or risk losing Sophia forever.

Maybe a woman like her needed two men behind her. Trouble followed her wherever she went. He and Cayden were more alike than different. They understood each other and had one very important thing in common—their love and devotion for Sophia.

Cayden opened the door, and someone passed him a black duffel bag. He couldn't hear what they were saying. Just before he closed the door, the other person tossed a set of keys to Cayden. He caught them in a tight fist.

"I'm going to get dressed. I have a long drive ahead of me," said Cayden.

As he passed, Hawk put a hand to his chest to halt him. "Sophia doesn't want you to leave."

"And?"

"So, stay," said Hawk. "You have somewhere else you need to be?"

Cayden laughed without humor. "You're just as bad as her. Are you telling me you think her little threesome fantasy is a good idea? It's called a fantasy for a reason. It's bullshit and bound for disaster."

"So, you'll run from what you love? Maybe you should take a good look at yourself and decide it's time to stop running."

Hawk knew Cayden was damaged goods. They all were in their own way. He had a good sense for people, and he knew Cayden loved Sophia unconditionally. And he had a conscience. A rare commodity in their world. Everyone he'd grown up with was ruthless and shallow. Hawk wouldn't trust anyone with Sophia. Cayden proved himself different time and time again.

"What do *you* want, Sophia?" asked Cayden. "Don't tell me you think Hawk has a great idea here."

"None of us having anything left. Why not stay together? Is it so bad?"

"You want to be one big happy family?" Cayden dropped the duffel bag on the coffee table. "You think it will be all rainbows?"

"No family is perfect," said Sophia.

They were all orphans, all alone in the world. Why the fuck not? Hawk wasn't insecure with himself or his body. He just needed Sophia's love. As much as he wanted her for himself, filthy images of sharing her kept creeping into his thoughts.

"So, who gets Sophia in this arrangement?" asked Cayden.

"We both do. That's the point. If she can't choose, that means she loves us equally."

They turned to Sophia at once. She stood quietly. Listening. Wide-eyed.

Cayden brushed the hair from his eyes. "You've known Hawk all your life. You can't love us equally. I'll always be your second choice."

"He was my babysitter until my father died. Everything happened so fast. My feelings aren't in question for either of you," she said.

"This is ridiculous. It would never work," said Cayden. He threw up his hands, but Hawk could tell he was intrigued. Looking for confirmation that it was possible.

Hawk knew one way to test this arrangement.

"Come here, Sophia." Hawk used a curled finger to beckon her closer. She came within arm's reach. "You know that sharing means taking both of us, right?"

She bit her lower lip. The sexiest thing he'd ever seen.

"At the same time?"

"Maybe."

"Yes," said Cayden. "That should be enough to scare you."

"It doesn't," she said. "It's what I want."

Hawk looked to Cayden. "We won't know until we try. Or are you too weak from your gunshot wound?"

"Hey, it was just a scratch."

"You do have my blood inside you," said Hawk. "Must be that."

Cayden huffed and walked away, leaning against the closest wall. He ran a hand through his hair again, his expression hard. "Neither of you have thought this through. What happens after today? Antonio Jr. is still a threat. Where are we supposed to live? How can it work?"

"You've never had a real family. You'll get used to it," said Hawk.

"That answered none of my questions."

Cayden exhaled, appearing to settle down slightly. Hawk almost laughed out loud, but held it in. He was trying to convince another man to fuck his woman, to live with them under the same roof. He wasn't sure why he felt so confident in the arrangement, but it felt almost natural, like it was exactly what was supposed to happen. It fixed all the problems.

Since realizing Sophia had a thing for Cayden, it tore him up inside. But then the other man grew on him, and he could understand what Sophia saw in him. He'd give her the fucking world, his life, so why not the unorthodox relationship she craved? Their lives had always been far from normal.

"I need you, Cayden. Please stay," said Sophia. She approached him but kept her distance.

"How can this not bother *him*?" Cayden waved a hand in his direction.

"I'm right here, you know? It's not exactly my first choice," said Hawk. "But I know what I bring to the table, and if she says she loves me, too, I have to believe it."

He was confident in his prowess. Hawk was a man, not a boy, and having another guy in the family wouldn't make him feel insecure. He was willing to make it work—for her.

"I'll stay the night … but only to recuperate a bit more. I still need to think about things, so don't think I've agreed to anything."

****

Sophia awoke to a whisper against her ear. Was she dreaming? She rubbed her eyes and twisted in the blankets. It was still dark outside.

She'd been sleeping alone. Hawk was in the second bedroom and Cayden on the sofa. Cayden said he'd stay on one night, but one night had turned into three. They all seemed to be avoiding the topic and keeping their distance from each other. She was tired of walking on eggshells around the suite.

She *could* love them equally.

She knew that.

Not a doubt in her mind.

Sophia was just grateful Cayden was even considering a ménage relationship. *Ménage.* It sounded wrong and crazy and taboo, but the reality couldn't be further from the truth. It was her ultimate fantasy. The only answer for her in this situation. She'd inadvertently given her heart to two different men.

It already surprised her that Hawk had changed his tune so quickly. She remembered his tone of voice when he mentioned double-fucking her in the ice room. It intrigued him.

"Come with me."

Cayden had one knee on the bed as he hovered over her.

"Where? What's going on?"

"I need to be alone with you. We have to talk. Just you and me," he whispered.

"Okay…"

She sat up, still partly in a daze. He was fully dressed, his jacket and boots on, ready to leave. She'd taken her usual shower before bed, so she just pulled on some clothes and tied her hair into a ponytail. Only the moonlight gave her enough light to see. As soon as she was dressed and had her flats on, he took her hand and led her to the front door.

"What about Hawk?"

"He's sleeping like a baby. We won't be too long."

It felt good to hold Cayden's hand, so strong and warm. She hadn't really been close with him since she left the trailer. She missed him—their talks, the silliness, their growing connection. It had all been building into something beautiful when he cut their time together short.

The light in the hallways stung her eyes. She cuddled against his side as they walked down to the elevator, only the sound of keys jingling in his free hand. He smelled so damn good, a mix of woodsy cologne and leather. Although she had no clue what he was up to, she didn't care. She trusted him and wanted him to trust her in return.

They exited on the lower level, and he led her to a motorcycle. She stared at the beast, black, chrome, and badass. He handed her a helmet.

She shook her head. "I can't, Cayden. I've never been on one of those."

He smirked, putting the helmet on her head and buckling it up. "We can't waste time. I need to show you something. I won't let anything happen to you."

"Do I get to know where we're going yet?"

"You'll find out soon enough." He put his own helmet on, then straddled the Harley, bringing it to life. The roar of the motor echoed in the underground garage like an angry dragon. He nodded behind him, and she reluctantly climbed onto the back. She wrapped her arms around his waist, loving the feel of him so close to her.

"Hold on tight, princess."

Then they were gone, racing through the narrow rows in the garage before bursting out onto the street. He hit the highway, the sky still dark and a chill in the air as it chased through her hair and up her pant legs.

She slid her fingers under his leather jacket, feeling his bare skin and the hard grill of his abs. Sophia dared to reach lower, cupping his crotch and giving him a squeeze. He hit the gas in response, making her squeal and wrap her arms around him again in fear of flying off the back.

They kept driving, mile after mile. As her nerves subsided, she savored the freedom, the speed. She'd wonder where they were heading on occasion, but she mostly stayed content resting her head against his back and holding on.

"Sophia, look," he said a while later.

She peeked around him at the sky ahead. The sun was making its debut, a brilliant red sphere appearing on the horizon. Like magic, the sky began to transform into a canvas of pink, orange, and red. She was awestruck, staring as the world continued to shift from night to day in a spectacular display of color. Even the clouds became things of beauty.

If only she had a canvas and full set of acrylic paints. She'd try to capture the beauty forever.

Cayden turned off the next exit, taking a sharp right onto a rough dirt road. He knew precisely where he was going. Her body jostled as he navigated down the uneven trail. He finally came to a stop, his foot coming down to support the bike. Silence settled in once he cut the engine.

"Where are we?" she asked. There was a dilapidated cabin of sorts, but it was on the edge of a narrow river where she could still get a clear view of the sunrise. It was stunning. "Another one of your hideouts?"

He helped her off the bike, and they removed their helmets. Cayden took her hand and led her toward the river. "I used to come here when I was younger."

They carefully stepped over the loose stones. She held onto his arm for balance. "To fish?"

"To escape."

She swallowed hard. Sophia knew he'd had a hard upbringing, but they never talked too much about it.

"When things got too hard, I'd come here to get away. To think. It was my therapy. Sometimes I'd sleep in that cabin. I'd close my eyes and pretend my life was anything than what it was."

She touched his face. "Cayden…"

"It's okay. Now I don't have to pretend. Because I have you." He combed both hands into her hair, securing her head as he stared into her eyes.

Her breath caught.

"Please don't hate me."

"Trust me, I've tried. It's not so easy." He stepped back, then squatted down to skip a flat stone across the water. He glanced up at her. "Are you happy, Sophia? Is this the life you want? What's enough?"

"Are you talking about Hawk?"

He went back to skipping stones, and she couldn't help but stare at his broad shoulders and his thick hair starting to fall into his eyes. She thought of him as a little boy, here, escaping his living nightmares. Sophia wanted to be the change he needed.

"What if it doesn't work?"

She squatted down next to him. "It will. I won't let it fail."

"Right, you're used to getting everything you want." He winked at her but couldn't hide his pain.

"And I want *you*, Cayden."

"I've been thinking about everything for the past few nights. It's been like having a fucking devil on my shoulder. I'm used to having things my way, and in this situation, I'd normally tell both of you to fuck off. I have no problem being on my own. It's all I know."

"Don't say that."

He ignored her. "But things changed somewhere along the way, you know? I did something I promised myself I'd never do." They stood up. He was so much taller. "I fell in love with a girl. And everything changed."

Her lips parted as her breathing picked up. She could feel him all the way to her marrow—everything Cayden, the good and the bad. Sophia wanted all of it. "What's going to happen now?" she whispered.

His jaw clenched. "When I was a kid, grade five, one of the foster fathers did something to me that changed me forever. I'd already been through countless fucked-up homes. The beatings, the burns, the neglect—

nothing compared to that. I wanted to tell my teachers, but it was too embarrassing. I was just a kid. I felt dirty. Humiliated. Disposable. People never cared about foster kids. I did the only thing I knew that would get me out of there. I stabbed him when he was watching TV. He survived, but I ended up in juvie, exactly where I wanted to be. It was hard to give a shit after that, impossible to trust." He took a breath. "Once my feelings changed for you, I didn't feel worthy. You were too pure. Too perfect for a piece of shit like me."

"Don't say that, Cayden. It wasn't your fault. You know that, don't you?"

"Doesn't change the past. Doesn't make me whole."

She cupped his cheek, finally understanding all his broken pieces. Sophia's love only blossomed. He deserved a happily ever after. "My feelings haven't changed. You're still the same man I fell in love with. Strong, kind, and perfectly imperfect. I'm glad you told me."

"How can it not bother you?"

"Cayden, I only care that you're still hanging onto all this pain." Everything made sense. She knew he'd been keeping something bottled up, something that really messed with his head. He trusted her enough to tell her, and she hoped it would help him heal.

"I never told anyone before. Still not sure I did the right thing telling you."

She interlocked her fingers with his. "Thank you for telling me. I don't want anything coming between us," she said. "And nothing from your past will change my feelings for you."

"I wanted you to see the sunrise," he whispered.

"It was perfect."

He blurted the next words. "I'll give what you

want a chance."

"Oh God," she murmured, her relief instantaneous. "Thank you." She tried to kiss him, but he held her at arm's length.

"I was worried I'd fuck things up because of the shit I've lived through. But I could never hurt you. Never." He held the sides of her head and massaged her temples with his thumbs. His features were set hard. "But it has to be equal. I'm tired of being second best. Do you love him more than me, Sophia?"

She shook her head emphatically. "If I did, I would have chosen him. Please never think my love is diluted because of Hawk. It's just different with all of us." Sophia closed her eyes and took a deep breath before focusing on him again. "I told you I'm fucked up."

He tugged her against him, his mouth coming down on hers, kissing with hunger and a claim so strong her knees became weak. She wrapped her arms around his neck, unable to get enough of him. It had been like pulling teeth to get his attention back at the cabin. This was real. Perfect.

"I need you," she said. "I want to be yours."

He licked his lips, and she saw the need glazed over in his eyes. "Remember the trailer? I still remember the taste of your pussy. Sweet as fucking honey."

"Cayden. Oh, please…" She unzipped his leather jacket, running her fingertip along the single gun holster he had over one shoulder. Everything about him turned her on, made her desperate and wanton.

He leaned close, his words a gentle brush against her ear. "Are you wet for me?"

Sophia's words caught in her throat. She wrapped her hand around his belt and tugged his hips toward her.

"You're not a virgin anymore, are you, baby doll?"

Her cheeks flushed.

"That's okay. For now."

"Cayden, I want you. Take me and never let me go."

Chapter Nineteen

There was nothing Cayden wanted more, but he wasn't going to fuck Sophia in the nasty shack by the river. That place had its own set of twisted memories attached to it. He wanted to enjoy her in a proper bed. With his cock rock hard, his mind scrambled for options.

His neighborhood was close by. He'd take her to his apartment. Claim her in his own bed.

Then they'd return to the hotel, and he'd have equal ground with Hawk. Right now, Sophia belonged to the other man. Once Cayden had his way with her, she'd belong to him, too.

His secret was out in the open, and she hadn't run the other way. There was no reason for him to push here away any longer.

The morning had already brought the city to life, but there on their way to the seedier end where Cayden grew up. He'd wanted Sophia to see a sunrise through his eyes, to have some time alone to express how this arrangement was screwing with his head. Part of him wanted to stab Hawk straight through the heart. Another part was curious, willing, and ready to commit.

The engine settled as he eased up on the throttle, parking his motorcycle in front of his shithole apartment. Maybe she'd think twice about him after seeing how he lived on a daily basis.

"Let's go," he said.

Cayden kept his guard up as they walked to the stairs to his basement apartment. He was on edge just being here again. It was different with Hawk there because they had the power of numbers and the burning desire to rescue Sophia.

"What is this place?"

"It's my apartment," he said as they descended

the concrete staircase. "Or it was. Can't exactly live here anymore after Hawk put me on the radar for every asshole in the city."

"Should we be here?"

He turned to look at her. "Don't think I can protect you?"

She shrugged. "Just saying."

Cayden unlocked the door, then pressed a hand to her stomach, pushing her back. "Wait here a sec."

He pulled out his Glock and did a full sweep of the small apartment. It looked ransacked, but that was how they left it. Cayden ushered Sophia inside and secured the door.

"Home sweet home," he said, raising his arms to the sides before realizing he was still holding his gun. He holstered his weapon. "What do you think?"

"I think you need to hire a housekeeper … and a handyman." She pointed to the numerous spots with drywall damage.

"I don't like people in my space."

"What about me? I'm here."

He clenched his teeth as he watched her wander around, her little fingers touching everything in reach. She roused the beast in him with just her smile or the sound of her voice.

"You're different. I plan to keep you."

"Yeah?" She ran her hands up his chest, hooking her fingers behind his neck. He leaned down and kissed her on the mouth. They kissed, and the world went away.

He backed her up to the nearest wall and raised her arms above her head. Her pulse raced as he pinned her wrists high. "Stay like that. Just like that." Cayden lifted her shirt. She'd gotten ready in a rush, so she wore no bra beneath. Her tits were perfect, her nipples tight little buds. "I remember these."

"It's not a game anymore," she said.

He covered her nipple with his mouth. She mewled, dropping her arms, and combing her fingers into his hair. He suckled the other tit, thoroughly enjoying her sweet, young body.

"Only twenty-five. I'm a bastard for what I'm about to do."

Cayden tugged her shirt off all the way and scooped her up into his arms to carry her to his bedroom. He tilted her to the side as he went through the doorway threshold, like newlyweds on their honeymoon. His bed was unmade.

He settled her down on the mattress and immediately tugged off her pants. She crawled backwards to the center of the bed.

"Scared?"

"I trust you," she said.

"You shouldn't."

She leaned back on her elbows, her eyes roving over his body.

Sophia was right.

There was no fear in her eyes.

He liked that.

She only wore a little pair of white bikini panties, nothing else. If he thought he wanted to fuck her back at the trailer, that need was nothing compared to right now. This was going to happen. His whole world was about to change, but for the better he wasn't so sure.

He shrugged off his leather jacket and holster, resting them on the dresser. After tugging off his shirt, he bunched it up and held it in his fist as he crawled onto the bed.

"Are you the big bad wolf again?" She smiled at him, and he knew there was no turning back. She'd stolen his fucking heart.

239

"Do you like wolves?"

Sophia nodded. She parted her legs, her chest rising and falling in heavy waves.

He pushed her knees open wider and mounted her, his jeans rubbing against her little panties. She arched up against him, her eyes closed.

Cayden nipped her jawline, kissing all the way around her ear and neck as he worked his hips to rub her clit.

"That feels so good," she murmured. Her hands were all over his shoulders and back, her nails gently scraping his skin.

"I don't know what it is about you. You're everything I usually avoid, but I can't stay away."

"Good. I never want you to leave me again." She held him tighter. "I'm tired of this life. The death. The blood."

He wanted to be here everything, her knight in shining armor. "I'll keep you safe."

"I just want to be loved. To fly away. To forget everything." She cupped his cheek. "I miss painting."

He felt tears prick his eyes. Cayden never cried. He didn't recognize himself. All he cared about was making this girl's dreams come true.

Cayden kissed down the center of her chest, shifting lower down her body. "You'll paint again."

He planted kissed all the way down to her panties, giving her pussy one kiss before standing up at the end of the bed. She watched his every move. He unfastened his belt and stepped out of his jeans. Cayden palmed his erection over his boxers. She appeared fascinated.

"I know you've seen at least one of these before," he said.

"Not yours."

He tilted his head. "Take off your panties. Let me see if I can fit in your little pussy." She wiggled out of her undies and set them aside, keeping her knees closed. "Don't tell me you're shy now, princess. I've already had my head between those legs. Or have you forgotten?"

"I remember."

"Then show me. Drop your knees." She did as told. *So obedient.* He couldn't help but growl deep in his chest. Everything was coming back. "Spread your folds for me. I want to see it all."

She used one hand to open her pussy lips, all pink and glistening.

He removed his boxers, his cock springing free. She watched in rapt fascination as he climbed back on the bed. Cayden licked his finger and pressed it into her hot little cunt, nice and slow. He pulled out and reinserted two fingers, fucking her until she gasped for air.

She reached for him. "I don't want your fingers."

"What do you want?"

"Your cock."

He smirked. "Such a filthy mouth for such a pretty girl."

Cayden settled between her legs again, this time nothing to separate them. He kissed her on the mouth. It wasn't just the desperate need blazing inside him, but pure, unadulterated love. He wanted to consume her, own her, never let her go.

He didn't deserve her.

But he'd take her anyway.

He'd wrestled with his conscience and concluded that no man was good enough for her. All Cayden knew was he'd spend the rest of life trying to be what she needed.

Her kisses made him ache. They squirmed

amongst the blankets, kissing, necking, devouring. He didn't hold back this time. Things felt different now.

"Cayden, please. You're killing me."

He poised himself, reaching for his cock. As he ran the firm head up and down her wet slit, she writhed, mewling with need. The sound turned him on. Everything about Sophia drove him nuts.

"Tell me to stop if I hurt you." He pressed in an inch, then another. She gasped, her body stiffening. "You okay?"

"I never said to stop."

He continued to fill her with his dick, the tightness of her pussy making it nearly impossible to behave. Skin to skin. Sophia naked in his arms. It was fucking heaven.

He began to piston his hips, pumping in and out, building up a faster rhythm. Cayden could go on all night long. It seemed like forever since he'd messed with a woman.

Sophia wasn't a whore. She was a fucking angel.

The bed began to shake, the cheap frame clapping the wall each time he filled her with cock. She held onto him, her legs wrapped around his waist. Her sounds grew louder, echoing in the quiet apartment. She was tight and sweet and perfect.

"You like it, baby?"

She nodded, too breathless to speak.

"Tell me what you want."

"Harder," she chanted. "Faster."

He delivered, no holding back. Hawk had already deflowered the Morenov princess, so he didn't have to go slow and gentle. He could savor her, enjoy her tight little cunt squeezing the shit out of his dick. She was slick and receptive, her body arching up for more.

His thoughts briefly flitted to the future—when

he'd be sharing Sophia with Hawk. He was surprised the idea didn't repulse him like it should.

****

Sophia felt complete. Cayden's big dick was deep inside her, claiming her, joining them together. They were bonded now, body and soul. She'd never thought this day would come after he dropped her off at the hotel. She'd never felt so alone and desperate that day.

Cayden had unwavering control, and she never expected he'd break and give her what she wanted. Give them a chance.

"You're mine now," she said.

"You do always get what you want, don't you?" He kissed her temple, then shelled the rim of her ear with his tongue.

"Today. Yes." She squeezed her pelvic muscles, making him groan. The deep, masculine sound made her wetter. "Promise me something, Cayden."

"What is it?"

"Promise you'll never leave me again. You won't get pissed off and disappear."

She wanted him to stop running, stop being the victim for the rest of his life. He was a grown man, strong, and had so much life ahead of him. There was more to him than his fucked-up past.

"I'll try."

Sophia shook her head. "Not good enough. Not if you love me."

"Such a bossy little thing." He began to fuck her harder, his thick cock stretching her in the most delicious way. She could feel her orgasm building, but she wanted to enjoy him for as long as possible. His body was hard muscle, scars, and ink. Beauty and pain intertwined. She never wanted to stop touching him. Exploring him. Unraveling all his secrets.

There was nothing that could shock her, not when her own thoughts could get so dark they suffocated the air right out of her.

He pulled out when she was so close to orgasm. Before she could complain, he flipped her body over, tugging her hips up into the air. Within seconds, a strong hand pressed her back down and his cock filled her up again. The new angle brought more sensations to life. She gripped the sheets in both hands, stabilizing herself as he rammed her from behind.

He was a machine.

All man.

Cayden fucked her, slamming in and out of her pussy, the sounds of sex filling the small room.

"Come for me, Sophia." A moist thumb circled her asshole, making her choke on her own cry. It felt so damn dirty and impossibly good. He impaled her with this thumb, still thrusting his cock in her pussy. "And next time I'll be taking you right here, filling your cute virgin ass with my dick. This will be all mine."

Just thinking of him taking her ass, Hawk and Cayden double fucking her, sent her hurtling over the edge. Her orgasm detonated in her womb, making her see stars. The pleasure rippled out to all her extremities, making her feel like she was floating, flying. Cayden had taken her there.

He growled and pumped his hips a few more times, then crashed down on the bed next to her. She collapsed to her stomach, still trying to catch her breath. Her body was pleasantly sated, the afterglow of sex still surrounding her, warm and comforting. After so many days trying to win him over, craving him like a forbidden toy—he'd finally given her what she wanted.

Sophia rolled to her side, running her hand over his hard chest. Even now, she wanted him again. She licked the moisture off his shoulder, cuddling up closer.

"It feels different when you love someone," Cayden said. He stroked her hair absently, staring up at the ceiling. She studied his features—his strong jaw, thick lashes, and the scar on his cheek from that day she kept trying to forget.

"Love?"

He smirked, and she noticed a dimple she hadn't seen before.

"You're thirty-five. Have you ever thought about settling down, having kids?" she asked.

Now his brow furrowed. "I can't have kids."

"What do you mean?"

"You need good role models to be a good father. I guarantee I never had one of those," he said. "I'll gladly break the cycle. It's not worth the risk."

"What about Frank? You respected him, looked up to him. Why can't he be your role model? The others don't count. They don't deserve to be in your head."

"It's hard enough worrying about one day at a time. I shouldn't be talking about bringing another life into the world. Especially our world. Did you have a happy childhood?"

She shrugged. Sophia had some beautiful memories, but most of them came from painting or her imaginary escapes. "You're a better man than my father was."

He kissed her on top the head, not saying anything more.

A police car passed in the distance, the siren making her bristle for a moment. Cayden was right. Being raised in a crime family was dysfunction at its finest. But they could do things differently. Love harder. Learn from their parents' mistakes.

"Hawk will be worried," she said.

He groaned. "You're thinking of him right now?"

"If he brought me here, I'd be thinking of you, too."

Cayden pushed up on an elbow. "I told you we wouldn't be gone long. I wanted to show you the sunrise, but I'd say it turned out much better than expected, no?"

She smiled and he gave her a kiss on the lips. "It's been a perfect day. For the first time in a long time, I can breathe."

"Hopefully it's the start of a new trend. It's time to start living," Cayden said.

"I agree."

They got cleaned up and dressed. She puttered around the small apartment, looking for more clues into Cayden's life. There were no photos, trophies, trinkets. His life had been so empty, and she wanted to change all that.

She heard the jingle of keys. "Time to go, Sophia. We need to beat the worst of the morning rush hour."

They walked up the concrete steps from the basement apartment. The sky was a crisp blue, massive numbers of seagulls swarming high in the distance. She pointed to them.

"There's a dump over there. On a bad day, it can get real ripe around here," he said.

Even though the neighborhood was in a sketchy area, she didn't care. She'd been so sheltered growing up that the new people, sights, and sounds intrigued her.

"That's far enough."

A man stepped out from behind the brick wall of the building, a gun discreetly trained on Cayden, partially hidden by his jacket. She turned her head and recognized the other man from Antonio Jr.'s house. She grabbed onto Cayden's arm.

"Damn, Antonio can't take a fucking hint, can

STACEY ESPINO

he?" said Cayden. "I'm kind of embarrassed for him right now."

"Both of you get in the car." There was a black sedan with heavily tinted windows parked on the street. A sense of dread weighed heavily in her gut. She was going to be sick.

Antonio Jr. had no reason to keep Cayden alive. He'd kill him for stealing her away and force her to marry him. Then he'd murder her, too, and make it look like an accident.

This wasn't good.

"You going to shoot us in broad daylight?" Cayden asked, still refusing to budge.

"I doubt anyone would notice around here," said the man in front of them. "I bet they won't even call the cops."

The man behind them rammed the butt of his gun down on Cayden's shoulder, bringing him to one knee. He cursed under his breath.

"Leave him out of this!" said Sophia. "I'll go with you quietly, but only if you forget about him. I'm the one you want." She couldn't live with herself if they killed Cayden. At least she knew they wanted her alive.

"Not happening," said Cayden. He reached for the gun in the back of his jeans as he stood back up, whipping it out to aim at the man in front of him. The other man pointed a gun at him in response.

The first man chuckled. "Just drop it. You're outnumbered. Kill me and you'll both join me within seconds. You know how this works. Even you're not that fast, Mr. Walsh."

She held Cayden's outstretched arm, but he was too focused, his arm rock hard and unwavering. He had nerves and balls of steel.

"Antonio Jr. would never approve of you killing

247

Sophia. You go home and tell him she's dead, that asshole will skin you both alive for ruining his wedding plans. No, this is what happens—I shoot you in the fucking face and your friend will do me the same favor. Sophia walks away."

"Cayden, no, stop it!" she said. Her nerves were frayed, her heart jackhammering in her chest.

"Sophia, go back to the apartment. Just walk down the stairs and lock yourself inside. Call Hawk and tell him where you are. No one will hurt you." He used his free hand to pass her the keys, his blue eyes never leaving his intended target. Once she was out of sight, he'd kill both men, not caring if he was killed in return. How could this be happening?

"I'm not leaving you!"

"Neither am I."

Everyone turned to the new voice. The second gunman collapsed to his knees, then fell to the ground, his neck at an unnatural angle. Hawk stood in his place, a gun aimed at Antonio's other man.

"Hawk!" she blurted. It was hard to contain her excitement. Both men were ready to die for her. She loved them more than she could ever express.

Chapter Twenty

"Baby, down the stairs. Now," said Hawk.

Sophia did as told, walking backwards and using the railing as she slowly descended.

He turned to Cayden. "A heads-up would have been nice."

Hawk had woken up to an empty hotel suite. He had a strong feeling Sophia was with Cayden, but he had to know for sure. Just like Cayden had traced his car, he'd returned the favor and put a tracker on his Harley. It brought him here, to the old apartment where they staked out together.

The black Mercedes had been out of place in the rundown neighborhood, so he'd shifted gears and moved in on foot to investigate.

"I never planned to come here. It just kind of happened," said Cayden. "Nice to see you, by the way."

"You know this place is hot."

"Like I said, unplanned. And stupid." Cayden focused on the last man standing. "Why are you still pointing that shit at me? Toss the gun, then get your buddy down the stairs."

Once they were back in Cayden's apartment, the body in the bathtub, he tied the other man to a chair in the kitchen. Sophia was in the bedroom, the door closed, because interrogations were never pretty.

They roughed him up a bit. His name was Renzo, and he worked for Antonio Jr., which was no big surprise. Sophia had told them that Antonio Sr. didn't know about the kidnapping. Apparently, the old man thought the wedding was planned, and he looked forward to uniting the two powerhouses of Morenov and Baretti.

Antonio Jr. was a fucking little prick with no self-respect.

"Where's he staying? Last chance to speak up," Cayden said, pacing back and forth in front of the man.

Blood ran from his nose. "I told you I don't know. He only comes to the house once in a while. He only saw Sophia a few times, and then he'd leave."

"Someone knows," said Hawk.

The bedroom door opened, and Sophia came into the kitchen. He recognized the look on her face. It was the mask, the one she wore when nothing fazed her, when she had no choice but to be strong. She was a Morenov, after all.

"Back in the bedroom, Sophia." Cayden pointed to the door.

She shook her head. "I'm tired of this. All of it. Ever since my father was killed, I've been on the run, hiding, and wondering if we'll all survive from one day to the next. I've found out things that will give me nightmares for the rest of my life. I'm done."

"Sophia…" Hawk stepped toward her, but she put her hand up to stop him.

"Give me that," she said, reaching for his 9mm. He handed it to her, looking to Cayden with apprehension. Sophia pointed it at Renzo, her eyes welling up with tears, but she angrily wiped them away with the back of her free hand. "Where's Antonio Sr. staying? He's the only one who can end all this bullshit. I'm tired of hiding. Tired of being everyone's pawn."

When the man didn't answer, she shot him in the fucking foot, squealed, then dropped the gun on the ground and jumped back into Cayden's waiting arms. Renzo cried out, rocking in the chair as his foot bled all over the cheap laminate floor.

Hawk bent over and picked up the gun. "She asked you a fucking question."

"He hasn't gone anywhere. The boss lives in his

mansion. You'll never get to him."

Sophia was broken and crying as Cayden held her close. This world was killing her. He didn't want her to lose her unique innocence. One good thing about Vasily was his drive to shelter her from the dark life they lived.

The louder Renzo screamed, the more Sophia retreated into herself. He ended it with a head shot. Silence settling down on them.

Hawk pulled out his phone, getting someone to handle the mess. They wouldn't be coming back here again.

Sophia was right, of course. Antonio Sr. was the way to end it all. Once he realized what his son was up to, he'd put a stop to it. The so-called devout Catholic would never hear of a fake wedding, one where his son planned to kill his bride for power. It was sleazy, and the old-school gangster would never approve. Certain lines were not to be crossed. Vasily Morenov was gone, off the map, so there was no threat or opportunity left to exploit.

Sophia was going to disappear.

They'd keep her safe and get out of this city for good.

"Take her in the car. I'll follow on my bike," said Cayden.

He took Sophia's hand and cautiously made his way to his car in a nearby alleyway. "You okay?"

She reminded him of the way she acted on the day of her father's murder, zoning out completely. When she didn't respond, he picked up the pace. He strapped her into the passenger seat and got in the driver's side. Cayden was already behind him, revving his engine. It felt good to have backup.

They got back to the hotel, the one they should have been at all morning. Cayden had really fucked things up, but Hawk's record wasn't the greatest, so he kept his mouth shut.

"Now what?" asked Cayden. "How the hell are we going to get an audience with the boss man?"

"I'll think of something," said Hawk. "We don't need to do anything tonight. Sophia's been through enough."

Cayden turned to look at her curled up on the corner of the sofa, staring out the windows.

"The house sold for just under asking price. The Morenov Empire is gone, and everything is in the process of getting liquidated," said Hawk. "Once we deal with Antonio Jr., we're free. All of us."

"And then what?" asked Cayden, keeping his voice low so Sophia couldn't overhear.

"No one read fairy tales to me. All I know is Sophia wants a different life than this, a cute little house, security, and apparently both of us fucking her."

Cayden's jaw clenched. "She wants the happily ever after, and she needs to paint again."

"You're right," said Hawk. "We'll finish this and give her what she deserves."

It was unnerving how they thought so alike. Hawk began to realize he *wanted* Cayden to be part of their lives. He wanted their triad to work.

They both kept turning to check on her.

"And us? Her whole fantasy with the three of us. You think that's realistic?"

"I can't say no to her."

Cayden nodded. "I'm not fucking you, if that's what you're hoping for." He smirked.

Hawk shoved him. "Keep your dick to yourself."

"So, we're doing this. Okay," said Cayden. There was a new air of acceptance around him. The usual resistance was nowhere to be found. "We'll have to get eyes on the mansion. Tail the family. Let's give it a couple days. Sophia's been through too much."

"I'll get in touch with my contacts. And we have some girls working for the Barettis."

"This morning has been a bit of heaven and a bit of hell. I'm taking a shower. Can you order pizza?"

****

Cayden wouldn't say anything to Hawk, but he was getting used to the high life. Living in the posh hotel for the past couple days was growing on him. He couldn't complain about being holed up with Sophia, and the constant stream of room service was his kind of living. It was better than his empty fridge and fending for himself every day.

They needed a couple days to get things together, to devise their plan to deal with Antonio Jr. once and for all. Now the waiting was almost up. They'd had two nights in the suite. Everything was coming together.

He didn't want to go out in a blaze of glory any more. Cayden had something to live for. Purpose. Love. People who understood and accepted him. Maybe Sophia and Hawk could be his unorthodox family.

"Tomorrow's the day," said Hawk, clapping him on the shoulder as he passed.

"In broad daylight again?"

Hawk shrugged, leaning against the kitchen counter. "We know his routine. He'll be at the gym at ten in the morning. It'll make it easier to get to his father." He wiped at apple on his shirt and took a bite.

"When did we get fruit?"

"I ordered it. Money talks," said Hawk. "We're not in the ghetto anymore."

He would tell him to fuck off, but he had no more desire to deprive himself. After opening up to Sophia, he realized a lot of his actions were fueled by self-hatred and the inability to grow and move on. He had to put his nightmares to rest if he wanted to enjoy the rest of his life.

Sophia came out of the bedroom, her hair wrapped up in a towel. "What are you two talking about?" she asked. She sat on a kitchen chair opposite Cayden. He could smell her sweet shampoo wafting in the air.

Hawk spoke up. "We were talking about making this threesome official."

Cayden looked at him but didn't say anything. He waited and listened.

"What do you mean?" she asked.

"You said you want both of us. Forever. No?"

"Of course."

"You love both of us?"

"With all my heart."

"Then you know what that entails. We won't know for sure if it'll work until we share you," said Hawk. He took the last bite of his apple, acting too casual when Cayden's heart was already racing. Would he even be able to go through with this? He'd fucked around a lot, but he'd never had a threesome, and certainly hadn't shared Sophia.

"Now?"

He tossed his apple core. "Why not? We've both kept our hands to ourselves the past two nights. I guarantee Cayden feels the same way."

She turned to him, her dark eyes questioning. "Do you? Want to do this, I mean?"

Hawk had already set things in motion. He was right about needing to test the waters. Sex could make or break their well laid plans. Cayden wouldn't be a pussy and back out. And it would be a lie if he hadn't been thinking of Sophia naked and under him every hour of every day since coming back to the hotel.

"Getting cold feet?" he asked.

She shook her head.

"You may be getting more than you wished for. Get on the bed. Lose the towel and robe," said Cayden.

Sophia glanced at both of them one more time before returning to the bedroom and closing the door behind her.

He stood up, his chair legs scraping the tiles. Cayden braced both hands on the table. "I don't know if I can fucking do this," he attempted to whisper.

Hawk paced, unbuttoning his shirt. "Relax. We're doing this for Sophia. We love *her,* not each other. I don't plan on crossing swords with you."

"Good to know." He pulled off his t-shirt and rolled out his shoulders. "One rule."

Hawk cocked an eyebrow. "Oh?"

"You stole her virginity from me, so I'll be taking her ass first."

"Fine. I can play nice."

Cayden got everything they'd need. They approached the master suite. Would she be scared or naked and waiting? If this all fell apart, he'd have nothing. No woman. No family. Nothing.

He'd gotten a taste of a life without feeling unworthy, lonely, and rejected. Cayden didn't want to go back to those days.

Hawk turned the handle.

Cayden gave the door a little push. The room was dark, only the lights from the other downtown hotels offering a soft wash of light from the window. It took a minute for his eyes to adjust.

She was sitting on the bed, only her face visible from under the white duvet.

"I thought I said to take your clothes off," said

Cayden.

Sophia unfolded the blanket to the side, revealing her sitting cross-legged in the nude. Her nipples had pebbled. "I did as told," she said, her voice faint.

Hawk finished removing his shirt, setting in on the back of the lounge chair. He began to unbuckle as he approached the head of the bed. Cayden followed suit, kicking off his jeans, leaving him in just his boxers. Sophia watched his movements.

"Are you afraid, princess?" Cayden asked.

She shook her head. "I trust both of you."

"Can you fit two cocks in that tight little body of yours?" asked Hawk. He climbed on the bed behind her, kissing her bare shoulder.

Sophia closed her eyes and bit her lip.

"You're both so big, but I'll try."

"She knows the right things to say, doesn't she?" said Cayden, climbing towards her on his hands and knees. He wrapped his lips around her perfect sloping tit. She gasped but didn't move.

He expected this to be more awkward, but once they started exploring her body—kissing, touching, sucking—it felt like the most natural dance in the world. They moved like a team, working together to pleasure their woman.

Cayden removed his boxers, no longer caring that Hawk would see him naked. He was way beyond caring. They lowered Sophia to her back and both of them parted her at the knees.

"Such a pretty pussy," said Cayden.

Hawk ran his finger along her slit. "Look how wet she is. She wants to get double-fucked."

Cayden couldn't hold back. He lowered his face between her legs and lapped at her folds, fucking her with his tongue. Hawk suckled her tits, his hand on her stomach to keep her grounded. She writhed on the sheets, moaning, and begging. It was the sexiest thing he'd ever experienced.

"Who do you belong to?" asked Hawk.

"Both of you."

"Anyone else?"

She shook her head. Cayden looked up from her pussy. "Say it," he said.

"No one else. I belong to both of you."

"That's right. No other men will know this body." He suckled her clit until she bucked off the bed, squealing for relief.

Hawk pinned her arms to the side of her face, forcing her to accept the pleasure, kissing her to drown her moans.

Cayden continued to eat her pussy, careful not to let her go over the edge just yet. Cayden twirled his tongue around her tight little asshole, making his cock even harder. He could already imagine how tight she'd feel when he speared her virgin hole.

Next time he glanced up, Hawk was kneeling by Sophia's head, his cock down her throat. She worked him up and down as Hawk directed her actions with a hand secured in her blonde hair. He wanted to feel that same pleasure.

Cayden got to his knees and joined Hawk at the head of the bed, on the other side of Sophia. "Don't tease Cayden," said Hawk. "He wants your mouth, too."

She turned her head and opened her mouth, waiting for his dick. He nearly came on the spot. Her eyes were glassed over, her nerves faded to nothing. What really impressed him was Hawk not trying to control this party.

The moment her hot, wet mouth covered the head of his shaft, he groaned aloud, grabbing the headboard for stability. For being innocent, she had a talented tongue.

"She's got a wicked mouth on her," said Hawk. "Such a naughty little girl."

And naughty girls needed punishment.

He finally had to grab her hair and pull her off his dick or he'd be finished before they started.

Hawk lay on the bed next to her, his cock erect. Cayden returned the favor. "Sophia, sit on Hawk's dick." He helped her up as she twisted on the bed to straddle the other man. "All the way down. Nice and deep. Take it all and lean forward."

She mewled as he filled her.

It was like a mix of sex and porn, watching and participating. He never expected it would be like this. They both loved Sophia to the point they'd agreed to this in the first place. Now he was fully invested, and glad he hadn't driven off into the sunset.

Hawk had his arms around her as they kissed, passionately making love.

Cayden grabbed the tube of lube, coating his shaft. Then he poured a generous amount over the crack of her ass. He pressed her down against Hawk, skin to skin, as he swirled one finger in the moisture and impaled her tight little hole. He carefully scissored his two fingers, stretching her, preparing her for what was to come.

"Are you ready for me, sweetheart? We're about to make you ours," said Cayden.

"Yes," she chanted.

He pressed the tip of his head against her tiny asshole, Hawk already deep inside her cunt. "It's going to hurt for a minute. You need to relax for me. Don't clench."

He held her hips and forced his cock past her

tight anal ring, then gave her a break. It was impossibly tight with Hawk sharing her body, but also the best thing he'd ever felt.

"Such a good girl," Hawk cooed. "You're taking two grown men. We're sharing your beautiful body, just like you wanted."

Cayden sank all the way in, only a thin membrane separating him from Hawk's dick.

"Fuck, that's tight," he said. "Tell me if you want to stop."

****

Sophia had no plans on ending what they'd started. She was flying, soaring, drifting further and further from reality. They'd been smothering her with delicious foreplay for what felt like forever. Their mouths and hands were everywhere, sharing, no apologies.

She loved every minute of being their plaything.

Loved their dirty talk and control in the bedroom.

Now they'd taken her, sharing her body in the most forbidden way. The initial intrusion into her virgin ass had been painful, the pressure unbelievable. She nearly tapped out, but Cayden had her well lubricated, making it easier. Hawk pinched her nipples when she clenched.

Cayden gave her time to adjust, and once her anxiety faded, she became obsessed with the fact two cocks were deep inside her pussy and ass. Hawk and Cayden, the two men she loved, were destroying her innocence in the best way imaginable.

She wiggled her hips a bit, getting a reaction from both men. "More," she said. "I want more."

They worked together like a finely tuned machine, pumping in and out of her, taking turns. One cock in, the other out, over and over, creating enough beautiful friction that she could scarcely breathe. Cayden's strong hands were on her hips as Hawk kissed her, making all her thoughts vanish. It was only about pleasure now. Seeing how much she could handle. The filthier, the better.

"She's too fucking tight, I'm going to come," said Cayden. He fucked her ass harder as Hawk stilled beneath her. She gagged, unable to speak, and shocked at how intense the pending orgasm felt as it grew deep in her cunt.

Cayden groaned like an animal as he came, filling her ass with his cum. He slipped away, and Hawk immediately rolled her over, dominating her from above. "All mine now, baby. Hold onto me."

She held his biceps as he pistoned into her like a beast, his pubic bone stimulating her clit with each pump of his hips. "Oh God, Hawk, I'm going to come."

"Do it, Sophia. Come all over my dick."

There was something perfect about them talking dirty to her. It aroused her in crazy ways. She stopped fighting, relaxing enough that the wash of orgasm could spread all through her like a firestorm. Her body jolted, her pussy tightening around Hawk as she detonated, her body contracting in deep waves. It was the most intense orgasm she'd ever experienced.

Hawk fucked her harder, pulling her hair to the side as he growled in her ear. She felt the moment he came inside her, his cock pulsing as the tension in his muscles eased.

His breathing was rapid as he rolled his strong body to the side. Cayden was back, a washcloth in hand. He'd been away in the bathroom, now wearing a pair of navy workout shorts, his hair casually slicked back.

"Open your legs, Sophia."

She relaxed her legs, and he stroked a warm wash

cloth over her inner thighs and between her legs. Her body was still extremely sensitive, and she jolted with each swipe. When he was finished, he joined them on the bed.

"You realize we're going to need a huge bed," she said.

"So, does that mean this threesome experiment of yours passed the test?" asked Hawk. He shifted to his side. She felt completely enveloped by the men, and half expected to wake from a dream at any moment.

"I never doubted it. Sex isn't a factor for my love."

"It helps," said Cayden, brushing the moist hair from her forehead.

She smiled, savoring their attention, and the knowledge this could actually work.

Chapter Twenty-One

The house reminded her of home. Antonio Baretti had the same expensive taste as her father. The entrance had massive stone pillars and statues of lions guarding the main door. Hawk and Cayden flanked her as they walked up the steps.

She needed this to go smoothly. If any of Antonio's men started something, she knew Hawk and Cayden would take them all down to protect her. That was way too risky. Being diplomatic was her top priority.

As planned, one of the maids that used to be on her father's payroll opened the door for them. She pointed in the direction of the Antonio's office, whispering to Hawk in Russian. He nodded and continued down the hallway. Her heart raced. They were inside the dragon's den now. She was certain something would go wrong. Every time she found happiness, it seemed to get ripped away.

The heavy mahogany doors looked ominous. Cayden leaned his back against the wall, just outside the doors, to stay on watch. Hawk entered without knocking.

The old man sat behind his desk watching porn on the big screen mounted on the wall. She was thankful he was alone. Her father had rarely been without at least one of his men. She remembered Antonio Sr. from some old events her father made her attend. He'd been kind and respectful to her in the past, but that could have been due to her father's influence.

"Sophia?"

He stood and fumbled with the remote to turn off the television, before sitting back down in his chair.

"Mr. Baretti. It's been a long time," she said.

"I sorry about you father. He was good man."

His English was rough, and her Italian was even

worse, so Hawk took over. She only caught bits and pieces of what he said, but the plan was to expose his son. Antonio Jr. had kidnapped, threatened, and planned to kill her. The entire wedding was a front to get his claws on the Morenov Empire's power and money now that her father was dead.

"He's disappointed you won't be his daughter-in-law, but he won't allow his son to go through with the wedding." Hawk translated for the old man. "He apologizes for the actions of his son."

She nodded her thanks. "*Grazie.*"

After a bit more talking, they said their good-byes and returned to the hallway. She wouldn't be able to breathe until they were driving away from the house. The place gave her a bad vibe, and she knew better than to trust anyone.

Cayden took his hand out of his jacket once they exited. "Everything good?" he asked.

"Too good," said Hawk. "Let's get out of here."

They walked straight to the main doors. She kept her eyes forward, not even daring to take a breath. Daylight streamed in through the glass doors, a beacon in the dim hallway.

So close to freedom.

As Hawk turned the handle, the shadow blocked out the sun. Sophia's entire body tensed.

The door opened to reveal Antonio Baretti Jr. and three of his men.

Fear ripped through her, and memories of him tormenting her came back with a vengeance. Every time he came in the room, she didn't know if he was going to hurt, rape, or kill her.

"You have balls," said Antonio.

Hawk shrugged. "You should have taken *no* for an answer."

"We had to involve mommy and daddy," said Cayden. "Guess they need to teach you not to take things that don't belong to you."

"You shouldn't have come here," said Antonio. "This is my fucking parents' home. It should be off limits."

Hawk laughed out loud. "You kidnapped our fucking woman. Where would that sit in your books?"

Antonio's men spread out, circling them in the foyer. Hawk grabbed her hand and shoved his way to the expansive front porch. Cayden kept his hand inside his coat, and she knew he wouldn't think twice about pulling out his gun and raining down on them.

"Does she belong to *both* of you?" Antonio leaned against the doorframe, looking too casual and smug for a man who'd single-handedly tried to ruin their lives.

"Yes, I belong to both of them," said Sophia. She was tired of the fear, of keeping to the sidelines while everyone around her played with her life. "My father's empire is dead. I don't care about his legacy, his territory, or anything he controlled. It's all gone, and all I care about are the men I love."

Antonio cocked an eyebrow.

"Does it shock you she's fucking both of us?" asked Cayden.

Hawk kept his body between her and the doorway. "And she still wouldn't marry the likes of you."

"Go check on my father," said Antonio, turning to one of his men.

"Your father's fine," said Sophia. "We're not animals. And thankfully he doesn't feel the same way you do about forcing a woman to marry."

"Go your own way. Stay out of ours," said

Cayden.

It was broad daylight as they backed away from the house. Hawk opened the passenger door of the car, and she got in her seat as Cayden got in behind her. Once Hawk was in the driver's seat, he glared over at Antonio Jr. once more before hitting the gas. The tires squealed as they raced up the street.

Sophia's knuckles grew white as she gripped both sides of her chair, her heart in her throat. It was only when Cayden's strong hand squeezed her shoulder from behind that she remembered to breathe.

"Is it over?" she dared to ask. "Really over?"

Hawk glanced at her in between watching the road ahead. "Doesn't matter. We're getting out of this city. Away from everything."

She twisted in her seat. "But you said this city is all you had, Cayden. I won't leave if you won't."

"Wherever you are, that's where I want to be," he said. "I thought my fucked-up memories made me who I was. But they only brought me down, made me feel like a nobody. You make me want to live."

Sophia saw the sincerity in his eyes, and her mind went back to their first days together, to all the progress they'd made in their relationship over this crazy journey. She cupped her hand behind his neck, bringing him closer.

"We're going to have the happily ever after. Our own kind, because nobody can tell us how this story ends." She kissed him, craving his affection, needing to feel grounded when everything felt so uncertain.

****

Hawk kept driving long into the night. He knew exactly the direction he was heading in. Over the past week he'd been doing a lot of research on the side, making sure they had plans A, B, and C depending on how things went with Antonio Jr. and Cayden.

It appeared they were going with plan A.

Antonio would be smart to keep off the radar for now, and Cayden was part of the package if he wanted Sophia. But he knew he could live with that. All that mattered now was making Sophia happy.

They needed to settle down, grieve their losses, and accept their new normal. Life had been running on full throttle for too long. Breathing for the second, hopping from hotel to hotel, and keeping in hiding—it was no way to live.

"Is that the ocean?" she asked, waking up in the early hours of the next morning. He'd taken turns driving with Cayden, only stopping for bathroom and coffee breaks. Hawk didn't want to stop. He wanted as much distance as possible between the three of them and everything they were leaving behind.

"That's right. What do you think?"

She sat up in her seat with wide-eyed wonder despite just waking up. "It's beautiful. It goes on forever."

He slowed the car when he reached his destination. Hawk parked along the side of the road by the water and got out, motioning her to follow. Did they stand out in this new place? He'd be paranoid for a while. Maybe forever. But it was part and parcel of his past. Vasily had raised him to be a killer, to protect the family … to be there for Sophia.

She walked toward the water. Gulls cawed above, and he heard children's laughter in the near distance. When she was out of earshot, Cayden came and stood beside him. Sophia occasionally turned back and smiled. The most beautiful thing in the world.

"This is where you fucking bring us?" Cayden palmed his pockets as he looked around the neighborhood.

"Looking for your smokes?"

Cayden scowled. "Just out of habit. You know I've quit."

Sophia kicked off her shoes and wet her feet in the water. Her blonde hair fluttered loose in the breeze.

"She loves art, so this neighborhood is perfect for her," said Hawk. There were a couple local galleries, and every weekend there was a market by the dock with art for sale.

"Are we hipsters now?" Cayden touched the gun under his jacket, then interlocked his fingers behind his head as he paced back and forth. "I want to kill everyone here."

"Relax. You'll get used to the change of pace. We all will."

Cayden looked like a fish out of water, but he'd adapt. Hawk knew he would because he was making the same sacrifices for Sophia. Hawk didn't know the first thing about playing house, but with their fucked-up threesome, they needed a place that was open-minded. That eliminated much of the map.

"This is why you wouldn't show me the house, isn't it? Where are we going to live, a damn hostel?"

"No, Cayden, it's a real home. Not a hotel, not a rundown apartment, and not a place for a stakeout. That's what we should all want. I mean, neither of us had that, so we should give that to Sophia."

Cayden looked off at the ocean. "One day she'll mourn and remember I killed her father. She'll remember and hate me."

The lull of the waves replaced their voices.

Hawk turned to the other man. "Then I'll remind her of everything we've all been through. Remind her that she loves you."

Cayden smirked. "You're all right, Hawk. Sophia has good taste."

"Come on." He clapped Cayden on the back. "And don't worry. You'll approve when you see our man cave in the basement."

They walked down to the water to get Sophia. He had the keys to their new home in his pocket. This was going to be the first day of the rest of their lives. They both needed to learn how to play nice, to take out the garbage, and mow the lawn.

There'd be a major learning curve.

"I love the smell," she said. Sophia closed her eyes and took a deep breath.

"Smells like brine and dead fish," said Cayden.

She opened her eyes and scowled. "Does not. If I remember, your old neighborhood smelled a lot worse."

"You get used to it."

"Let's go, we have something to show you," said Hawk.

They practically had to drag her from the shoreline, the bottoms of her pants already damp. Soon her pale skin would be sun-kissed. No more hiding the princess in the castle.

It was only a five-minute walk to the house. Waterfront, of course. Hawk had to compromise on wanting the best and providing the simplicity Sophia craved. The life Vasily provided was never meant for him. His real parents were poor immigrants struggling to keep their store open. Was that the reason slumming it terrified him so much? He wasn't sure, but Hawk needed to remind himself to look forward and not back or it would drive him crazy.

"Mr. Tesino. I have everything prepared like you asked."

One of the real estate agents they used to use

waited on the sidewalk near the house, a file folder in hand. Hawk had left very specific instructions. He wanted this to be perfect for Sophia.

Cayden appeared less than impressed, but that only made two of them.

"Thank you. Will you give us an hour? We'll handle the signatures after that."

"Of course, sir."

He walked out front. Cayden held Sophia's hand as they followed. The flowers he'd requested were colorful and overflowing the gardens and planters. He stopped at the side entrance of the house and turned around.

"What do you think, baby?"

She cocked her head to the side. "What do you mean?"

"It's home," he said. "The little house by the ocean."

Sophia kept quiet, looking from the house to him and back again. "I don't understand."

Hawk handed her the keys. "Open the door, Sophia. It's your house. *Our* house."

"For all three of us?"

"All three of us."

She unlocked the door, her hands slightly shaking. "This can't be happening."

"Wait," said Cayden. "Be a fucking gentleman. Let's carry her over the threshold."

"Right."

They scooped her up from each end and carried her inside, setting her onto her feet again. Cayden's cat, Rosie, rubbed up against her leg. She smiled. Hawk shrugged when Cayden raised an eyebrow.

"And then there were four," she said.

Sophia was off before he could close the door,

dashing in this direction and that. The wall facing the ocean was mostly windows, and an easel had been set up with a stool at the perfect vantagepoint.

She ran her fingers over the blank paper, then over the new brushes, one by one. When she turned her head, her eyes were filled with unshed tears. "You thought of everything, didn't you?"

"We both want you to paint again," said Hawk. "It's time to live our lives."

Sophia spun in a slow circle, her arms at her sides. He wasn't sure if she was losing her mind again. She was always an enigma.

"You okay?" asked Cayden, sitting on the arm of the sofa.

When she stopped spinning, he couldn't find the joy he expected. Only sadness.

"This is too perfect. It's everything I've ever dreamed of."

"Then what's the problem?"

"It's what *I* want," she said. "I can't imagine either of you living here. You're like oil and water."

"You're wrong," said Hawk. "We both want this, or we wouldn't be here."

"Is that true, Cayden?"

"I've been at the bottom, princess. I've lived my nightmares. One thing I've never experienced is real life. Life how it should be. I'm not saying it'll be easy, but I want the same thing you do."

She smiled, a barely-there smile, and it lit up the room.

"You won't miss the chaos, Hawk? The contracts?"

He shook his head so he didn't have to lie. Cayden was right. It wouldn't be an easy adjustment, but it was his dream, too.

"Then shouldn't we christen our new house?" she asked.

Chapter Twenty-Two

At least it wasn't a monstrosity like the Morenov mansion. It was small, simple, and relatively private. Cayden could deal with it.

When he saw the happiness in Sophia's eyes, every sacrifice he'd make in the future was already paid in full.

Cayden and Hawk were going to have to put their pasts behind them and become the typical men next door. Normal. Do domestic shit around the house. Maybe they'd build a fucking shed.

He was feeling slightly overwhelmed by everything until Sophia suggested they christen the house. She was exactly what he needed to clear his head and make everything better.

"Truth or dare, Sophia," Cayden said.

She tried to hide her smirk. "Dare."

"Show me your tits."

This time she pulled her shirt right off and unfastened her bra, letting it fall to the tiled floor. She ran her hands over her breasts, teasing and taunting.

"Stunning," said Hawk. "Turn around. Let me see you."

She spread her arms to the side and spun around slowly. When she faced them again, she slapped her hands over her breasts and gasped.

"What is it?" asked Hawk.

Cayden turned to the door.

His old friend, Randy, was standing in the foyer.

He got to his feet and pointed to Sophia. "Hawk, get her covered." Then he turned to Randy. "What the fuck are you doing here? How the hell did you find me?"

"Your keys."

Randy had brought him his Harley, clothes, and keys when they were staying at the hotel. Why would he try to trace him? Cayden tried to think of all the best intentions. Randy was his childhood friend, after all. But his instincts screamed at him that this was too fucked up.

They'd been clashing ever since he took Sophia.

"We're not around the corner. We've been driving for almost twenty-fours straight."

"No shit," said Randy.

His expression said it all. This wasn't a housewarming visit.

"Stop playing games. What do you want?"

"You were the best, Cayden. You were going places. I swear you could have owned the city, if you wanted it, but ever since she showed up in your life, you turned soft."

"Doing the right thing is soft?"

"I don't even recognize you. You gave up three million. Three million! At least I can probably get something if I return her to Antonio Jr. It's better than nothing."

"Did he send you?" asked Cayden.

"No, this is all me. I know what I'm doing."

"Antonio's father already nixed the wedding plans, buddy. There's no bounty to collect. It's over." Cayden felt the betrayal all the way to his bones. He tasted the bitterness on his tongue. "I love her, and you'd try to sell her to my enemy?"

"You're brainwashed, and apparently jumped ship without a word to me. I've been your errand boy for over a decade, and not even a good-bye."

"It doesn't have to be like this, Randy. We've been friends since—"

"I don't want to hear it! I've made up my mind.

Unlike you, some of us have to earn their living."

"For your habit."

"Whatever. Just stay back because I'd rather not kill you when I take her ... but I will."

Someone knocked on the door behind him making him jumpy.

"Who is it?" Randy asked Cayden.

He shrugged. "Probably the agent. Obviously, he's not a threat to you."

"A Morenov real estate agent? He's a threat."

Hawk had Sophia, so Cayden could breathe. He'd have to kill the closest thing he had to a best friend. It wasn't fair, but when had life been fair? All he needed was Sophia and Hawk now. Anyone else who wanted to fuck with his happiness had to be eliminated.

"Not in the house, Cayden," said Hawk as if reading his mind.

Right. They didn't want their new home tainted with blood and bad karma. He'd take this party outside and finish it. Once this lone wolf was out of the picture, they'd be free to live their lives in peace.

"Let's talk outside," said Cayden. "Like men."

"I know you better than that. Give me the girl or I'll shoot her in the leg. You can both watch her bleed out. Or are you willing to test my shooting ability?" Randy aimed at Sophia, but Hawk shoved her body behind him.

"How about I shoot you in the leg, asshole." Hawk fired, bringing Randy to his knees.

"Shit, Hawk. I thought we weren't going to shoot in the house," said Cayden.

"Right. Sorry."

Cayden pulled Randy up by the collar, making him groan when he was forced to his feet. He opened the door. "Get inside," he said to the agent.

The agent kept his arms up as he shuffled inside.

"Don, call cleanup. I want them here within the hour for the body. Leave the papers on the table and you can pick them up in the morning," said Hawk.

The man nodded and rushed out of the house.

Cayden dragged Randy from the foyer to the back garage of the house as he half limped his way along.

So he had to handle it.

Randy was right about Cayden, though. He wasn't the man he used to be.

****

"In the bedroom," Hawk said.

She did as told. Sophia knew he was trying to keep her from seeing the blood, but she wasn't as weak as she used to be. Her father was dead. The life she once knew was a thing of the past.

But she was okay with that now. She accepted their reality, anyway.

He closed the door behind him. "I'm sorry about that, baby." Hawk cupped her face and kissed her. She closed her eyes and melted against him, getting lost in his kiss.

Cayden burst in moments later. "Everything good here?" he asked.

She stepped back, resting both her hands on the dresser behind her. "I thought you both said you could live a regular life, no killing, no craziness?"

"We can," said Hawk.

"That was a brief hiccup," said Cayden. "Straight sailing from here on."

Maybe she didn't want them to change at all. Their dangerous sides turned her on because she knew they'd never hurt her. They had good hearts, but there was nothing normal about any of them.

She started undressing again, removing her shirt

and tossing it on the corner of the bed. That's when she noticed how huge the bed was. It was built for three.

They watched as she shimmied out of her pants, leaving her in just her panties. "What happens if one of our neighbors plays the music too loud when we're trying to sleep?"

Hawk scratched his head and turned to Cayden. They both kept quiet.

She couldn't help but giggle. Sophia knew they'd want to smash the stereo and threaten the neighbors at gunpoint, but they were struggling to come up with a politically correct answer and failing.

"Just don't kill anyone, okay?"

Cayden tugged off his shirt, and she couldn't help but stare. "No promises," he said.

The men kept undressing and moving in on her. Tanned skin, ink, scars, and raw male need. She felt completely enveloped as they surrounded her.

The heat from their skin scorched her bare breasts. Their hands were on her, everywhere, removing her panties, smoothing over her curves. She didn't know who was touching or where, but it didn't matter. She loved them equally, and they both knew exactly how to pleasure her.

Cayden sucked the pulse at her neck, then whispered in her ear. "I like your little house, Sophia. But it's about to lose its innocence." He slowly moved down to his knees, kissing and tasting her as he descended.

Hawk cupped her breasts from behind, her nipples hard and aching. She dropped her head back onto his chest. "That feels so good," she said.

He rolled her nipples between his fingers. She felt his erection tapping her back, reminding her she was about to get double-fucked again.

Two men.

Two cocks.

Cayden got up and ran an arm across the low dresser top, all the decorations falling to the carpet in one swoop. He hopped up and sat on the wooden surface, his cock bobbing, hard and virile between his legs. Her mouth salivated looking at him, so needy and fierce all at once.

"Give her to me," said Cayden.

Hawk cupped his hands under her shoulders from behind and lifted her up into Cayden's arms. She straddled Cayden's waist, her knees on the dresser top.

She had a view of the ocean from the large bay windows in the bedroom. If anyone walked by on the beach, they'd get a clear view of them fucking on her dresser.

"Put it in," said Cayden.

"I'm not fucking touching you," said Hawk.

"Not you. *Her.*"

Sophia pushed up on her knees, reaching between their bodies to grab hold of Cayden's big dick. It was hard as steel, and her fingers could barely reach around his girth. She positioned him at her entrance and lowered her weight down on him. Her pussy was slick from arousal, easily taking him inside her, inch by thick inch.

"Oh yeah, just like that, sweetheart." Cayden squeezed her hips with both hands, motioning her to fuck him. She rose and fell over his cock, her arms loosely draped over his shoulders so she could look at him. Stare into those hard, blue eyes. "Tonight, I want to watch you swim naked. I'll lick all the water off your body."

She moaned, driving down harder over his cock, savoring the explosion of sensation cascading through her. Then Hawk's rough hands ran down her bare back all the way down to her ass. She never stopped riding

Cayden, even when Hawk pressed two lubed fingers into her asshole. Sophia began to fracture from the dual stimulation, so much delicious pleasure to the point of overload.

Building.

Spreading.

Growing hotter.

She impaled herself up and down over Cayden's erection with Hawk's fingers buried in her rear, stretching her, fucking her.

"Hawk, I need you," she said. Her orgasm was already blossoming. She wanted him buried to the hilt with his cock. It felt immeasurable better to come when she was stuffed full.

Sophia heard the spurt of lube before the wide tip of Hawk's cock speared her tight hole. She groaned from the pressure, leaning into Cayden.

"Her ass is fucking tight," said Hawk.

"I told you," said Cayden. "You won't last long."

She braced herself as both cocks slid home, pistoning in a filthy rhythm, the sounds of wet sex filling the room. She felt so full, so completely owned by these two hitmen. They'd do anything for her, and she was nothing without them.

"More," she chanted.

They fucked her harder. Squeezing, suckling, dominating. She screamed their names, begging for release. Hawk pounded into her ass, coming inside her seconds later. She felt the moment he swelled and released, finally slipping from her body.

Cayden slid off the dresser, his cock still deep in her cunt. She kept her legs wrapped around his waist as he carried her out of the bedroom into the kitchen.

"Time to christen the next room," he said, lowering her back onto the wooden slab kitchen table.

She jolted from the coldness, but soon his body was close, his arms tucked under her shoulders as he began to pump his hips.

He rocked the table, the legs scraping the tiles as he ravaged her body. She kissed his rough jaw, combing her fingers into his hair as he fucked her. She loved him, and he was hers. Finally, she didn't have to beg.

"I love fucking you," he said.

Hawk was back, he pushed Cayden out of the way so he could suck on her tits. The double-teaming was too much when she was already hanging by a thread. The two hulking men crowding her, devouring her, brought her orgasm racing to the surface. She blossomed, a perfect rush of heat and energy washing over her as she detonated. Sophia milked Cayden's cock, on and on, forcing him to come along with her. She arched and screamed as they doted on her until every ounce of her energy was spent.

"Look how her cheeks flush," said Cayden.

"Our little Russian princess."

One of them carried her to the big bed in the next room. Her eyes were closed, her body limp and beautifully sated.

Someone slid open the window, the sound of the waves filling the bedroom with the calming song of the ocean. She sighed contentedly as the men settled in on either side of her.

The odd seagull cawed, and she remembered the desperate feeling of being trapped when she lived with her father. No love. No future.

How things had changed.

Now she knew what it felt like to fly.

Hawk and Cayden had given her a family, a future, hope. They'd given her wings.

The End

www.staceyespino.com

EVERNIGHT PUBLISHING ®

www.evernightpublishing.com

Made in the USA
Coppell, TX
20 May 2021

56037655R00163